Advance Praise for *Cerulean Isle*

Cerulean Isle opens with a powerful and dramatic scene, and moves on from there to weave a wonderful story with colorful characters skillfully brought to life. Browning's descriptions of life on board the Obsidian are excellent.
        Bob Steele, *Spin and Conflicts of Interest*

From the intriguing opening onwards, *Cerulean Isle* is vivid and compelling, rich in atmosphere and enigma. The overlap of historical fiction and fantasy is extremely effective. It's tempting to think of this as a highly cinematic narrative, but I don't think cinema could really do it justice.
        Ivan Phillips, *Johnny Face-Ache*

Powerful, punchy writing that puts me in mind of *Treasure Island*. The sights, smells and sounds of Santiago ring clear.
        Cas Peace, *King's Envoy*

A great start, good meaty writing, fabulous characters. I was instantly reminded of the books I loved when I was younger - Robert Louis Stevenson in particular. G.M. Browning has a terrific feel for the period and the skill to put it all on paper. All in all, it's an exciting, gripping, hugely enjoyable yarn.
        S.A. Sterling, *Will's Treason*

G.M. Browning obviously has done his research, and it shows in the effortless authenticity of his scene painting. I feel like I'm there as I read. I even sway in my seat during the scenes on the sea. This is an engaging story.
        David McCaffrey, *Green Ore: the Guardian*

More Advance Praise

I recommend this book to all adventure, fantasy fans who will be thrilled by how Browning brings his mythological characters to life....It is a swashbuckling pirate adventure, laced with visually stunning details of the enchanting and effervescent 'Merlords' and 'Mermaidens' that inhabit the Cerulean Isle.
 Hannah Fraser, *Professional Mermaid Performance Artist*

Rarely have I had the pleasure of reading such a riveting tale of adventure on the high seas. *Cerulean Isle* delivers page after page and seems to have it all, from bloodthirsty pirates to the mesmerizing 'Mermaidens' of the deep. I highly recommend this book to anyone who has even a passing interest in those bold adventurers of old who called the heaving deck of a ship their home and declared war on the world around them.
 Robb "Hurricane" Zerr, *Pirate Re-enactor*

Cerulean Isle

Camryn,
Enjoy the story.

[signature]

2015

Cerulean Isle
G.M. Browning

WiDō Publishing • Salt Lake City

WiDō Publishing
Salt Lake City, Utah
Copyright © 2011 by G.M. Browning

All rights reserved. No part of this book may be reproduced or transmitted in any form or by any means, electronic or mechanical, including photocopying, recording, or by any information storage and retrieval system without the written consent of the publisher.

This book is a work of fiction. Names, characters, places, organizations and incidents either are products of the author's imagination or are used fictitiously. Any resemblance to actual persons, living or dead, events or organizations is entirely coincidental.

Cover design: Rusty Webb
Book design: Don Gee

ISBN: 978-1-937178-09-3

www.widopublishing.com

*This book is dedicated to my mother,
Nancy J. Browning.
The love in her heart is as endless as the sea.*

...Part One...

A New Life

Prologue

"Still waiting, Jacob?"

I sat on the western docks at the edge of the harbor. The sun had dipped below the horizon. The Caribbean Sea reflected the orange and purple sky as the veil of night crept over the island. I turned to my friend, Grant. "She'll come. She said she would."

Grant smiled and extended a hand to help me to my feet. "Give her some time. We all suffered a great deal of hardship. She has a duty, like we do. She'll come when she can."

We walked down the docks and along the waterfront. The harbor bells chimed in the distance and moored ships creaked as if anxious to be free of their restraints. The sounds of the harbor always made me remember the ordeals of my youth.

I was twelve years old in the year 1746, when my life changed forever.

Chapter 1

Captive

The dark stare of the pirate captain made the townsfolk turn their backs. "Gangway," he hollered.

As we passed the crowded market, more men joined our group. Some carried baskets of fruit, slabs of smoked meat, or bundles of bread. There must have been thirty dressed in a similar fashion: crudely sewn, dirty tunics and pants. All had some type of belt securing their knives and short swords, but only their captain had a pistol.

As he forced me onward, I recalled the horrifying events of that morning.

My father didn't say why we had come to the port town. Before that day, I had never joined him on any of his errands. We sat at a table in the center of the saloon. When a disheveled man approached, my father stood to greet him. The man placed a brown pouch in my father's hand. He did not open it, but weighed it in his palm.

Two bruising hands took hold of my underarms and hoisted

me high off my seat. The room whirled around me. Two foul men in tattered tunics forced me across the smoky room. I kicked. I writhed. I screamed—to whom, my father?—I looked back for him, but he was gone.

As my new master hurried me through the bustling roads, he continued calling for his crew. This was the port town Santiago on the island of Cuba, not a common stop for the good of heart. The very sight of the pirate captain was intimidating. His face was dirty and browned from the sun. He wore a faded red scarf over his head to hold back his long black hair. His lips were cracked and his teeth rotten. A large gold ring dangled from his left ear and glinted in the sunlight.

A white, long-sleeved tunic flapped loosely on his torso and tapered down to a tight leather belt. This belt was home to a long and blemished dagger and twelve-inch Flintlock pistol. His crudely sewn brown pants were tucked into muddy, black boots.

My underarm throbbed from his iron grip and my tired feet could hardly keep up with his stride. I stumbled once, but he did not slow. He dragged me until I scrambled back to my feet, the skin on my palms and elbows scraped. I looked for help. I glanced toward a stableman and sent him a pleading look; he shook his head in refusal and went back to shoeing his horse.

We passed a brothel, and outside the swinging wooden doors, two busty women taunted a light-haired man. When the man noticed me being dragged down the road, I reached for him, wordlessly begging for his help. I imagined how I looked: a young man of twelve, thin build with olive-toned skin, and short brown hair being pulled down a dusty road. The light-haired man came forward and, sensing the approach, the pirate stopped and turned to face him.

"You there," called the man, "what do you mean by handling the lad in such a manner?"

The man was taller than the pirate captain, who looked up

at him and grinned. He kept his grip tight around my arm. "I'll do with him as I please."

"Are you his father? I fail to see any resemblance in his troubled face."

"Do you always meddle in the affairs of men more powerful than you? You, with your fancy clothes and golden locks."

The good man looked down at me. "Release him at once."

The pirate said nothing. He looked to his left and to his right, his right hand painfully clamped above my left elbow.

"Did you hear what I said, you foul vagrant? Release the boy."

"No one challenges me and moreover, no one insults me. It has been your fortune that I have stayed my blade for so long. Now, I'm afraid, your luck has run out."

With those words, he pulled his dreadful dagger. With a groan, the man doubled over and fell, his face slamming against the ground.

The pirate let out a hard laugh. He reached down, still clutching my arm, and rolled the body over. With ease, he withdrew the blade from his stomach. Blood rushed from the open wound.

He spoke coldly to me. "Check him."

I did not understand.

His jaw tensed. "A man lies before us dead. *You* have killed him. Now check him. Take whatever money he may have. Do as I say or this patch of road will be a grave for two."

The man had a small pouch on his belt. I took it off and handed it over. The pirate opened it and poured several silver coins into his hand.

"Not a bad prize. Come, we must make haste to the harbor."

I kept up and sent glances to no one.

We passed several saloons much like the one my father had taken me to. As we passed, drunken men often peered out the windows and came out to follow us. On we walked.

Soon we came to the harbor of Santiago. On the looming

hillside, I saw the smooth walls of Castillo del Morro, the newly built fort meant to protect the bay's entrance from people like my captor. Its stone walls, though armed with massive black culverins, looked like gold in the morning sunlight. The ocean spread out from it, blue and green with lapping white waves that sparkled like so many tiny diamonds. The pristine beauty of the sea enchanted me and brought back memories of my mother.

"There she waits," said the pirate, disturbing my trailing thoughts.

He pointed to the left, and resting off the coastline, anchored beyond the reefs of coral, was a three-masted ship larger than any I had ever seen.

"Behold my worthy ship *Obsidian*. She'll be your new home and the pride of all that you do. Serve her and you serve me."

The pirate captain led me down a sloping rocky hillside and over a narrow road leading to the water. His followers clambered down the stony trail. The harbor was enormous; a resting place for several boats and ships. As we passed smaller fishing ships, I watched men roll barrels of fish down the planking and onto the docks. One of the vessels was in the process of loading cargo. Muscular slaves struggled with large boxes and crates marked with the names of far away places like Grenada, Bonaire, and Puerto Bello. The merchant ship creaked as the heavy freight was hoisted aboard.

We stopped at a stretch of docking, moored to which were several long rowboats. His men filled three of the boats. We took our place in the center of the third; the pirate captain sat at my right and a dirty bald man worked the oar to my left. The rowboats swayed as the men heaved and pushed.

Soon the docks and harbor were far behind us. The blue sea rolled and rocked under our boat, gently lifting and lowering us with each passing wave. With every pull of the oars, we drew closer to the *Obsidian*.

Chapter 2

Welcome Aboard

The *Obsidian* loomed over me. Our rowboat drifted close to the sharp, towering bow and soon we passed under the twenty-foot bowsprit. The sprit was as thick as a fallen oak. It tapered away from the ship to become a terrible point.

The figurehead mounted to the massive beam was a wooden carving of a man's corpse, its wrists tied to the bowsprit and its feet nailed to the prow of the ship. His long tunic was torn from his shoulders and hung around his waist. The giant wooden corpse had lean muscular features, but his head hung lifelessly. Where his eyes should be were two gaping holes. As we passed under him I looked away, still seeing his distorted, reflected face in the moving water

The men rowed along the ship's starboard bow. The lofty masts scraped the sky and sent long shadows over the waves. The hull was clean and dark brown with a deep red line painted across its length.

The rowboats stopped parallel to the ship. The crew

onboard the *Obsidian* looked gaunt and sullied, like common thieves and beggars in ruined clothing. They tossed long rope ladders down to each boat. The pirates climbed up the swinging ladders and onto the ship. The last man off each tied two separate ropes to the rowboat; one on its bow and one on its stern, and tossed the free ends to the men on deck. The crew hoisted the empty boats from the water and secured them aboard the ship.

Tired, sore, and weak, I struggled to climb the rope ladder. The men shouted at me.

"Land legs troubling ya, boy?"

"Let the sharks have him, he's useless."

I slipped on the smooth wet decking, falling hard on my backside. The men laughed, jeered, and cursed at me.

When the captain spoke, the laughing stopped. "Be it known to all that this boy is here to serve our lady *Obsidian*. He knows naught of the tasks and customs. Be mindful of the shipboard articles of conduct you've signed. Now, where's the quartermaster?"

An older man with curly gray hair came forward. He wore a blue ruffled blouse with a black belt and black pants. He was barefoot like the others. His piercing green eyes studied me.

The captain released his grip on my bruised arm. "Ah, Christoff. Top of the morning."

"And the rest of the day to you, Captain."

"I'm entrusting Jacob to you. Get him accustomed to his new home. Assign him as you see fit."

"Indeed," replied Christoff. "Tell me, other than this boy, what provisions were you able to secure in Santiago?"

"The men have brought aboard new arms as well as fresh bread, meats, and fruit. There are two barrels of rum and a carton of cheese. I did not make a full invoice."

"Why not?"

"There was an unexpected turn of events. I killed a foolish would-be hero. He insulted me and tried to take the boy. You needn't worry, Christoff. There is enough to last, and should it turn out otherwise, I'll see to it that the stock be replenished. For now, take the boy and prep him to work under the boatswain."

"As you wish, Captain." Christoff turned to me. "Let's get you something to eat. You'll need your strength if you are to be of any use."

Christoff was the same height as his captain, six feet, perhaps. He had thick forearms and rigid shoulders. He walked with confidence. The men on deck nodded to him as we passed, and he greeted them with a wave. His bare feet were calloused and scarred, as were his hardened hands. His gray swirling hair looked like the smoke that used to billow upward from my father's cottage.

A lump of sadness filled my throat as I let my gaze wander over the sea to the island of Cuba. *My father is out there somewhere, walking around with a pouch of money. How could he abandon me? What did I do to dishonor him so?*

Christoff led me toward the ship's stern and down to a lower deck. When I smelled the food, my mouth watered. We entered a small room where a one-armed man salted a boiling stew. Two long wooden tables stretched out before me.

"Sit," ordered Christoff.

I obeyed and watched as he went to the cook's bubbling pot and scooped out a hearty portion of the stew with a wooden bowl. Christoff dropped a rusted spoon in the bowl and placed the meal before me. The stew was hot, foggy, and brown with chunks of meat, corn, peas, and cabbage swirling around. It smelled of ground pepper.

"Thank you, sir," I said.

Christoff nodded and sat across from me. He ran his fingers through his hair and rested his elbows on the table. "Eat. Captain Jean L'Ollon expects you to be strong."

I snatched the spoon and began to eat. The steaming broth ran down my throat. It was a good and comforting meal.

"Why was I taken from my father? Why did he agree to this?"

"Only your father knows why. Perhaps he was tired of caring for you."

My mother died shortly after giving birth to a lifeless infant. She had worried when the baby seldom kicked or squirmed. I recalled many times when she tried to tell my father, but he would not listen, refusing to believe her.

I always listened to her. I listened to the bedtime stories she told and the songs she sang as she combed her hair. I listened when she cried out as the quiet baby was pulled out of her.

So it was that I always understood. Every word she spoke meant something to me, but it was her dying words, her promise, that would mean the most.

"Are you a captain as well?" I asked him.

"No, lad. I am the quartermaster, second in command of this vessel. My role is to oversee the actions of the captain and fellow crewmates. I make sure there is order while at sea. I am the only crewmember the captain must consult with and only man aboard with authority to challenge his decisions. As much as L'Ollon prefers to keep his affairs private, I prefer to be in the know. What else do you want to know about your new life?"

I shook my head, afraid to ask all that I wondered about.

The quartermaster prompted me. "Go ahead, lad. You better ask me your questions than another who would beat you as soon as look at you."

I swallowed hard and asked, "Are the men aboard this ship slaves?"

"The men who work the *Obsidian* serve her by choice and proudly at that. Captain L'Ollon's crew consists of dangerous men, each capable of guiltless violence and unspeakable cruelty. With men like this, organization and respect is essential. I, the quartermaster, give this respect and in turn, I gain their trust. I am their spokesman, their representative to L'Ollon."

As Christoff spoke, I relaxed. "How did you get so much authority?"

"I was elected by the crew. You see, there are many positions that must be filled aboard any ship, lad. Captain, quartermaster, navigator, and boatswain are but a few. Some are voted upon, others are appointed by the captain. All crew members agree to a contract of rules and a code of conduct. As wicked as these men are, they have all sworn peace at sea and camaraderie; well, as much as can be expected.

"You are aboard the ship *Obsidian*. A grand ship, indeed. A three-masted barque fitted with twelve powerful cannon, the *Obsidian* has become known as one of the fastest and fiercest ladies on the water today. Captain L'Ollon has made it his life's work that his name be spoken with dread on every shore. We are proud to sail with him."

"How can you be proud of someone who can kill so easily?"

"Ah, you have a sharp tongue and much to learn, lad. You must first understand a man before you can pass judgment. Captain Jean L'Ollon is the grandson of the most ruthless pirate to ever set sail, Jacques Jean-David Nau, known throughout by his professional name, Francis L'Olonnais. Do you know anything of him?"

I shook my head.

"Well then, there's a yarn to be shared, but I've rambled on for too long. There's work to be done."

"What will become of me?" I had heard stories of how slaves were treated on distant lands, starved, beaten, chained and killed when no longer needed.

"You are the property of Captain Jean L'Ollon. He has ordered me to assign you as I see fit. You will work, lad. You'll begin your service among the cabin boys helping them clean the ship from deck to bilge. The cooper will teach you how to make barrels, and while doing so, you will answer to the boatswain. He is in charge of inventory and repairs. You will do all that you can to keep the hull free of rats and insects and you will frequently inspect the provisions, ensuring the quality. Perform these tasks without fail. Be it known, lad, the consequence for failure is dire. Do you understand?"

"Yes, sir."

"Good. Follow me."

Christoff led me down a narrow companionway to a lower deck. Light streamed in through iron grates overhead, but even so, the corridor was shadowy and dank. A heavy musk filled my nose and my bare feet splashed through cold puddles. The floorboards creaked.

I heard harsh arguing from pirates above. "Testing me patience again, heh?"

"Stay your dagger, mate. I won, right as rain! To the victor go the spoils."

"Take the prize and deal another hand before I cut yours off."

The ship pitched and yawed. At times I held the walls for stability. Christoff was surefooted and needed no assistance. His body moved with the subtle rocking while I wobbled and staggered behind.

We stopped at a wooden door. A deep voice barked and cursed, then I heard a slap and a thud.

"Damned scallywag!" Christoff kicked open the door. A boy lay on his side clutching his left ear. Thin streams of red trickled through his fingers. A greasy man with stringy brown hair recoiled as Christoff entered.

"What goes on that justifies such an outburst?" Christoff demanded.

The pirate did not answer. He looked down at the bleeding boy, then over at me. I froze under his dark eyes. I recognized him as one of the men who had pulled me from my father's side. He had carried me out of the tavern and thrown me in the alley.

"You can answer to me or you can answer to the captain," said Christoff. "Make your choice."

"The boy don't do what I tell him. I speak and speak but he listens to naught. Teaching him a lesson is all, sir."

"Is that so?" Christoff walked over to the boy, shoving the pirate as he passed. The man toppled backward and landed hard among a stack of empty barrels.

The others in the room made way for Christoff. They watched me, a few of them nodding a silent greeting.

"Easy now. Let me have a look." Christoff pulled the boy's left hand away from his swollen, bloody ear. Christoff touched it with his thumb. "You're from San Juan. Am I not mistaken?"

The boy did not respond. He cupped his wounded ear.

"Speak up, lad. I say you're from San Juan. Is that so?"

No response. Christoff hardened his jaw. "Answer me!"

"I am," the boy muttered incoherently in a slurred, flat voice. "I am deaf."

Christoff reached into one of his pouches and produced a small clean rag, which he folded and pressed to the bleeding ear. The boy bowed his thanks and backed away. A groan came from under the barrels.

"Strike the lad again and you'll answer to L'Ollon. Now all of you listen here," he said to the room of young men, "the lad in the doorway is named Jacob. Be fair to him, as you would have fairness in return." Christoff turned to me and said, "You'll do as the cooper instructs and as the boatswain commands. The cooper is the older of the lads, an experienced barrel maker, and the boatswain? Well, he is the one under the barrels."

Christoff made for the doorway, but before exiting, he turned and looked me square in the eyes. "Welcome aboard, lad."

Chapter 3

A Friend

The stale, salty air was tinged with body odor. Barrels of all sizes, some sealed and others broken, were stacked along the walls. Piles of wood scraps and metal bands lay on a large worktable. The cold floor was free of puddles.

A hand touched my shoulder, and I spun around. A young man stood before me. Behind him the other children gathered, the deaf boy among them.

"Good day, Jacob," said the young man, extending his hand for me to shake. "My name is Grant. I am the cooper, the barrel maker. Welcome aboard."

A man emerged from under the barrels with a groan. He rubbed his head and glared at us. Muttering, he left the room.

"That's Beelo. He's the boatswain, down here as punishment. No mates want to work the lower decks."

"What is a boatswain?"

"The boatswain looks after the stock and tends to the ropes, rigging, and equipment."

"What did he do wrong?"

"He got drunk a few months ago and insulted the captain. Captain L'Ollon commanded him to serve below deck, so the crew calls him 'Beelo.' Despite the conditions, we take care of each other down here."

I nodded. I guessed that Grant was two or three years older than me, fifteen, perhaps. He had a pale complexion with curly red hair that came just below his ears. He wore a patched gray shirt and tattered brown shorts. On his feet were crude but sturdy- looking wooden sandals. All the children here wore them.

"Your sandals," I said. "Where did you get them?"

He smiled and wiggled his toes. "I made them. Would you like a pair?"

"Yes, indeed."

Grant nodded to one of the boys among the crowd. The boy hurried to a barrel, opened the lid, and withdrew two wooden sandals. He tossed them to me.

I put them on at once. A soothing feeling overcame my entire lower half as I stood in my new sandals. No more cold floor. No more sharp splinters jabbing my toes.

"No worries. Come, there is work to do, and you must learn quickly." He pointed to a stack of wood on the large worktable. "A good barrel is tight and strong to hold food, drink, and powder. The captain wants the food barrels replaced every six months. Great care is needed when constructing a barrel. The stock must stay fresh and free of rats."

I nodded.

"Watch as we build. Ask questions if need be and then take up a hammer. Beelo will want you working when he comes back."

I watched them bend the metal ties and cut the boards to size. They pounded the bottoms with rusted mallets and soon had two new barrels. The finished barrels were cleaned and stacked, ready to mark and fill.

The boys sang a simple rhyme while they worked.
Hard at work, deep in the hull
A cooper's nail is never dull
Be it morn' or noon or night
The work will always be done right
And should the cap'n come he'd find
A brow of pride that drips with brine
Let's set sail and all will know
The food is fresh but the rum is low.

Their cheerful song reminded me of a celebration for my parents to honor my mother's pregnancy. I recalled the night clearly. There was dancing, music, singing, and roasted pig. The three of us danced and feasted all night. I laughed and sang and when it was over and the fires were nothing more than dwindling embers, we retired to our cozy house. I listened to my father tell stories of pirates and tribal clans, until my mother came in and warned him not to fill my head with frightening tales. They kissed me goodnight, and I slept warm and happy. I couldn't have imagined the betrayal that would befall me.

We spent the afternoon working the barrels and repackaging the provisions. Grant painted labels for each stocked barrel: fish, salt, meat, cheese, nuts, lime, hard-tack, rum, wine, and water.

We worked quickly to clean the room in time for the boatswain's return.

"Floggin' rats did good afta all," he said. "Keep it up and I may get me old job back and be rid of ya. Have suppa and be ya off to sleep. The morrow will be coming early and we'll be setting sail for Curacao."

I joined the other boys in picking food from the barrels. I took a hard-tack biscuit, two bananas, and a wedge of smoked cheese. I ate everything but the biscuit.

Grant laughed. "Hard-tack is a last resort, friend. You couldn't eat it without a pitcher of water to soak it in. It's as hard as a hammer's head."

As night fell, the chamber grew dark. Pale light from the upper deck poured in through the grates over the main passage. Grant handed out dusty gray blankets to the boys, who set their beds throughout the room. Grant tied my blanket around one of the pillars and then attached the other end to an iron spike that stuck out of the wall, making it into a crude hammock.

"The hammock is the most comfortable way to rest, but not the warmest. If you get cold, take it down and sleep on the floor."

"Thank you. You've been kind."

"We're all in this together. You'll get used to this life."

"That's hard to believe. I don't understand how men like Christoff and L'Ollon could want a life at sea."

"L'Ollon wrote the rules that he lives by, Jacob. That's what a seafarer loves about it."

I climbed into my crude hammock. "What do you know about Captain L'Ollon?"

Grant swung in his hammock with his arms folded behind his head. "Captain Jean L'Ollon is the grandson of Francis L'Olonnais."

"Christoff told me that Francis L'Olonnais was a ruthless pirate."

"Indeed. He was known throughout as 'the Flail of the Spaniards' because he targeted Spanish ships with unmatched cruelty. Francis L'Olonnais thought nothing of cutting off a man's head or tearing out his heart. And he was richer than you could imagine."

"Captain L'Ollon must be rich as well."

"Not anymore. Francis L'Olonnais was killed in 1668 by Darien Indians, and his fortune was lost. His son, Jacques L'Ollon, came forth years later to carry on the legacy. He made it his goal to slaughter the Darien Indians and reclaim his father's treasure.

"When he accomplished that, he built an impressive fleet of ships: the mighty galleon *Hydra,* the barque *Obsidian,* and the sloop *Cutlass*. Seamen from all corners of the world spoke of him. The son resembled the father so much that people said the wicked Francis L'Olonnais had returned from the grave."

One of the boys turned out the lantern, and the barrel room went dark. As my eyes adjusted, I made out small beams of moonlight shining through cracks in the floor overhead.

Grant lowered his voice. "Jacques L'Ollon fathered Jean. He taught him everything he knew and raised him to the malevolent family name. During Jean's eighteenth year, Jacques grew very ill and died. But not before he had signed his pirate empire over to his son. Jean loaded the inherited money, the entire family fortune, aboard his three ships."

"And where are the other two?"

"Well, from what I've heard in the pubs and markets, L'Ollon sailed with the trade winds and met a terrible storm. The *Hydra* and the *Cutlass* were bested and destroyed. Many men died, but Jean escaped with the *Obsidian*. The great fortune of his forefathers was lost at sea."

"How is that possible?"

One of the other boys called out, "Go to sleep before you earn us all a flogging."

Grant shifted in his hammock. "I'll tell you more another day."

The others snored and muttered while they dreamed. My mind was restless and my body ached. I felt the ship moving with the ocean. The entire room tilted to the left, then to the right. There was a constant creaking and the patter of pacing footsteps overhead. From time to time, I heard a cough somewhere in the distance and the faded fragments of conversations resonating through the ship.

There was never complete silence on the sea. I closed my eyes to see the small house my father built in the nameless village on the outskirts of Santiago. It consisted of shacks and hovels clustered around a common area packed with outdoor

Cerulean Isle

markets. A single road coursed through the center of our town. Travelers and peddlers passed through daily. Would I ever see my village again?

The ship swayed, and my hammock swung. Two warm tears rolled down my cheeks.

Chapter 4
Setting Sail

Grant roused me from my sleep. "Wake up, Jacob! You don't want to miss it."

"Miss what?" I rubbed my eyes and rolled out of my hammock.

"The hoisting of the riggings, the setting of the sails. The *Obsidian* is preparing to take wind."

He led me down the damp hallway, our sandals clopping as we hurried to parts of the ship I had not seen yet. Sunlight spilled through cracks in the deck and grains of sand and dust sprinkled down from passing feet.

We came to a ladder leading to a square hatch.

"Go up and lift the hatch. You can see the main deck and all that goes on. But don't let them catch you."

I nodded, swallowed my fear, and climbed the ladder. I pushed open the creaking hatch to a blazing morning sun that nearly blinded me.

The wide deck gleamed and seemed to stretch out

endlessly. In front of me loomed the powerful mainmast, like a tree sprouting from the center of the ship. Though it looked like one mammoth trunk, it was made of three separate beams fitted perfectly together. Four other wooden beams intersected its length at varying heights. These sturdy arms, the crosstrees, held the ropes and bundles of sail. I watched as men climbed these riggings to the tops of the swaying arms. They crawled out onto the limbs and let loose the heavy fabric that would catch wind.

Captain L'Ollon stood under the mainmast looking upward at the men. He wore a knee-length brown coat with bright gold buttons and wide square sleeves. His gray pants were tight on his legs, and he wore the same black boots. His pistol remained around his waist, as did his blade. The lengthy red scarf was tied over his head, the ends twirling in the wind.

"On my word," hollered the captain.

The men readied themselves.

"Main topgallant."

Near the top of the great mast, a wide white sail began to fall and flap in the wind. I could hear the rippling of the heavy fabric and the whipping of the lines.

"Make fast," L'Ollon called.

The sail tightened to a crisp yet billowing square as the men pulled and secured the rigging. The first of the sails was set.

"Top and studding sail," yelled L'Ollon.

From the second and third beams, four magnificent sails spread outward and fanned together.

"Make fast."

The men pulled the lines, drawing the corners of the sails tight to the crosstrees.

"Main course."

The largest of the mainsails opened. The white and slightly tattered sail was enormous. It took several men to ready the fighting fabric. The wind seemed to give it a life of its own as it writhed and resisted their efforts to keep it under control.

"Make fast the main course!"

Slowly, the great rippling sail was pulled into submission and the corners secured. The white sails bloomed, full of wind. The massive barque *Obsidian* began to move.

L'Ollon watched the sails flap against the bright morning sky. When his eyes fixed on me, I recoiled and closed the hatch, hurrying down the rungs of the ladder.

Grant waited below. "No going back now. We're off to the island of Curacao. Come on, we'd better get back to our quarters before Beelo comes around."

Once back in the barrel room, we each took a broom and began to sweep. I asked Grant where he came from, how he came to be here.

"I was born in Nassau on the island of New Providence, north of Cuba, a wild and lawless port town. My family cared naught for me. I left them when I was ten and took to thieving. I was cunning, patient, and no one suspected a mere child.

"One day, not too long ago, I stole a loaf of bread from a docked merchant vessel and went to the beach to eat. I saw a mysterious and wealthy-looking ship in the distance. Its three masts were strong and tall, the white sails blooming like clouds, and as it drew near, I saw the figurehead of the corpse dangling from the bowsprit. I knew there was only one ship with a figurehead like that—one ship, one crew and one captain that everyone spoke of in whispers. It was the *Obsidian,* the last of the great L'Ollon's fleet. I felt drawn to it. I waited until it furled its sails and entered the harbor. You see, Jean L'Ollon and his never-ending quest is known by all, and I—"

"What quest?" I asked suddenly.

"You don't know the story?" asked Grant, eyes wide with surprise.

I shook my head.

"Well, then. I'll tell you tonight when the others sleep. For now, let me just say that when I saw his ship coming, I knew I wanted to join his crew. L'Ollon's shipboard articles guarantee the best pay, not to mention the glory of being a part of the toughest crew on the Caribbean."

"How did you get Captain L'Ollon to take you aboard?"

"It was Master Christoff who brought me. I followed a few of L'Ollon's men around town and into a pub. I watched them. I saw an older man talking to a woman. This man had a huge pouch tied to his belt. Being a thief, I could not resist. I approached and attempted to make my move, but the man twirled around with a finesse I had never seen, and the next thing I knew, a sharp knife was pressed to my throat.

"'Do you know who I am, lad?' he asked me. 'I am the *Obsidian's* quartermaster. You've made a big mistake, but you're young and foolish. I will give you a choice.' His knife cut me only a little. 'Take my money and run as fast as you can, and we'll see if you can elude my flying dagger, or you can put your sticky fingers to use. Captain L'Ollon could use a bold scrap like you. Make your choice quickly, lad. My knife knows no patience.'

"I agreed to go with him and here I am. I am just a servant, but I was given the title cooper. I hope to one day become a fully articled crewmember, a pirate of the *Obsidian*."

Grant leaned on the shaft of the broom. With a flick of the wrist, he twirled the broom up and around, holding it aloft like a sword. He lunged in attack, then spun to deflect another imaginary attacker. The boys laughed. Grant turned and thrust once more, the tip of the broom handle smashing against a barrel. The wooden handle snapped in two. He shrugged and tossed the broken broom aside.

"That's enough sweeping for one day," he said. "Come, let's have something to drink." Grant lifted the lid of a water barrel and scooped two cups. He handed one to me and we sat down at a workbench.

"What do you mean by *articled* crew member?" I asked.

"Jacob, you have much to learn," he chuckled. "All pirate

crews sail the seas working as a team, a family. There are written rules that everyone agrees to and obeys. This document is known as the Shipboard Articles. The Articles define the many jobs and rules pertaining to them. Pensions, earnings, and shares of loot are defined therein to insure fairness. All along the edges of the document you will find the signatures of every man aboard, even Captain L'Ollon."

"Along the edges?"

"Indeed. No man signs above any name, thus no man may be deemed more important. I hope to sign my name one day, and then I won't have to steal. I'll be guaranteed a monthly stipend as well as a fair share of every prize."

"You work hard down here. You have a title and everything. You mean to say that you are not paid for your labor?"

"No pay, Jacob. But ah, no worries! Food, shelter, and the protection of the crew are the reimbursement for my services. This is true for you, too. Only crewmates get the reales."

"If we are so protected, why did the boatswain hurt the deaf boy?"

"This is not an easy life. We are servants here among vile men. Captain L'Ollon seeks three things when recruiting crewmates: health, character, and skill. He looks for men with an edge, a temper, an aggression that will flame in battle—a true fearlessness of death. A good captain looks to recruit musicians, cooks, surgeons, carpenters, swordsmen, marksmen. Most importantly, experienced sailors. I was brought aboard because I am a talented thief. Though assigned as a barrel maker, I am sure they have other plans for me."

Hours passed. The ship rocked and bobbed over the water. I imagined the *Obsidian* gliding over the waves, rising and falling, pitching and yawing. It brought to mind the memory of my mother's coffin being sent to sea.

The flower-laden box drifted out of sight as the sun rose over us. My father fell to his knees on the muddy shoreline, his eyes red and his face sunken and tired.

I did not cry that morning. My mother's promise gave me strength. I spent the hours before her death at her bedside, and when it was only her and I, she said, "My son, in my heart I know this is the last time I will look upon your handsome face. No longer does your brother stir in my belly. He is asleep, you see. He will never wake. He is making me sleepy, too, and when I close my eyes I will not open them again. Before I rest, son, I want you to hear me and remember my words."

"I hear you, Mother. I'm listening."

"I promise that I will watch over you always. I will be the sunlight that warms and the wind that cools. I will be the rustle of leaves and the stir of the sea. Feel these things through all of your days and know I am with you. You will have my love so that you may overcome even the hardest of times. I promise to protect you from harm and Death itself."

"We are moving slow," said Grant, his voice pulling me from my memory's grip. "Sailing southbound, slightly against the wind. The trade winds come from the east and sweep northwest into the Caribbean Sea. Merchants do all they can to plan routes with the wind. It makes for a faster voyage. A voyage with an eastern or southern destination takes much longer, since a crew must cut angular courses southbound rather than a direct line. That's what the *Obsidian* has been doing."

"You will make a fine seaman, Grant, if not an expert barrel maker."

I tried to understand Grant's ambition to sail under L'Ollon and wondered what the captain was searching for. What could have taken down his fleet? A simple storm could not sink two strong ships manned by such an experienced crew, nor could it kill so many seamen.

Chapter 5

The Quest

It was hard to breathe in the dark barrel hold. The entire room swayed, and I could hear the cargo shifting. The beams creaked and popped as if the ship would cave in at any moment. I could not sleep in my makeshift hammock and tried to find comfort on the damp wooden floor. A rhythmical clashing filled the corridor and rumbled my ears as the ocean waves broke over the body of the *Obsidian*. In the lower quarters, its tempo was like a sleepy song.

"Jacob." Grant's voice startled me. "Are you asleep?"

"No. Tell me about L'Ollon and his quest. I have been waiting all day."

"All right, but don't ever tell anyone that I told you this. Agreed?"

"Agreed."

"Good. Where did I leave off? Oh yes. Captain L'Ollon lost his fleet, all but the *Obsidian*. His entire fortune was aboard when the storm fell around them. L'Ollon knew better than to make it known that he was sailing with such riches. Other pirate fleets would have certainly attacked. Before he set sail, he told only one other pirate of his plans, a man named Captain James Shanley. L'Ollon trusted Shanley and paid him a heavy purse to ensure L'Ollon's route be left clear. James Shanley is quite powerful, you see, and he agreed to keep L'Ollon's wake free of rival pirates.

"L'Ollon, entrusting the safety and secrecy of his voyage to Shanley, left the harbor of Curacao. L'Ollon plotted a northern course; where to exactly, I do not know. He sailed fast, and five days out, the storm hit. All good captains know to furl the sails and batten down in a heavy storm. He did so, and held his ships steady over the raging water. The waves roared with the wind. The sails, though hoisted and furled, flapped and beat against the great masts. But the explosion of sudden gunfire made L'Ollon take arms and race across the deck. Near the starboard bow stood one of his crew, pistol in hand and rambling in panic. Two other men stood nearby, each with readied guns.

"'What is the meaning of this?' cried L'Ollon. 'Have you gone mad?'

"The crew members were frightened. They pointed overboard at the dark waves. L'Ollon looked over the edge of the ship but saw nothing.

"'What are you firing at? Speak up!'

"Then one of the men yelled in terror and pointed out at the churning sea. 'There, Captain. Heaven help us!'

"L'Ollon peered out across the swirling black water and saw a large gray fin crest upward and then slip silently under the waves.

"'You fools, we be in the midst of a storm and you waste shots on dolphins.'

"'Nay, Captain. The devil himself has taken fin,' ranted the fear-stricken pirate. His pistol trembled in his wet hand.

"L'Ollon was angered by his crewmate's reckless behavior.

He struck the man in the face. The pirate wobbled backward from the blow and stumbled over the edge of the ship, falling into the furious water. L'Ollon looked down at him.

"'Say hello to the devil for me, matey! Ask him for one of his fins, why don't ya?'

"To the captain's shock, the man was pulled under the water. A blast of bubbles followed by a cloud of crimson bled in the waves like dreadful red ink. L'Ollon readied his pistol and watched as a figure took form and emerged. A man appeared in the water. He had smooth, leathery skin and long hair that clung to his neck and shoulders. L'Ollon looked down at the stranger in the waves. He seemed to float effortlessly. He did not flail his arms in fear of sinking, his solid chest did not heave with gasping breaths. He was a part of the water, and as he looked up at L'Ollon, his shadowy eyes glimmered as if filled with starlight. L'Ollon raised his pistol but the man in the waves leapt from the water. His body was not all human, and when L'Ollon saw the fishlike lower half, he dropped his pistol overboard.

"Yes, Jacob, I tell you that the man from the water was not a man at all. A magnificent fin bloomed where legs should have been; a fin much larger than that of a dolphin. It was the Water People. L'Ollon saw them with his own eyes."

"My father used to tell me stories of the Water People. I never gave them much thought. After all, I've never seen a Water Person."

"You wouldn't. However, that is not to say that one has not seen you."

"I've heard the Water People are a peaceful race."

"I've heard other yarns. Some say they're wicked and unforgiving, that if a ship sails into their territory, nothing will save them from their wrath."

"And just where did you hear such stories? How did you come to know L'Ollon's tale in such detail?"

"I was a thief, Jacob. I spent many days at the markets

and waterfront picking pockets and eavesdropping. Gathering information is a basic survival skill. People talk, and many times too loud."

"Have you ever seen a Water Person, Grant?"

"No. However, if L'Ollon succeeds, maybe we will before our adventure is over."

Grant yawned. He rolled onto his back and tucked his hands behind his head. "I'll tell you the rest another time. Get some sleep, friend, and have no worries. The morrow comes early."

Chapter 6

Swordplay

The *Obsidian* held true to its course. From our chamber below deck, we heard the many conversations of the crew above. On our fifth day at sea, I heard one man tell another that six days remained until we reached Curacao. Our destination was the harbor at the town of Willemstad.

Willemstad was a Dutch-built settlement where one could buy anything for a cheap price. Grant told me it had been one of Captain L'Ollon's favorite places. Now it was the territory of Captain James Shanley. The men spoke of their apprehensions in confronting such a formidable opponent, yet they were eager to best Shanley and his men. A victory would guarantee L'Ollon's pirates a heavy stipend of the reclaimed L'Ollon fortune.

"Gold and silver is the root of piracy," Grant told me. "No man risks his life for free."

We worked hard at the barrel making and kept up with inspecting the provisions. The boatswain made his rounds and took inventory often. He checked every barrel and ordered us to store them in the appropriate holds. When the barrel making was complete, Beelo tasked us with sharpening knives and blades, supervising us with a loaded pistol while we handled the weapons.

I learned the careful practice of refinishing a sword. Holding the edge of the blade at the correct angle against the grinding wheel was awkward at first, but I mastered it. Sparks of bright yellow streamed from the stone wheel and dissolved on the damp, wooden floor. When I finished a blade, I examined its sharp edge. I liked the way the short swords, cutlasses, and foreign scimitars felt in my hand—balanced and light. When I tossed a sharpened sword into the pile of readied blades, they clanked and chimed like deadly bells.

Beelo sat in a chair in the corner of the room, drinking from the barrel of wine. After several mugs, he wobbled over to me.

"Say," he said, "have ya ever wielded a sword?"

I shook my head, afraid to antagonize him.

"Well, see here, boy!" Beelo grabbed a sharp sword from the pile and held it aloft. He looked at the clean blade and smiled. "It'll be your death if ya never learn." He belched loudly and shook his head. The ship swayed and he staggered to regain his balance. "Now," he went on, "pistols are nice and all, don't misunderstand, but this here sword is quiet in the killing. She never runs out of shot 'cause she don't have any. No reloading, to be sure. Just a steady slice, and a man will fall. No one has to hear nothing. Stand up, boy."

I obeyed. He handed me the sword.

"Hold it in front of ya with the right hand. That's it. Keep your elbow bent and knees loose. Right leg forward, yes, that's it. Left hand ready and relaxed; keep them eyes looking at me. For the sake of the lesson, I'll be the man—" another rancid belch escaped him, "—that wants to kill ya."

Beelo picked up another sharp blade, larger than the one

I held. "Now, then," he said in slurred voice, "when a man lunges forward, ya be having two choices. Ya gets out of the flogging way, or meet his moving blade with yours and force it away. Understand?"

I nodded. My mouth was dry and sweat beaded on my forehead.

He lunged at me. I was hardly prepared. His shimmering blade shot forward like an arrow. I sidestepped at the last moment; the tip of his sword tore through my dirty shirt, missing my stomach by less than an inch. My quickness surprised the boatswain, who chuckled as he pulled the piece of cloth off the sword tip.

"Not bad at all, boy. On to the slash. Since I want to kill ya, pretending of course, I will try to swing my blade across your body, hopefully spilling your insides. When I try this…ya listening, boy? Ya look a little sick."

"I— I'm listening, sir." My hand grew numb from clutching the handle so tightly. My legs wobbled, and the sweat stung my eyes.

"Right, then, as I was saying, when I slash at ya, you should stop my attack with your readied blade. Block it, I say. It'll take some strength but you seem fit enough. Block my attack if there not be enough room to get out of the way. Ready then?"

I nodded.

Beelo's attack came quicker than the one before. His swing was wide and swift, and I seemed to see it all in a dreamy slow daze. I heard the blade cutting the air as it swooped toward me. The sword grew larger as it closed in on me. I could not block such a strong attack, knowing there wasn't room enough to jump back and out of the way. I ducked as low as I could, feeling the cold wind of the unforgiving sword blow over my head.

The momentum of his swing carried his unstable drunken body forward, and he landed hard on the ground. He hurried to his feet, confused. Still crouching as low as possible, I looked up at him. His face filled with anger. I had embarrassed him in front of the others. This was no longer a lesson in swordplay.

Beelo growled. Strands of his oily hair fell over his face. He lifted his sword, the sword I had sharpened to perfection, high over his head. He charged forth, leaving me seconds to decide what to do. The sword came swinging downward; my only escape was to roll out of the way. I heard the blade slam and stick into the floor. Beelo growled again and tore the sword free. I scrambled to my feet, short sword in hand, and readied myself as he had shown me for his next attack.

A terrible, empowering anger overcame me. My grip on the handle loosened enough for the warm blood to flow back into my fingers. I felt the swaying floor under me, and I let myself move with its rhythm. My shoulders were at ease as I stared at my attacker with teeth clenched and sword pointed forward. I was ready for him and ready for my death. The pirate lunged at me with deadly precision.

I saw his attack coming. When his tip streaked forward, I moved to the right and slammed my blade hard on top of his. I forced his attacking sword to the ground. The blades clanged loudly, a song to my ears. I pinned Beelo's sword to the floor with my left foot and pressed my blade tip to his throat.

The drunken pirate looked pleadingly into my furious, hateful eyes. He didn't know what had happened. I wanted to kill him for how he had hoisted me from the tavern, tearing me away from my father. I hated him with my first real taste of bitter rage and sword-wrought power. I imagined thrusting forward with my sword and feeling the spray of his blood.

Instead, I turned my sword around and struck him in the face with the pommel. His eyes crossed and blood streamed from his nose. The impact of my strike made him fall backward. As he landed, I saw a steel blade break through his chest. Behind him sat the deaf boy, eyes wide from the horror of the accident, the sword handle he clutched dripping with Beelo's blood. A gasp erupted from the boatswain, followed by a series of choking gurgles. Beelo reached up and touched the blade that protruded from his breast.

Beelo looked at me with clear eyes. "Ya see, boy, quiet in the killing. No one has to hear nothing." His head fell to the side, the face pale and lifeless. His dead eyes seemed to peer into my frightened soul.

All was silent except for the constant creaking of the ship and the sloshing of the waves. The deaf boy released his grip on the fatal sword and moved out from behind the boatswain. Beelo's body crumpled to the floor. A steady stream of blood seeped from his mouth and pooled around his face.

The boy began to cry. His hands dripped blood, and he tried to wipe them clean on his shirt.

Grant turned to me. "Listen, Jacob, we're in a lot of trouble now. You have just defeated one of L'Ollon's best swordsmen."

He and the others dragged the corpse to the side of the room and covered it with a blanket. They left the blade in because if they removed it, more blood would flow. They mopped the floor and tried to get back to work. It wouldn't be long before someone came down to our quarters looking for the boatswain.

Chapter 7
The Chart and the Book

No one could concentrate with a dead body so near. Everyone left me alone. I sat atop an empty barrel in the far corner of the room. It was past noon. The sun would be bright and hot overhead. The heat of the day fell through the cracks in the floorboards. Beelo's body began to smell.

My heart raced each time footfalls rumbled the deck. I couldn't help but watch the doorway, expecting an enraged group of pirates to storm in, blades drawn and pistols in hand.

Grant busied himself with a broom. He swept the room, humming softly, but I could see his fear. His face was pale and beads of nervous sweat trickled down his brow. He looked over at me, then continued sweeping.

My hands began to shake as I recalled every second of the fight. The pile of swords on the workbench gleamed as if silently calling to me. Despite the horror of Beelo's drunken game, the sword gave me bravery and evened the odds.

I stood up, planning to take up another blade for protection, when a barrel streaked across the room. It shattered, spilling its contents of lemons and limes about the floor. Captain Jean L'Ollon, Quartermaster Christoff, and another pirate stood in the doorway.

L'Ollon's coat was as brown as the wooden floor, and his heavy boots clopped like the shoes of a horse. Kneeling down, he pulled back the blanket and held his hand over Beelo's bloody mouth. He turned to Christoff. "No breath. He is dead."

L'Ollon approached Grant, his left hand resting on the pommel of his long dagger. "Speak, Cooper. What treachery has come to pass?"

Grant's eyes met mine, a grave mistake. L'Ollon struck him hard. Grant staggered back but did not fall. Regaining his posture, he looked squarely into L'Ollon's eyes. A thread of blood trickled from his nose.

"We were tasked with sharpening the swords, Captain. The boatswain took to the wine. He engaged young Jacob in a round of swordplay but was enraged when he could not win. He attacked Jacob with the intent to kill but fell backward, landing atop a blade the deaf boy was refinishing. It was a terrible accident, Captain."

L'Ollon looked around the room and found the deaf boy cowering in fear, traces of blood still on his hands. The captain turned to Christoff.

"Christoff, bring Grant and Jacob to the office at once. I will deal with them in private."

"And what of Beelo, sir?" asked the other pirate in the doorway.

"Wrap the mate in clean linen and give him to the sea. Take the sword out of him. I don't want to lose a sharp blade. As for the deaf boy, clean him up and lock him in the cage. Leave him there till we reach Curacao."

"Aye, Captain."

"There's not enough work to keep you rats busy," said L'Ollon. "Swordplay and murder, eh? Is that the way of it here in the barrel room? Henceforth, the provisions will be checked four times daily. I want twenty new barrels made before dawn and if this is not done, I will kill every last one of you."

The captain left and the sound of his angry cursing echoed in our ears.

The quartermaster said, "Grant, how could you let this happen?"

Grant said nothing. Christoff glanced over his shoulder at the corpse. The other pirate tugged on the sword protruding from Beelo's body.

"Beelo was our finest swordsmen." Christoff looked at me. "How be it you bested him with a blade? Beelo was fast, ruthless, even with the wine in him. Come you two, and may God help you."

Christoff led Grant and me through the damp, dim corridor to a narrow companionway. These stairs took us up to the main deck. The sun was warm on my face and the fresh wind smelled of sea salt. As we followed Christoff, the other pirates stared. Did they know their boatswain was dead?

There were pirates everywhere. The three masts stretched overhead and men clung to the crosstrees. They climbed the rope ladders and swung down from the lines with incredible finesse. Others worked vigorously with mops and buckets while their shipmates coiled extra line around thick wooden cleats. The sails took the wind and moved the barque swiftly over the sapphire water. The brilliant sun was white-yellow and its endless light set fire to the tips of the waves. The Caribbean Sea glittered around us like a jagged and living crystal creature. I wanted to stop and take a deep breath, feel the sunlight on my face, and pray to my mother one last time.

We made our way toward the stern and through two large wooden doors that led to the crew cabins. A short corridor stretched ahead of us with four rooms on each side, making eight small resting quarters. At the end of the corridor, we stopped at the last room on the left. Christoff opened the door and motioned us to enter.

Several lanterns lit the room. The thick red carpet gave a fiery contrast to the brown, wooden walls. Swords and pistols hung from brass hooks. Sturdy shelves crowded with dusty books were nailed to the walls. A large table dressed in clean linen was set with fresh bread, fruits, vegetables, and wine.

Captain L'Ollon sat behind a desk opposite the table. He was scratching some words on a parchment with a tattered quill. When we entered, he paused from his writing and stared at us coldly. The desk was adorned with stacks of parchment, candles, inkwells, and maps. A faded blue sea chart hung off the edge of the desk, and I could see fine lines, words, and numbers scribbled all over it.

"Come closer, boys," L'Ollon ordered. "Christoff, close the door."

Grant and I approached the captain's desk as his eyes remained fixed on us.

"You have aided in the committing of an irrevocable crime aboard my ship. The penalty, under my articles, is death."

A small part of me welcomed the thought. At least I would be with my mother again.

L'Ollon stood and took a sword off the wall. It gleamed dreadfully in the yellow glow of the lanterns.

"Listen to me, you ungrateful galley rats," he said. "Your deaf friend will spend a few nights in the cage—a cold iron cell in the bowels of the *Obsidian*. Under normal circumstances I would have him gutted for his deeds, but he's the leverage in my plan. Now you two are leverage as well." The sword glimmered and flashed as L'Ollon paced about the room. "I shall offer you a choice. You can either do as I instruct henceforth, or die by my blade."

Grant looked squarely at L'Ollon. "We will serve you, Captain, loyally and without fail."

L'Ollon smiled at me. His rotted teeth looked like kernels of corn caked with soil. "It seems that there is more to you than I thought. A real bargain. I should thank your father next time I dock in Santiago. Tell me, where did you learn to wield a sword?"

"With the boatswain was my first time, Captain."

His rancid breath puffed in my face. "Well, your talent will be put to the test in due time. As for you, Cooper Grant, your thieving days have just begun. Sit, I shall tell you what lies ahead." Captain L'Ollon pointed to a small bench not far from the desk.

We sat down. I watched his sword. Christoff sat in a plush chair near the doorway. He reached for a nearby carafe of ale and poured some into a silver mug. He relaxed in the chair with his drink and listened intently as L'Ollon spoke.

"We make for the island of Curacao. We will dock in Willemstad. That town is home to a fellow pirate, Captain Shanley. He is a floggin' traitor and a lying, backstabbing thief." A deep distance formed in his eyes. His brow dipped in anger and his lower lip curled. He was remembering something, and Grant and I knew what.

"You see, a few years ago, he and I arranged a deal. I paid him a heap of gold and gave him a copy of my sea chart; he was to keep my voyage free of followers. Not long after I set sail, my fleet met a terrible storm. I lost my fleet in that tempest." L'Ollon looked away and set his gaze toward the window. Deep in thought, he looked out at the rolling waves. "The *Obsidian* is all I have left."

I watched L'Ollon stare out the window. *Are the Water People out there, somewhere in that beautiful blue water, following, watching, and listening?*

"My gold fell to the bottom of the sea, and it was Shanley who set out to comb the ocean floor. He still has my sea chart. I need it so I can return to the place of my ruin. Curse that galley-rat. He has made several voyages and has recovered much of my fortune. It is my gold that he spends. My father's gold. My grandfather's gold!" He slammed his fists on the desk.

"I will get that chart and reclaim the empire built by my forefathers. Shanley will pay with his blood, and once in Curacao, we will not leave until he is dead and his ill-gotten fleet destroyed."

The sunlight spilled through the window, creating a bright red square on the carpet. L'Ollon stepped into the sunbeam, his black boots shining like wet coal.

"The two of you will play a critical role in my game. Willemstad is riddled with Shanley's crew. I will send Christoff into town, as Shanley's men do not know him. You two will go with Christoff to Shanley's guarded villa. Christoff will pretend that he is interested in purchasing one of Shanley's smaller ships, a sloop. While he deals with the rat, you, Grant, will sneak into the villa through the rear entrance. Your orders are to steal the chart bearing my signature. Do not be discovered. Jacob will be with you throughout and if you are seen, he will utilize his new-found talent in swordplay with orders to kill."

"I don't understand, Captain," I uttered.

L'Ollon loomed over me. Strands of oily black hair fell into his face. "I will give you a sword, Jacob. You will protect Grant's life. You will kill anyone who hinders the success of your mission. Just remember what you learned in Santiago when that man tried to take you from me. Remember what you did to Beelo." He smirked. "Death just seems to follow you, doesn't it, lad?" He stepped away from me and motioned for Christoff.

"Once you have stolen the sea chart," Christoff began, "make for the harbor. I will lead Shanley there. He will think he is about to make a grand sale, but *Obsidian's* crew will be there to capture him and bring him aboard. He will answer to Captain L'Ollon for his crimes."

L'Ollon threw his heavy sword across the room. The tip of the blade stuck into the wooden wall. The pommel wobbled from side to side.

"There is time yet," he said, now sitting on the edge of the desk. "Four days, to be precise. I want you both to work the main deck until we reach Curacao, so I can keep an eye on you. Once land is on the horizon, I will provide you with fresh clothing and the necessary tools to help you accomplish the mission. Now I ask only once, do you have any questions?"

"When the job is over, Captain, what of Jacob and I?" asked Grant.

L'Ollon's brow arched. He stepped close to Grant and peered down at him. Strands of his black hair sprouted from under the red scarf and dangled over his eyes. "Are you asking, Cooper, for a reward? You want a share of the gold, do you?"

"I desire no gold, Captain."

"Then what, in the wrath of Neptune, do you ask?"

"To sign, Captain. I want to be official on board this great ship. I desire to be an articled crewmember. That is all I ask."

I could not understand Grant's passion for the pirate life. Why would Grant desire to serve the ruthless L'Ollon? I wanted freedom. I wanted off the *Obsidian* and to be rid of Jean L'Ollon forever. I imagined asking for that. I envisioned myself standing tall and proud as Grant and asking the vicious pirate to let me go.

"I'll tell you what, Cooper," said L'Ollon. "There is something else I want. If you can steal this item along with my sea chart, the shipboard articles will be spread out before you and you can sign your worthless name with my quill. How does that sound?"

"Excellent, Captain. What more shall I obtain for you?"

"A book, young cooper."

"A book, sir?"

"Yes. In the private quarters of his villa, you will find a small library. Among the dusty tomes waits a book, small and crudely bound in sun-bleached brown leather. It is tied with a dark blue ribbon. Shanley has this book. I want it. You must get it but do not open it."

L'Ollon walked over to the window. The sunlight shone on his face as he stared out at the endless water. His left hand fell on the handle of his pistol. Silence filled the cabin and several long minutes passed. The ship creaked as it swam over the waves.

"Christoff," said L'Ollon suddenly, "set them to work on the main deck. Instruct them as you see fit. Teach them anything you desire. As for the deaf one, leave him in the cage until we reach land. No food, only water."

"Understood, Captain. Come along, lads."

Chapter 8

Young Pirates

So it was that Grant and I began our work on the main deck among the crew.

Christoff showed us many things over the next several days and instructed the other pirates to share their knowledge when needed. There was excitement in Grant's eyes as he worked alongside the pirates. Every chore he was given, he performed with a smile and hardly took time to rest. The other pirates liked his eagerness and energy. They took full advantage of him, using him to lighten their loads.

I did what I was told. My life depended on it. Captain L'Ollon made his rounds and often stood on the forecastle looking down at the working crew. I could feel his eyes watching me. My misery was obvious, and he reveled in making matters worse.

During midday, the Caribbean sun always shines the hottest. L'Ollon commented, "You look overheated, Jacob."

I nodded, not sure how to respond.

"Give me your shirt, then. You'll feel better with the spray of the sea on your back."

I obeyed and handed him the garment. The edge of his mouth curled to a devilish half grin. He left me to my work without saying another word.

At first, I did feel better. The cool spray of the waves was refreshing, but it wasn't long before I realized that I had been made a fool. I suffered terrible burns on my back and neck. The skin on my back cracked and bled.

Apart from the maltreatment, I continued to work as hard as I could. I found that if I focused on the labor, I forgot my woes, if only for a little while. Though terrified, I climbed the highest rigging to the top of the mainmast to check the condition of the lines. I handled buckets of volatile gunpowder, served the pirates their food and drink, and held watch over the sea so the ship's navigator could take a few moments rest.

After several days of working the main deck, I grew fond of the sounds of beating lines and flapping sails. The pull of the wind, the rolling of the water, the moonlight casting a web of shadows on the deck—I enjoyed this part of life on the sea.

In the few fleeting moments I was permitted to rest and eat, I went to the starboard bow to look out over the beautiful azure sea. The tips and swirls of the dancing waves sparkled like my mother's eyes. In my heart I could hear her last words to me: *I promise that I will watch over you always. I will be the sunlight that warms and the wind that cools. I will be the rustle of leaves and the stir of the sea. Feel these things through all of your days and know I am with you.* Remembering her comforted me. I pressed on with strength.

~~~~~

"This isn't so bad, Jacob," Grant said.

We were down in the barrel hold helping the others check the food and other provisions. The stock was dangerously low.

"Better than being thrown overboard, I suppose." I

answered. "I like not being confined to the barrel room, but I don't share your allure of the pirates' life."

"For many years, I picked pockets to survive. I lived alone, and when I lost my way, there was no one there to help me. I dreamt of sailing, dreamt of being free. This is it, my friend. The *Obsidian* can go anywhere."

"Your devotion will not be rewarded. You'll see. L'Ollon means to use us and then we're dead. If not for his plans in Curacao, we would be dead right now."

"When we get there, we'll see how…" he paused, and then tensed. "Today is the day, Jacob. We should be entering Willemstad Harbor this afternoon."

Grant and I stared at each other, suddenly frightened. A part of me wished we had another week to sail, another week of working the main deck instead of committing thievery with the possibility of being killed at any moment.

"Aye," said a deep voice from behind us. Christoff looked imperial in his fine russet blouse and shiny black boots. His leather belt held a magnificent cutlass enclosed in a gold trimmed scabbard. On his fingers he wore dazzling jeweled rings that sent beams of color dancing on the walls. He needed to impress Captain Shanley, to convince him that he was a wealthy seaman interested in purchasing a ship. He looked the part as he stood in the lantern light of the barrel room.

"Come with me," said Christoff. "Captain L'Ollon wants you cleaned up and readied for land."

We went to the main deck where the crew was hard at work furling the sails. At dizzying heights, the pirates dangled from taut lines and swaying beams. They hollered and grunted as they hoisted the heavy, wind-catching fabric to long bulging rolls. As the sails were raised, I felt the *Obsidian* slow. Soon, the three great masts looked like naked trees, and the pace of the mighty barque was reduced to a drift. I looked over the starboard side and saw Curacao resting on the horizon. The island looked long and flat; we were close enough that I could make out the pointy roofs and colorful paint of the Dutch-built homes.

We followed Christoff to a small storeroom. He opened a long wooden chest to reveal bundles of clean clothes. Christoff drew out two clean, white linen shirts and handed them to us. Next, he gave each of us a thick black belt, a pair of soft leather shoes, and light brown pants made from soft dyed cotton.

"Dress," he said. "Forget your tattered garments. These clothes are yours to keep."

The pants were soft on my tired legs and the linen was cool on my burned back. The shoes fit perfectly. The soles cushioned my footfalls.

"Ah, an improvement to be sure, lads! Now follow me, Captain L'Ollon awaits us. You'll be given your orders one last time."

We found Captain L'Ollon standing tall at the bow in his knee-length brown coat and red scarf. He was peering out at the island through a small collapsible spyglass. When he heard us approach, he closed the glass and put it in his pocket.

"Yonder waits Curacao," began L'Ollon, "and in its midst is Captain James Shanley. He owns several ships, all of which are docked in the wharf. Shanley only sails two of them these days: his new brigantine *Kraken's Bane* and the schooner *Eternity*. There are four other ships in the harbor belonging to him; two sloops, another schooner, and a fishing boat. These vessels are for sale.

"Christoff will take you to the island in a rowboat; I don't want anyone to know you have come from my ship. The *Obsidian* will approach the harbor an hour after you have made it to land. Once in the town, you will go with Christoff to Shanley's villa." L'Ollon reached in the left pocket of his coat and took out a bundle of thin, metal strips. He handed them to Grant. "You will use these tools to assist in accomplishing this mission."

"Lock picks," exclaimed Grant in awe.

"When Christoff leads Shanley away, use them to enter the villa and private quarters. Retrieve my sea chart and the leather book, and then make for the harbor immediately. Christoff will turn on Shanley and take him aboard the *Obsidian* where the bastard will suffer for his betrayal. And as for you—" He pulled the long curved dagger from his belt. He turned the blade away and handed me the hilt. "Take my blade. May it serve you well, young swordsman, but if you fail, this steel will be your death."

With a trembling hand, I accepted the heavy weapon. I realized it was more than a long dagger; it was a short sword. I tucked it in the left side of my belt. L'Ollon reached in his pocket again and withdrew a bulging coin purse, reminding me of the brown pouch my father weighed in his hand. My left hand tightened on the handle of the blade.

He tossed the pouch to Christoff. "Enough gold to buy the larger of the sloops should Shanley want proof of payment. Don't give him so much as a reale. Bring back Shanley, and that purse is yours."

"Understood, Captain."

"Now, ready yourselves in any manner you see fit. Christoff, feed the boys and round up a few men to row you to Willemstad." L'Ollon shifted his gaze to us. "Good luck in Curacao, and while you're skulking around with Death chasing your heels, remember poor Beelo. Ha! The fall of Shanley's empire has begun." Turning back to the bow, he peered at the island through his spyglass.

Christoff, Grant, and I were secured in one of the rowboats and lowered to the waves. Four pirates joined us and they worked the oars steadily, pulling the rowboat away from the ship's dripping, barnacle-laden hull.

As the boat swam roughly over the water, I looked back at the *Obsidian*. Its gruesome figurehead seemed real, its lifeless arms tied at the wrists to the bowsprit, its dead head drooping sadly and defeated with that gaping mouth and those empty eye sockets. Jean L'Ollon, the *Obsidian,* and the legacy encompassing it meant three things to the people of the Caribbean: wealth, power, and death.

The island of Curacao grew larger as we approached. Grant's freckled face was pale as he nervously fiddled with the bundle of lock picks. I looked down at the blade that rested in my belt, a blade that had undoubtedly killed many men. Today I would kill or be killed.

Chapter 9

Thieves

L'Ollon's pirates rowed our boat into the wharf. All around us were glorious ships of varying shapes and sizes; some bore red flags, others blue and yellow. Crests of distant countries adorned the banners, and as we drifted in, I heard an assortment of languages.

The harbor was deep enough to accommodate even the grandest of vessels. Christoff pointed at one of the finest ships in the bay. "There is Shanley's brigantine, *Hydra's Bane.* A brigantine is very similar to a barque. There isn't much difference between *Hydra's Bane* and the *Obsidian.* Our barque is a bit shorter in length but our masts make up for it. The brigantine and the barque are the preferred ships for our trade, you see. Shanley's fleet is fast and maneuverable. His ships are all large enough to hold a tough crew, several cannon, and room for cargo."

Grant turned to me and whispered, "Trunks of gold and jewels, I'd say."

"I've seen many modified ships, as well," continued

Christoff. "Some seafarers employ carpenters to alter the forecastles, quarterdecks, and holds to suit the needs of the captain."

"Some pirate captains even build prisons in the lower holds," Grant said to me.

"Now look yonder, lads," Christoff directed. "There rests a mighty galleon. Jean L'Ollon had one just like her years ago. The galleon is built to hold large quantities of cargo and a large crew. It is a warship to be sure, lads, but speed it does not have. It takes heavy firepower to best a ship like her. 'Loot her and leave her if you dare get close,' say the best pirates, 'she won't be giving much chase.'"

The wooden dock wobbled under us. The afternoon was warm as the sun began tilting to the western sky. We found the main road connecting the harbor to the town.

Curacao was not much different than Cuba. The streets were littered with peddlers. Peasants and nobles alike crowded the taverns; the sounds of the smithy's hammer-falls rang like church bells. Fragrant fruits and flowers sweetened the air. I could hear music, laughter, and cheers coming from a nearby square. The townsfolk paid us little mind. They brushed by, unaware of our criminal intentions.

No one seemed to notice the dreadful sword hanging from my belt. It was commonplace for a boy to carry the arms of his father or master—a symbol of faithfulness and pride to follow behind bearing his trusted weapon should he need it. Perhaps Grant and I looked like Christoff's sons. Walking with him in the far away town of Willemstad was like walking with a powerful lion. I felt safe now that I was away from Jean L'Ollon. Even the feeling of the solid, un-moving earth beneath my feet was rejuvenating.

We entered a smoky tavern. Christoff instructed us to sit at a round table and speak to no one. He weaved around the drunkards and servers in the hazy room to a lone man sitting in the far corner, a fat man wearing a patched gray shirt. His arms were tanned and his grimy face was round. He and Christoff shook hands. Christoff took the chair across from him and they spoke for several minutes. I watched their mouths and tried to guess what they were talking about.

Grant leaned over the table toward me. "Jean L'Ollon's quest has begun, and we are a part of it!"

"What about this quest? You haven't told me the rest of the story."

"Where did I leave off?"

"The night of the storm, L'Ollon's men opened fire on the Water People."

"Right… L'Ollon panicked just as his men had. He called for the cannon to be manned and set. Soon, the galleon *Hydra* let loose its terrible wrath."

"He shot at them? Why?"

"L'Ollon thought only of his fortune. He assumed that the Water People had come for it. The *Obsidian,* with its twelve shots, fired freely. The sloop *Cutlass,* with its six, blasted the dark waves. On they fired until they were out of ammunition. It was then that L'Ollon and his crew realized their mistake.

"A vicious boom rumbled from the bilge of the *Hydra.* The men working below ran up the companionways and onto the main deck screaming, 'The *Hydra* is taking water! The hull has been torn open!'

"The sounds of men drowning below deck filled the stormy night. L'Ollon looked to his other ships. The *Obsidian* drifted on the water unscathed, but the *Cutlass* was sinking, too. L'Ollon gathered his sea charts, filled his pouches and pockets with gold, and abandoned his beloved galleon. He slipped into a small rowboat and cast away over the water. He rowed alone and watched the warship sink. The *Obsidian* was his only chance for escape. The crew hoisted him aboard and L'Ollon immediately gave orders to make sail. They obeyed and took wind despite the raging storm. The Water People did not follow.

"Six days elapsed, and soon the island of Puerto Rico took shape in the distance. L'Ollon called for a feast before landing. He told his men that they deserved a good meal for their trials and faithfulness. The galley prepared a fine stew using the last of the provisions, provisions that L'Ollon had poisoned."

"Poisoned?"

"Ah, Jacob, keep your voice down."

"Sorry."

"He wanted to kill the remaining crew. You see, they had seen the Water People. They were all on the brink of madness, even L'Ollon. He knew his crew would begin telling of the horrors they had witnessed to anyone who would listen. By killing his crew, L'Ollon would be the only one who knew the truth."

"Did they die?"

"From what I've heard along the waterfronts, yes. They drank the stew and died in minutes. In Puerto Rico, L'Ollon made repairs to the *Obsidian* and bought slaves to help him sail to Jamaica's port town of Kingston. Kingston is full of seafarers from the fallen Port Royal, and L'Ollon found it easy to recruit another ruthless crew. He set sail once more and pirated the surrounding waters.

"After some time, L'Ollon began to catch word that one of the crewmembers survived the poison and told the officials what had happened at sea. The man was locked away and labeled mad, so little harm was done. You know who else heard the news that the gold-laden *Hydra* and the *Cutlass* sank?"

"Captain James Shanley?"

"Precisely. Now L'Ollon is on a quest to reclaim his fortune. It begins with Shanley and will end with the Water People."

Christoff came back and we followed him out of the tavern.

"That man was one of Shanley's crewmates," said Christoff as we walked along the main road. "I paid him an eight for directions to Shanley's villa. I told him I wanted to buy the sloop."

"How did you know he was one of Captain Shanley's men?" I asked.

"Ah, it's a skill that comes with time, lad. Experienced pirates always recognize a man of the same trade. Certain mannerisms tell a lot. Also, there is the scent."

"Like sweat or old clothing?"

"No, lad. Though there is truth in that as well. I mean the scent of the sea, the perfume of the ocean air; the smell of a lifetime of sun, salt, and booze." He paused. We had come to an intersection. "We must go left and then make our second right. The road will take us up a hill, and there among a coppice of palm trees waits Shanley's villa. Come now, we are in need of haste. The *Obsidian* will make for the harbor in a half hour. The town will recognize her and Shanley's men will come running to warn him."

~~~~~~

Captain Shanley's residence had two levels, a sharply gabled roof and wide clean windows. It was painted bright yellow with white detail around the doorways, rails, and windows. Near the main entrance stood two armed pirates, one with a sword and the other with a pistol. They tensed as we made our way across the lush green garden and over the smooth stone walkway. Christoff did not seem worried. We followed close behind him.

"What business do ya have 'ere?" asked one of the guards.

"Good day," answered Christoff. "I am looking for the owner of the sloop."

"Captain Shanley owns them ships. Is he expectin' you?"

"No."

The pirate's brow dipped in disapproval. "Shanley don't meet wit' unexpected strangers."

"I arrived by a charter ship three days ago. I am new to the Lesser Antilles and I mean to buy my own ship. If you'd rather I leave, I understand, only let your captain know that you stopped him from making a good deal of money."

The two guards muttered to each other, then turned to us again. "Now see 'ere," one began, "you speak like a wealthy seaman, so we'll give you a chance t' buy your way in, but your little monkeys will be waitin' out 'ere. Got it?"

"Indeed."

Christoff opened the brown purse and took out four silver coins. He held them in the sunlight. They gleamed, as did the eyes of the pirate guards. With a flick of his wrist, the coins flew through the air and landed at the feet of the men. They chimed as they struck the wooden porch. The men rushed to gather them up. After a brief moment of examination, they nodded to each other, stuffed the silver in their pockets and stepped aside, letting our quartermaster proceed through the wide front door.

"Go on," yelled the guard with the pistol, lifting it and pointing it at us. "Me eyes be sick of lookin' at ya!"

Grant and I ran down the walkway, through the garden and back onto the winding road. I expected the gun to explode as we ran.

"Gather your wits, my friend; it's time to carry out our end of the deal."

"Deal? There is no deal!"

"We have our orders, and if we don't succeed, we're dead, remember? I've broken into dozens of homes. This one will be no different. Besides, I have these lock picks; they'll make the job easier."

"What do we do first?"

"We sneak around to the rear of the house. Once inside, we listen for voices. Sound is a thief's best friend, Jacob. Whatever we hear will guide us. Ah, leave it to me. Just have your sword ready."

"I'll certainly use it if need be, but I cannot promise success."

"Remember how you bested Beelo?"

"Yes. But I—"

"No worries. You have a natural talent with a sword. Now

let's go, we've wasted enough time. We must recover L'Ollon's sea chart and that mysterious book."

Grant and I found a window in the rear of the manor. An iron lock kept the two shutters closed. After Grant picked the lock and parted the shutters, we entered the house, finding ourselves in a large storage room filled with stacks of crates. With tender steps, we made our way through, being careful to disturb nothing. Light spilled in through the square window. The dusty air made the rays of sunshine look like milky white bars. Weathered trunks were concealed in one corner of the room.

"Let's have a look," said Grant. "Got to make fair use of these picks."

"Let's do the job and get out of here."

"Don't be scared. You're the one with the sword."

Grant knelt beside the biggest trunk and took the rusted lock in hand. He inserted his metal pick. With gentle pokes, he picked at the tumblers systematically. The pick snapped. He cursed under his breath, then produced another one. After several minutes, the rusted lock opened in his hand. He removed the lock, and we lifted the lid. A tattered, stained bundle of rags lay before us.

I grabbed the bundle of rags and lifted them out of the trunk, revealing a mass of glimmering gold.

Grant plunged his hands into the money. Heavy coins chimed as they fell through his fingers. Gold: solid, cold, and real.

"We can do it, Grant."

"Do what? Oh, yes, the chart and the book. Yes, we can do it."

"No. Not that. Let's fill our pockets with as much as we can carry. We can make for the town, book passage to anywhere, and be free."

"But I…" His voice trailed as he looked away.

"What is it?"

"I don't want to escape. I am so close, don't you see? We'll soon be able to sign L'Ollon's articles and become official members of the *Obsidian's* crew."

"Don't you know what kind of man Jean L'Ollon is? A tyrant, a murderer!"

"What else could he be? That's what makes him so infamous." Grant reached into the pile of gold and scooped out a handful of coins. He put them in his pouch and then handed the pouch to me. It was heavy and could barely close. "Here, take this and go if you want your freedom. I'll be fine alone. I can finish the job."

The pouch in my hand held enough to purchase clothing, food, a room, and anything else to aid in my quest for freedom. My eyes went to the window. The hazy sunbeams lit the way.

I crept to the window, free to escape. Leaving Grant with the treasure trunk and his wayward dream, I stepped through the dusty sunbeam and touched the wooden sill. I heard the squawking of the birds and the rustle of the palms, the very distant churn of the ocean. I looked back at Grant, who stood alone, one hand on the door that would take him into Shanley's home. I wondered what he was waiting for, and then I realized why he remained. He was making sure I escaped safely. The pouch of gold felt heavier suddenly, too heavy for me to carry alone.

I stepped away from the window. "Grant," I called. "Wait for me."

Chapter 10

Captain Shanley

We stopped to listen for voices from within the manor and heard Christoff engaged in conversation.

"Christoff's voice is far and faint," said Grant. "Any sounds we make will be just as faint to them. It should be safe to go in. Take off your shoes."

The stone floor was cool and dry on our bare feet. We slipped out of the storage room and into the brightly lit hall.

The polished stone floor was pristine and smooth. The air smelled of sweet incense. To our left, a spiraled stairwell snaked up to the second level; to our right stretched a long hallway. The walls were finished with a shimmering gold paint and throughout the length of the hall stood marble tables with vases of bright flowers. Directly in front of us was a foyer boasting a circular fountain. Crystal water cascaded from a stone seashell. The stream created subtle rippling waves of light on the ceiling. The quivering beams illuminated the walls and filled the entire room with a warm yellow glow.

"You're asking a lot for such a small ship, Shanley." Christoff's voice was louder, likely a room away.

We needed to move on. As we started for the stairwell, we heard footsteps approaching. We raced for the stairs and began our silent ascent to the second floor. I clutched the handle of my sword to keep it from clanging against the iron rails.

Looking down from the second floor into the foyer, we saw Christoff. In front of him stood a partially bald man with a round belly and strong build. He wore a silly half smile as he spoke, making his face pleasant and likable.

"So that's Captain Shanley," commented Grant. "He's not what I imagined."

Grant and I crouched and waited, watching and listening.

"That is my final offer," said Shanley, his voice calm. He led Christoff to a small writing table.

"That can be arranged," answered Christoff. "I have two thirds of the cost with me now. I will need to meet my investor at the harbor. I welcome you to join me."

"What is your investor doing at the waterfront?"

"My bank is in Aruba, and I have made plans to invest in Curacao's bank. He brings my notes. If you'll join me in meeting him, I will gladly pay you in full."

"Will he be carrying gold? I don't trust bank notes from men I have just met."

"Indeed. My man will have a trunk of money. You can trust me, Captain. Allow me to prove it." Christoff took the bulging pouch off his belt and poured the contents onto the table. Gold and silver coins covered Shanley's writing area and spilled onto the floor.

"I thought that L'Ollon said not to give him so much as a reale," I whispered to Grant.

"Let's have faith in Christoff."

Shanley continued, "Let me prepare the papers for the sloop, and I'll join you in a walk to the harbor."

"There is just one other necessity," said Christoff. "Forgive me if you deem it an unreasonable request."

"Please, go on."

"I need a crew."

"Have you prepared articles a man would find appealing?"

"Indeed, my shipboard articles guarantee a fair stipend." Christoff reached into his shirt and withdrew a folded parchment.

Shanley read it through. "Enticing and fair. I released a band of men from my services not more than three days ago. They're strong and eager for work. Allow me to give these articles to my guard. He can deliver them to the men at once."

Shanley called for his guard. One of the pirates from the front door entered the foyer. "I have an errand for you. Take these articles to Waylin. You'll find him at the pub. Tell him to round up his men and ready them for the sea. They are to report to my sloop in ten minutes if they wish to sail under a wealthy captain. They have permission to board and ready her sails. Tell them the sloop is fully stocked."

"It looks like he just bought the sloop and a crew to sail her," Grant whispered. "What's going on?"

Shanley gathered some papers and took a few minutes to write. He poured hot wax onto the form and stamped it, creating an official seal. Christoff signed his name on the document.

The men shook hands and left. We listened to them walk away and heard the front door of the manor shut.

"Come," said Grant, "we'll get the sea chart and the book, then race back to the waterfront before the guards discover us."

We dashed across the corridor and crouched in front of the largest door, assuming it was Shanley's private study.

"Did you hear that? Someone's coming!" Grant quickly worked his picks. This time, the lock challenged him. I heard a snap. "Damn! It broke." He fumbled for another pick.

I heard the footsteps echoing down the hall, likely coming from around the corner. I guessed we had less than a minute

69

before the patrolling guard turned the corner and caught us.

"Hurry, Grant!"

"I'm trying! There must be something pretty valuable behind this door to warrant a lock like this."

Another snap.

The guard began to whistle. His awkward melody made him sound very close. Small beads of sweat formed on Grant's brow.

At last I heard the click of the final tumbler and the lock popped open in his hand. We pushed open the door and fell into the room. Grant shut the door quickly and we sat motionless, listening to the guard pass by.

Like the foyer, the walls of this room were painted gold. Thick candles rested on every shelf, table, and pedestal. Vivid paintings of ships and sunsets excited my eyes, but it was a magnificent tapestry hanging on the wall behind Shanley's desk that captivated me the most. I could not take my eyes off this work of art.

The tapestry depicted an enchanting woman, naked from the waist up, her skin as smooth and golden as the sunlight that fell on her shoulders. Her arms and abdomen were lean, defined, and strong. The face of this radiant creature allured me. Two glimmering, intelligent silver eyes looked at us. Threads of every color imaginable twisted and swirled together, creating a wet rainbow of hair. Her bright smile seemed slightly mischievous.

Blue water surrounded her. A delicate ocean mist swirled around her waist as she rested on a smooth gray stone. I reached out to caress the soft threads of the tapestry and follow the curves of her waistline down to where her female body began to change. Where two legs should have been was the lower half of what looked like a dolphin. The sunlight in the tapestry glowed on her aquatic body and made the glorious fanned fin glow a calming shade of lavender. The fin was wide, nearly the size of her entire lower half from end to end. It rippled and streamed like a lilac bed sheet, blowing in the wind as the sun forces its way through the fabric. Speechless, I forgot the reason we had come.

A silver plaque was mounted under the tapestry. I leaned closer to read the engraved words:

THE MERMAIDEN.

ANGEL OF THE OCEAN. EVER-WATCHFUL KEEPER OF SECRETS.

"Look at the loot in this place!" said Grant in awe.

Endless treasure filled the room. Precious amulets and jeweled earrings sat atop tables and shelves. Stacks of silver coins were piled neatly near brass scales. On Captain Shanley's desk waited mounds of valuable gemstones. Sparkling jewel-encrusted rings and diamond brooches were arranged in meticulous piles. Grant stuffed treasures into the pouch that hung from his belt.

"Take what you can carry, Jacob," he said, his eyes gleaming with excitement.

"You've already filled my pouch, remember?" I patted the heavy bag that dangled from my side.

My thoughts trailed as I searched through the belongings of Jean L'Ollon's enemy. I kept thinking of the Mermaiden. *Is she really out there? Was she one of the Water People who sank L'Ollon's fleet? She must be real. An artist must have seen her and woven the tapestry to remember her, to capture her for all to see.* It was then that a terrible thought occurred to me. I recalled Grant's words: *'L'Ollon is on a quest to reclaim his fortune. It begins with Shanley and will end with the Water People.'* If these beautiful creatures truly lived, if they were responsible for the ruin of L'Ollon's fleet, he meant to kill them.

I stood motionless at the realization of this. I looked back at the tapestry. Her eyes gazed at me. It was such beautiful artwork, such intimate craftsmanship. I could almost hear the wind and feel the salty mist on my face. I wanted her to come to life within the threadwork and slip into the water where no one could harm her.

"I found it!" exclaimed Grant. He lifted a painting off its mount to reveal a weathered chart posted to the wall. "This is it, Jacob. It has L'Ollon's name written on the bottom." With care, he took it down and folded it small enough to hide in his shirt. "All we need now is that strange book. Any luck over there?"

I shook my head and stepped away from the tapestry of the Mermaiden.

"No worries," he said, "I'll search that book shelf, and you search the drawers of the desk. Hurry, we've got to get to the harbor."

Bundles of parchment and scrolls filled the top drawer. I sifted through them and went on to the next. Bottles of ink and extra quills met my digging hands. In the last drawer was a small assortment of leather bound books, and in the middle of them, a shiny blue ribbon caught my eye.

"I've got it!" I tucked the book safely in my shirt and joined my friend at the door.

Chapter 11

The Waterfront

We retreated to the storage room and closed the door behind us. After putting on our shoes, we snaked between the stacks of crates back to the window. We slipped through the open window and stumbled out onto the soft warm earth.

"It's time for the hard part," said Grant. "We must hurry to the waterfront and meet up with Christoff. There is a good chance that blood will spill before night falls. Be brave and keep a readied will."

We dashed away from the villa and into the thick growth of palms and fern, the leaves and vines slashing at us as we ran down the jungle-like hillside. The money in my pouch chimed and the deadly short sword clanged against my thigh. Grant ran ahead with the rolled-up sea chart stuffed in his belt.

Soon the Caribbean Sea gleamed beyond the edge of the forest. We broke from the tree line and raced down a graveled slope and onto a dusty trail that brought us into the heart of Willemstad.

Rushing through the crowded market, we headed to the harbor. As the scent of the ocean grew stronger, the bitter taste of fear brewed in my mouth. I saw the dozens of masts jabbing the clouds and heard boarding bells ringing, along with the distant murmur of seamen. The waves lapped against the pilings of the piers, and I heard the creaking of old ships moored against their will.

When we arrived at the waterfront, it was hard to tell who among the sullied sailors was friend or foe. I searched the crowd for Christoff.

"Stay close and don't look anyone in the eye," said Grant.

We ventured along the harbor, passing crews working to restock and repair their ships. They rolled barrels of rum, provisions, and powder over wobbling planks and up to the gangway.

We found Shanley's beautiful sloop rocking softly in the blue water. It was moored with heavy lines that coiled around sturdy cleats on the port bow and wide pilings stemming from the dock. The sloop was single-masted, with a white mainsail and several tight jibs. The headsail flapped in the subtle wind. The hull of the ship was clean and a bright blue stripe—the boot top—ran from bow to stern, marking the waterline. The sloop had no name, and I wondered what I would call it if it belonged to me. The most intriguing feature of the ship was that the quarterdeck had been raised and a cabin area had been built under it. I guessed that there were three small rooms above the stern.

There were nearly thirty men aboard the sloop. They busied themselves coiling extra line and inspecting the rigging. A man with long yellow hair mopped the deck.

Grant stopped suddenly. Christoff was engaged in conversation with Captain Shanley. Shanley was pointing out features of the sloop to Christoff.

Cerulean Isle

"Notice," said Shanley, "that this ship is more of a small warship than a traditional sloop. I've outfitted her with four cannon, two on the starboard and two on the portside. Each fires a nine-pound shot instead of the traditional eighteen-pound shot. This cuts down on weight. She could probably take another four cannon, but you can alter her as you see fit. That's what makes these ladies so attractive in our trade, eh? A man can make her into whatever he fancies. I've had the finest carpenters in Curacao alter her stern. This beauty has three comfortable cabins below the quarterdeck."

"You've crafted a fine ship, to be sure," answered Christoff.

"Ah, see there, looks like you got your crew, my friend," said Shanley. "Your shipboard articles were hard to turn down. That yellow-haired man with the mop, that's Waylin. He knows the seas better than me, I'll admit. He'll serve you and the ship well. I almost hate to sell her, but I got me a good buyer, so all's well."

"All's well indeed," said Christoff. "Well then, without further delay, I would like to conclude this deal. It seems that my financial advisor has arrived." Christoff nodded a greeting to the man standing behind Shanley.

Shanley turned around and gasped, stepping back as he recognized the man with the long, greasy black hair and rotted teeth.

"Good day, James," said L'Ollon, his face gnarled with malice. L'Ollon moved forward quickly and pressed his twelve-inch pistol into Shanley's stomach. "You're coming with me, and if you make a sound I'll pop your belly right here on the dock."

"Kill me, then," said Shanley. "I have nothing to live for anyway."

"Oh? Why is that?"

"You know why."

"Ah, yes. Your deaf son. Somebody kidnapped him in San Juan. I wonder who that was."

"You worthless fiend," growled Shanley.

L'Ollon struck him in the face. Blood poured from Shanley's nose and dyed his teeth pink. He recoiled from the impact of the blow and would have fallen to the ground if it weren't for Christoff holding his shoulders.

"What do you want, Jean? I'll pay whatever I can. I'll give you *Kraken's Bane* and *Eternity*. My estate, I'll sign the deed over to you. Return my son, and I'll surrender."

L'Ollon grabbed Shanley's face with his grimy left hand, forcing Shanley to look at him.

"You are in no position to negotiate. I did not come all this way to commandeer your fleet or seize control of Willemstad. No. I am here for three things: my sea chart, the book, and—" L'Ollon broke off and turned his gaze on the quartermaster. "Christoff, where are those two vagrant rats, anyway?"

Grant and I took deep breaths and stepped forward. Captain L'Ollon noticed our approach but kept his pistol buried in Shanley's stomach.

"Grant," yelled L'Ollon. "Were you successful?"

"Yes, Captain."

"It's time for a family reunion. And then I will have my *third* desire fulfilled."

"And what is that?" Shanley's voice shook with hatred.

"Your death!"

As these words were spoken, the *Obsidian* came into view. Its sails rippled against the sun, and its wide body split the water as it entered the harbor. People began to flee. Men scurried away from their ships, taking whatever they could carry. Peddlers and merchants recognized the dreadful ship, gathered their wares, and left. The sight of this one ship struck fear into everyone in Willemstad. L'Ollon looked on as his mighty barque drifted to a halt roughly two hundred yards from the docks. The powerful cannon were readied and aimed at the wharf. No other ships in the bay were ready to combat the *Obsidian*. As panic broke out along the docks, the barque and its crew waited for a signal to open fire.

"You see, James," yelled L'Ollon, "today your empire falls. Today I reclaim the fortune that my forefathers amassed, the fortune that you stole. Today you will watch your son die."

A lifeboat was lowered from the gunwale of the *Obsidian*. Two heavily-armed pirates rowed it to the docks. The men took hold of Shanley and forced him into the craft. Christoff signaled for us to get in. Once all five of us were seated, the pirates rowed away from the dock. L'Ollon kept his pistol aimed at Shanley, who remained silent as the lifeboat bobbed and rocked over the choppy waves.

The row to the ship seemed to last for hours. I tried to remain calm and keep my thoughts together. I felt the warm leather of the mysterious book against my chest. *What story does it hold? What words could be inscribed within that are so important to Jean L'Ollon?*

The *Obsidian's* hull loomed over us. The pirates on deck hauled our boat out of the sea. I saw a calculating look in Shanley's eyes as he exited the lifeboat, no doubt piecing together a battle plan, a desperate and last strategy.

Instinctively, my left hand fell upon the cold pommel of the sword that hung from my belt.

Chapter 12

Vengeance

"I bid you welcome, old friend." Captain L'Ollon stood proudly under the mainmast. Dark clouds formed overhead, a storm approaching.

A large portion of the *Obsidian's* crew surrounded us. L'Ollon and Shanley faced one another in the center of the circle. Grant, Christoff, and I stood to the right of our captain. L'Ollon, with his pistol aimed at Shanley, ordered one of his crew to retrieve the deaf boy. The pirate nodded and hurried away.

Shanley remained ready. He did not cower. He focused on his adversary and maintained a poised posture. Dried blood flaked under his nose. "You have my son?"

"I am a lot of things, but a liar is not one of them."

"If he has suffered, I swear I will—"

"You will what? Have you so quickly forgotten that I am in control? You are aboard *my* ship, encompassed by *my* crew, with *my* pistol readied against your heart."

"And what will you do?" challenged Shanley. "After you have killed me, what's next for the great and terrible Jean L'Ollon?"

"I trusted you once with my plans. Never again."

"Then it is as I suspected. There is nothing left for you after my death."

"You dare speak to me in such a manner? My plans have only just begun. It is all in the book, is it not?"

The brown leather book remained hidden in my shirt.

"You have succumbed to desperate measures, L'Ollon. The once cunning pirate lord is chasing the ravings of a madman."

L'Ollon pressed the pistol under Shanley's chin, forcing his mouth to close. He spoke in a half growl. "There is more truth in that book than you will ever know. People should learn to listen to the mad." He lowered his weapon and let it hover over Shanley's heart.

"The Merfolk are nothing but wild stories brought back from sea by drunken sailors. That book will lead you in circles."

"You speak like one who has sought Cerulean Isle."

"Nay. I wouldn't waste the labor of my crew on such a ridiculous voyage. There is no Cerulean Isle and there aren't any Merfolk. My last thought will be of the *Obsidian* sailing the blue, hunting imaginary Mermaidens."

The circle of pirates broke when two men burst into the center with the deaf boy in their grip. They tossed him to the floor. His sunken eyes looked desperately at L'Ollon and then shifted to Captain Shanley. A weak smile cracked his dried lips as he crawled toward his father.

"Sebastian!" Despite L'Ollon's poised weapon, Shanley knelt to help his son. "This is madness!" He cradled the boy. "Surely you have some sensibility left in you, L'Ollon. Again, I offer you everything I own if you spare Sebastian. Please."

"Ah ha! The great Captain Shanley reduced to a beggar."

"My son has nothing to do with our business or the wrongs we have done to one another. Come now, Jean. We are pirates.

We share a common lifestyle that goes far beyond shipboard articles. I am talking about infamy and renown." Shanley paused to help his son to his feet. The pair faced L'Ollon and his pistol.

Shanley continued, "What is done can never be undone. Nay, old friend, and we *were* friends not long ago, I am not begging. I should not need to, not to you, at least. What will you accomplish by the murder of a child? Yes, I found your sunken fortune and took it for my own. You would have done the same thing. I will give it all back to you, and more. You have won."

A long silence fell over the ship. L'Ollon's eyes burned in his skull. Rain began to fall and the wind of the brewing storm blew his inky hair, the oily strands twisting and writhing like black snakes. His jaw tensed and the edges of his mouth curled, showing brown and yellow teeth.

"Is there no end to your cruelty?" asked Shanley.

"No."

The barrel of the pistol exploded. A yellow flash flamed for an instant and a cloud of smoke filled the air. I heard a thud, the unmistakable sound of a body hitting the floorboards. When the pistol smoke cleared, the boy Sebastian lay in a pool of rain and blood. Shanley let out a heart-wrenching scream.

L'Ollon took a long silver sword from one of his men and approached the defeated pirate. Shanley held his dead son loosely in his left arm. He lifted his maddened gaze to L'Ollon. "You will burn in the deepest regions of hell, I will see to it!"

L'Ollon pressed the sharp tip of the blade to Shanley's throat. "Now you die, Shanley. Farewell."

"Farewell, indeed." Shanley grabbed the blade with his right hand. Blood streamed from his grip as the steel cut into his palm. He forced the blade from his throat and lunged at L'Ollon, barreling into him, causing L'Ollon to drop his sword. The two fell and tumbled across the deck. The circle of men, at the sight of a brawl, closed in and jeered as the pirate captains struggled and fought.

Shanley pummeled his enemy with bloody fists. L'Ollon groaned from Shanley's punches and bled from the nose and mouth. The spraying blood did not slow Shanley's assault. L'Ollon's crew looked on and hollered encouragement for their captain.

"It's pirate code," explained Grant. "The men wait for the command from L'Ollon. When it comes, Shanley will die."

"What if Shanley defeats L'Ollon?"

"Then the *Obsidian* will be under new command."

The smashing of fist against flesh resonated throughout the main deck. The wind began to quicken and the sails rattled their riggings. The barque creaked and swayed over the stirring water. The rain fell in sheets over the ship as the thunder rumbled over the masts.

Grant pulled me away from the fight. "Follow me," he cried over the hollers of the men. "We're getting out of here."

We ran toward the stern, slipping on the wet wood of the deck, and stopped at a rowboat suspended from thick ropes on an arching rack. It swung from side to side with the rocking of the ship.

"Climb into the boat," said Grant. "I will lower it to the water."

"What about you?"

"Once you are adrift, I'll jump overboard and you can pull me in. Hurry."

The boat creaked as I climbed inside. Grant wiped the rainwater from his eyes and worked quickly to release the clove hitch. With a sudden jerk, the boat slid downward. Grant struggled with the weight of the craft but slowly let the line slip through his grip. The pulleys worked smoothly as he eased the boat overboard. I held tightly to the sides as it swayed. I glanced over the side of the boat and saw the dark blue ocean getting closer. I heard Grant grunting as he used all of his strength to lower me safely to the churning waves. Finally, the boat touched the bouncing waves and Grant let the line loose.

I readied the oars. "Now, jump!"

He climbed onto the railings just as a blood-curdling voice called out the fatal order. *"Kill Shanley!"*

A body was hurled over the bow rails, a thick rope attached to the neck.

The slack of the rope ended with a nauseating crack and James Shanley's body dangled lifelessly, spinning, swaying, and knocking against the hull.

~~~~~~

I heard Grant call for help and saw him caught in the clutches of L'Ollon. L'Ollon was a gruesome red mess, his face unrecognizable. The beady dark eyes were swollen and nearly closed; his lower lip was split, revealing the entire row of bottom teeth, a wound that made him look monstrous.

"Your freedom has a price," yelled L'Ollon, his voice slurred. He held his battle-tarnished sword aloft.

I pulled the leather book from my shirt and held it high for L'Ollon to see. The blue ribbon danced in the wind. "Let him go, or I destroy your book!" I held it over the water. L'Ollon's eyes widened and he loosened his grip on Grant. "Now step away from him."

Just as L'Ollon lowered his blade, his body hurled into the air. The captain flailed as he fell overboard, splashing into the stirring blue water. His sword fell into the waves after him. Up on the deck, where L'Ollon had been, stood Christoff.

"Go, young cooper," he said. Grant splashed into the sea and swam toward the rowboat.

The boat had drifted a challenging distance from the *Obsidian*. Grant swam as hard as he could. I reached to pull him in. The boat rocked and tilted dangerously as I pulled him aboard. Just then, a gnarled hand grabbed his ankle.

Grant kicked at the monstrous man trying to pull him back into the sea.

The saltwater had rinsed away much of the blood from L'Ollon's face. The two halves of his parted lower lip flapped as he yelled at us. "Give me the book! Give me what is mine!"

I stood up, enraged. I clutched the handle of the sword at my hip and drew it from my belt. "You want what is yours?" I yelled. "Here! This belongs to you!"

I plunged the blade into his chest. Thunder roared over me and a streak of lightning split the stormy sky. L'Ollon wheezed as the cold steel entered his body. I pushed the sword as hard as I could, using both hands to drive the blade through his chest until it broke through the meat of his back.

L'Ollon roared in agony. He released Grant's ankle and touched the golden handle of the sword. He coughed. Blood sprayed. He began to sink. His eyes remained fixed on us as he fell under the sea. The captain of the *Obsidian* sank deeper and deeper into the ocean, still staring at us until the shadows of the sea swallowed his hideous face.

Chapter 13

Escape

"Row, lads," Christoff shouted. "Row as fast as you can!" L'Ollon's pirates turned on Christoff, but he fought them off, cutting them down and knocking them overboard. Battle plagued the main deck; pirates fought alongside Christoff while others fought for the fallen L'Ollon. The deadly booms of pistol fire echoed over chiming blades.

A group of men filled another rowboat and rowed over the water toward us.

"You'll die for your crimes against our crew," shouted one. He lifted his pistol and pulled the trigger. The shot erupted with a cloud of smoke. The water to my left splashed from the round. As the pirates continued after us, he loaded another shot.

"Keep rowing," Grant shouted to me. "The rolling waves and rain will make it hard for him to hit us."

Another shot rang out. The water burst again, this time inches from our boat. I pulled my oars in cadence with Grant as the ocean swelled from the storm. Lightning cracked overhead just as the third shot exploded and tore through the side of our boat.

One of the men called out over the raging storm. "If the ocean don't swallow ya, the storm will." They turned around, rowing back to the *Obsidian*.

Water poured in and the torrent of rain helped fill our boat. The waves carried us farther away from the ship. We rowed on as the water pooled over our feet. It seemed we were being pulled into the heart of the storm. The surface of the water became a dark blue landscape of sharp hills and deep valleys.

"Better hang on to something," Grant shouted.

The angry ocean swelled as thunder clashed. A great wave emerged, like a mountain of water. It loomed over us, pulling our small boat atop its shoulders. The oars fell into the sea as we caught the steep incline. As the mighty wave hurled our boat off its crest, I fell into the foaming ocean, hearing Grant's calls only when my head broke through the surface. I kicked and fanned my arms, but the sea pulled me down. I rolled under the waves, losing my orientation of which way was up. My eyes stung and my lungs ached. I clawed and fought the fierce ocean until I became lost and my mind clouded. *So this is my end.* As my eyes darkened, I reached up one last time and felt a hand close around my wrist.

Grant pulled me to the surface. He held me above the water as I coughed and choked. "I've got you, just breathe." My head spun and my chest heaved. The storm raged on and the waves pushed us around. "Are you well enough?"

"I...I think so."

"The boat has overturned but is still adrift. We must get to it; it's all we've got to hold on to."

We swam through the churning sea while the rain hammered down. We reached the capsized rowboat and held on for our lives, caught in the violent wrestling of storm and ocean.

~~~~~~

After what felt like hours, the ocean settled and the clouds softened. I could not tell if the storm had subsided or if we had drifted out of its clutches. I felt sick and dizzy and my arms were tired from gripping the boat. Grant held tightly to the opposite edge, the keel of the rowboat arched between us. He looked tired and a large bruise colored the left side of his face. He reached into his shirt and pulled out Jean L'Ollon's sea chart. With a proud smile, he laid it on the boat.

"I suppose I should let this dry," he said. "Do you still have the book?"

To my surprise, the leather journal remained tucked in my shirt. I pulled the book and pouch of gold from my shirt and laid them on the boat.

The last of the storm clouds burned away and the sun revealed itself, only to fall behind the western water. Night fell and the stars took light, followed by the silver moon. The sea turned to ink that shimmered in the pallid glow of the night sky. I was very tired. I could feel my grip slipping and the sway of the sea was inviting, as though it wanted me to fall away from our boat.

"Take off your belt and give it to me," Grant instructed. "I will join yours with mine and we will tie our wrists together. This way, we can try to sleep and should one of us slip away, the other will be pulled and woken. A life-line for the night."

We tied our belts together to make one long strap. With my end secured around my wrist and Grant's to his, we pulled ourselves onto the over-turned boat as much as possible and closed our eyes to rest. Though uncomfortable, I fell into a dreamless sleep that only seemed to last a minute.

The blazing sun woke me. I could feel my skin beginning to burn and my legs starting to numb in the water.

"How are you feeling?" asked Grant.

"Glad to be alive," I replied with a weak smile.

"I sure could use some breakfast," Grant joked.

"How far out from land do you think we are?"

"I really don't know. The first thing to do is locate the four points. The sun came up behind you, so that's east. The west is at my back. That leaves north to my left and south to my right. Curacao is that way." He pointed to his right. "We should watch the south and east water for approaching ships. Can you kick your legs?"

"I can hardly feel them."

"Well, come to my side of the boat and we'll do our best to kick our way south. We don't want to drift any farther from land than we already have."

We clung to our ruined boat and kicked, forcing our drift southward. We stopped to rest every so often, but without food and water it wasn't long before the last of our energy was spent. The merciless Caribbean sun charred our skin. We kept the sea chart and journal out of the water and soon, both had dried. We watched the path of the sun and maintained our southern course. When night fell, we belted our wrists again and closed our eyes.

I was too sore, burnt, and afraid to sleep. I watched the dark horizon, hoping desperately for a ship. My thoughts wandered and in my exhausted delirium, I imagined the Mermaiden from the tapestry in Shanley's quarters coming to our aid.

Chapter 14

The Sloop

The ocean sparkled under the moonlight as if dusted with floating gems. As I stared out at the dark horizon, an orange light winked on. The light brightened as it approached; a glowing lantern. Soon the silhouette of a single-masted ship emerged under the dim starlight, its bow pointed in our direction. The moonlight illuminated its white sails, making the craft appear elegant and ethereal.

I pulled the strap that joined me to Grant. "Wake up. A ship."

We studied the ship as it came closer. Under the lantern's glow, I saw the faint blue of the boot top running the length of the hull. "I recognize that ship. There was only one ship docked at Willemstad with a blue stripe!"

The lantern light fell over us, and when the helmsmen spotted our craft drifting on the open water, he took the lantern and began to swing it from side to side, letting us know that he saw us. The large sloop eased toward us. From the deck a man called out.

"Ahoy!"

"Ahoy," called Grant.

A long rope ladder was thrown over the starboard bow.

Grant said, "Gather the journal and the gold. I'll take the chart."

With tired limbs and callused hands, we climbed the ladder. The helmsman pulled us upward, making the climb easier. Once on the deck, we collapsed.

~~~~~~

I awoke in a small bed. Grant rested in a bed next to mine. We were in a small cabin, and seated near the door, watching over us, was a man with long blonde hair. He looked familiar, and though tired and weak, I remembered him. He was one of Shanley's crew. When he saw that I was awake, he approached. Grant woke then and tried to sit up.

"Be at ease, friend. My name is Waylin. You are aboard a large sloop enroute to Grenada."

I fell back into a deep sleep filled with nightmares, images of Shanley's body dangling off the *Obsidian's* bow, the ghastly, distorted face of L'Ollon as he sank below the waves; and Beelo, lifeless under a gray blanket.

Grant shook my shoulders and I woke up. Waylin had left us alone in the room. I looked out of a small window over my bed and saw that it was night. I had slept through an entire day, and though hungry and sore, I felt that some of my strength had returned. Grant helped me sit up. "Where is the gold? Do you still have it?"

I felt under my shirt. The book and pouch of coins was still there. I gave them both to Grant.

"We need to hide this." Grant looked around the room. He tapped his toes on the wooden floor and listened, doing this in several places until he stopped and bent down.

He pulled up a loose floor board, gathered the pouches,

chart, and journal, then stuffed them into the small space beneath the floor. There was a knock at the door. Grant opened it to find Waylin holding a bundle of clean clothes.

"Get dressed, then report to the galley for food, drink, and to meet with our captain. You'll find the galley below deck." Waylin handed Grant the clothing, and left.

Grant gave me a soft cotton blouse, olive in color, with long sleeves and a drawstring under the collar. It fit loosely yet comfortably. It was long, with a hem just above my knees. The long sleeves would protect my arms from the harsh sun. I secured my belt around my waist over the blouse.

I slipped on a new pair of black cotton pants. The soft leggings were breathable and, like the blouse, covered my entire leg to prevent sunburn. Once dressed, and sure that our belongings were hidden, we left the small cabin and made for the galley.

We walked a few paces down a narrow hall and came to a large door. We opened it and stepped out onto the main deck of the sloop. The single mast stood strong and boasted a triangular fore and aft rigged mainsail. We had been resting in the quarters built under the raised quarter deck. The night overhead was clear. Crewmates rested about the deck as the anchored ship rocked on the water. Some men played cards atop an overturned barrel; others sat in groups and talked while passing around a bottle. The men paused to stare at us as we made for the hatch to the lower deck.

The galley was easy to find. The scent of spiced stew and boiled potatoes was our guide. Soon, we came into a small room with a round wooden table nailed to the floor. Christoff stood to greet us.

"Master Christoff!" exclaimed Grant. "I am glad to see you."

"Aye, lad. Now sit, both of you. You need to eat." He brought two large bowls of stew and split a loaf of bread between us. He then poured two tall mugs of water. We accepted the meal graciously and ate. Christoff and Waylin each took a bowl of stew and joined us.

When Grant finished, he wiped his mouth with the edge of his sleeve. "We saw you battling the crew. What happened?"

"I've spent my life on the sea and have sailed with many pirate captains. However, I keep a moral standard, to be sure. When L'Ollon killed Shanley's son, it was more than I could tolerate. My allegiance to him ended with that boy's life. I chose to help you, lads. And for turning against L'Ollon, I was subdued, knocked unconscious, and tied up. It was night when I came to. I cut my restraints with a bit of glass from a shattered bottle and dove overboard. I swam back to the harbor and met with Waylin, a man with whom I've sailed in the past. We boarded the sloop and sailed off under the cover of night. I had been planning on abandoning L'Ollon and his crew for some time. With his money, I paid Shanley for the sloop and here we are."

"The other night," I began, "Waylin said we were enroute to Grenada. Why?"

Waylin pushed aside his empty bowl. "I have a friend there who can help you begin a new life. We must hurry, though."

"Why?"

"Because, lads," replied Christoff, "L'Ollon's crew is after you. You killed their captain and by their code, you must die."

Chapter 15

The Madman's Journal

Grant and I stood at the bow of the sloop. It was a hot day, not a cloud in the blue sky. The endless ocean surrounded us, but on the eastern horizon the peaks of tropical mountains rose up from a distant island. I took a deep breath. The salty wind filled my lungs.

We gazed toward the land that waited in the distance. The rails of the bow were warm under my grasp.

"We are rich," said Grant. "We've got an entire pouch full of gold and silver!"

Grenada, I thought, *my new home.* It was odd; I did not feel excited. I felt the same—rigid and somewhat lost. The mighty ocean comforted me and when I thought of my mother's spirit dwelling forever in the waves, I knew I could indeed make Grenada my home. The same water that smoothed the shores of Santiago splashed over the coral of Grenada. My mother had kept her promise to watch over me. I looked over the bow and into the rushing water. I imagined the Mermaiden swimming beneath the surface of the sea, cutting the water as easily as our ship.

"How much gold will it take to rid my memory of all the terrible things I've seen? Blood, war, death. Will these things be with me forever?"

"I don't really know," Grant replied. He gave me a reassuring smile. "Let's stick together and figure it out in time. We'll see what the land life has to offer, but there is always the sea. We could buy our own ship and sail the world. Our luck has changed and for that, I am relieved."

"You're right, but I think our troubles are far from over."

I stepped away from the bow and went below deck to our quarters. I closed the wooden door and retrieved the worn leather journal from under the floor board and loosened the ribbon. I opened the front cover. The pages were yellowed and stained around the edges, and much of the ink had bled and smeared. I made out the first line. Written in black ink and with a shaking script, it read:

It can only be God's will that I have survived to document what I have seen and learned.

As I turned to the next page, the paper crinkled.

I write only truth and do so on this stormy day from my cell. I am uncertain of the year. I am uncertain of the day. Though, for the benefit of this record, I will pen that it is Seventeen Thirty Two, yes that will do. As for the day…oh, I will choose Saturday, I do love Saturdays!

Wild this may seem. As wild and as full of lunacy as the townsfolk believe me to be. I will be proved of sound mind one day even if that day should come long after I am bone in the earth. Secrets never remain so for long, hence, I shall be survived by the truth and perhaps one day revered and named a hero for this work.

Imagine that. Me, Owen, a hero.

The rain is falling and it is drafty in my cell. The iron bars are moist. I am used to conditions such as these. After all, I am a man of the sea. Though locked away like a parrot or a monkey, I remain a great pirate. Many colorful lands I have seen and many men I have killed. I have sailed under many flags, but the most feared captain I have served flew no banners. I have called many ships my home but have loved none greater than the one with a dead Spaniard on the bow. Oh, I remember how she swam over the waves...the great and powerful Obsidian.

This was the diary of one of L'Ollon's men. I closed the book and went to the door and secured the lock. I continued reading.

As treacherous as I used to be, Captain Jean L'Ollon was more so than any man. I hardly escaped that treachery. The other men who sailed the Obsidian with me cannot speak the same. They are all dead. L'Ollon poisoned them. Not me...as you see. I did not drink the tainted stew. Nay! I pretended by pressing my lips to the bowl but allowing nothing to pass. I watched them all groan and tumble to their faces. They gagged and choked. I mimicked this. My ruse was a success! L'Ollon believed me to be dead. Ha! As I wrote earlier...secrets never remain so for long. I tell now the secrets that Jean L'Ollon believes have died.

His fleet, Obsidian, Hydra, and Cutlass, were bested by two cruelties of the ocean: a vicious storm and those who dwell in the depths of the sea. The Water People are real! I fired my pistol at the man in the waves. I will never forget the light that shone from his eyes. It was like the very light of the moon. I will never forget the gleam of his golden plates of armor or the spray of water as his great fin broke the cresting waves, sending him arching above the gunwale and back into the black sea.

Mermaidens! Merlords! Merfolk!

That is what I write of as the rain pours outside. That is what I must tell before I succumb to the hardships of prison and surrender to Death. The Merfolk defeated L'Ollon, and he lost his empire of gold.

I have been deemed mad and locked away for both my ravings and my crimes. A criminal lunatic. A vagrant thief. A killer. Yes! That is who I am but it shall not be my legacy. I have been sentenced to life in a cage. How be it that I was not adorned upon the gallows? Bribery is how. The judge accepted two pieces of eight to keep the noose from my neck. Money well spent, indeed, and proof of the world's corruption. Onward to corruption, ahoy!

Captain Jean L'Ollon murdered his crew to ensure that the truth of the Merfolk would not make land and be his ruin. He feared the soiling of his legacy, a legacy built by his father and grandfather. Once Jean had recovered and restocked his only ship, Obsidian, with a new crew, quartermaster, etcetera…I watched him sail away from San Juan. I remained on the island and tried to tell my tale. No one would listen. I was homeless. I could not gain entrance to even the worst of taverns. I spent my days at the edge of the harbor staring out at the unending sea. I waited to catch sight of the Merfolk so that someone would believe me. None came.

I decided to leave San Juan. I journeyed south, hopping the island chain of the Lesser Antilles. I bargained my way aboard merchant vessels and private ships until I ended my travels on the island of Curacao. This island was no different than the others. No one believed my story of L'Ollon and the Merfolk. Once more I found myself alone on the shore watching the waves for any sign of the Water People. To my surprise, another great pirate, a man with a respected reputation, met me. Captain James Shanley.

Captain Shanley had a yarn to share. He told me that he heard the people whispering my story and he admitted my claims intrigued him. He confessed to meeting with Jean L'Ollon prior to the ill-fated voyage. He claimed to have a copy of Jean's sea chart. Shanley then told me his plans to follow L'Ollon's route in search of the lost gold. The thought of such a voyage seemed ridiculous, but he offered me a place among his crew if I agreed to provide a certain service. I asked what service he spoke of and he said he wished me to be the night watchman aboard his ship Eternity. I was to watch the night water for any sign of the Mer. My stipend would be more than the other crewmates. Reluctantly, I agreed and it wasn't long before we set the sails on the Eternity.

For this old salt, it felt lovely being back on the rolling sea. Eternity was a fine ship. Shanley was a fine captain. The nights were long and frightening for me, however. I kept watch over the blackness, waiting to spot the ghostly glow of the Merfolk. They did not come. The voyage was uneventful. No Merfolk and no gold. Shanley was frustrated.

Soon, the stock was low. We needed to re-supply the Eternity. Shanley ordered us to sail west to the Mosquito Coast. We obeyed and in three days we dropped anchor along the Nicaraguan shore. We hiked inland, set our camp, and spent the next few days gathering fruits and water. We were not alone on this distant land. Darien Indians confronted us but meant no harm. Our captain was skilled and quickly won their trust. I too won the trust of one of the natives. She was beautiful. With dark hair, black eyes, and olive-toned skin. We quickly fell in love. I was a fool.

This tribe had secrets they guarded closely. I sensed this, as did Captain Shanley. He spoke to their chieftain and asked about the Water People. I had never witnessed such uproar! They worshipped the creatures of the sea. Shanley laughed at this. The chieftain was insulted and commanded that we depart at once. Shanley refused to leave. He wanted more time to stock the Eternity. Alas, he had dishonored the tribe and lost their hospitality. The Darien's drew spears, but Shanley drew a pistol. I stepped in front of the tribe leader and ordered Shanley to lower his weapon. He laughed and fired at me, wounding my left arm. I fell and a violent, bloody battle began. Shanley and his men were driven back to the Eternity. I lay in the sand bleeding. I watched the Eternity hoist anchor and sail away. My love cared for me. She dressed my wound and the tribe honored me.

My beautiful lover shared the tribal legends of the Water People with me. This is how I have come to know so much about the Merfolk. Oh, yes. There is much more to write.

Ah, ha! Joy for me! The rain outside has ceased. The air remains dank, however. This cell seems to be shrinking around me, but they have been kind and have given me a window. Though barred, the light and wind come through freely. I will escape this cell. When I die, my body will rot to nothing more than a skeleton clutching this journal. Brittle will my bones become. To dust they will turn and when a warm wind blows into this wretched, stinking cell, the dust of me will ride the air and out I will go...through the barred window! Ha! Yes, I will escape then.

I am tired. I need to rest. I need to eat, but they bring me food as they see fit. Perhaps tonight they will bring me bread. It has been many nights since I have eaten. I shall continue this work on the morrow...if I wake.

My eyes heavy with sleep, I wrapped the blue ribbon around the cover and returned the journal to the hole in the floor.

Chapter 16

Sea and Song

One of the pirates aboard the sloop was older than the rest and could always be found sitting near the mast. They called him the Shanty. He played a small lute and sang with a coarse voice. When he saw me standing by listening to his melody, he waved for me to come close. "Aye! A lover of sea and song?" he asked.

"Yes, sir. In my village we cherished music."

"Sounds like a fine place to hail from, me boy. You be one o' the lads who overcame L'Ollon and his men, aren't you?"

"Yes. My name is Jacob."

"Well then, Jacob," he shouted. "Cause for a song if I e'er heard one. Have you any requests? I would be much obliged to play that which'll lighten your heart."

"Come to think of it," I said, a smile spreading on my face, "I've never heard any songs about…oh, never mind. Any song will do."

"Nay, nay. What is it you meant to ask? You ne'er heard a

song about what?"

"I've never heard any songs about the Water People."

He burst into a loud laugh. "You be speakin' o' the Merfolk, me boy. Come now, I know a cheerful tune about them. Indeed. Me old father learned it to me." He cleared his throat, then yelled out to the crew, "Ahoy! Lend an ear to *Fathoms Blue*."

The Shanty pressed the fingers of his left hand to the neck of the small lute and with his right he strummed the strings. The instrument filled the air with a stream of sweet, repetitive notes. He began to sing.

"In darkened tide,
In fathoms blue,
There'll be eyes
A' watchin' you.
Just jump right in,
Go overboard,
And swim beside the ole'
Merlord!
Ahoy! Ahoy!
To the island blue
If you don't drown
Where the women swim
In fish-mail gown.
So trade your feet
For a fin of weed,
The Merfolk gold
Is a Pirate's greed!"

When the song ended, the old Shanty rested his lute on his lap. "You see, me boy. The old seamen always know a song or two about the Merfolk. Some say that the Merfolk wrote them, stuffed the parchments into bottles and let the bottled tunes loose o'er the waves. They say that men found these bottles driftin' and hence learned the songs. Alas, it's just an old yarn from an old seaman."

Night fell around the sloop. We were close to Grenada, but the enveloping darkness forced us to anchor for the night. Grant and I made our way to the small cabin. I locked the cabin door, retrieved the journal from its hiding place and relaxed in my bed. I turned down the lantern so Grant could sleep. The yellow light dimmed to a soft glow. Shadows filled the room. I opened Owen's journal.

The vagrant in the cell next to mine has died. The buzzing of the flies woke me. The stench made me wish I, too, had ceased to live on this day. At the very least, the sun is hot in the sky. A lovely gold ray of light pours in through my barred window and in its warmth I now write.

The guards have not brought me any food or any drink. I suppose I do not deserve it, but dying slowly is a horrible thing to endure. The unending pains in my stomach and the dryness in my mouth are making me wish I had taken the noose. There is no looking glass in here but when I look down at my hands and arms, I see the beginnings of the skeleton that I am destined to become. I used to be strong. I used to be a lot of things…

Chapter 17
Owen's Yarn

As it were, I was left on the shore of the Nicaraguan Bay with a tribe of Darien natives. The elders amongst them concurred with the chieftain, and it was decided that I was to be told the secrets of the Mer. To be schooled in the way of the Water People was a privilege few outsiders ever received. My lover and I sat around a great red fire and the elder tribesman shared all that he knew and believed.

Trying not to sound disrespectful, I asked him a few questions.

"How have you come to know so much of the Water People?"

"The Chief of the Mer told them to me."

"The Chief of the Mer?"

"Indeed. Lord Sydin is his name. He is wise and has led his tribe of Merfolk for over a hundred years."

"Tribes? You say they live in tribes?"

"That is what I say. Merfolk have always lived in tribes.

Territorial they are, as we humans tend to be. The Mer of this part of the world rarely venture beyond the fringe of their domains. For example, a Mer tribe that inhabits the waters of the north will not be welcomed down in the tropics. The reverse is also true."

"There are different races, then?"

"Of course. Just as there are different races of humans. Why wouldn't there be different races of Mer? Humans that dwell in the lands of Asia resemble the Mer that inhabit the surrounding waters. The same can be said for the people of Africa and the people of the north. We are all exposed to the same elements, such as the sun and wind. These things change us, and so it is that ethnicity is not a trait exclusive to land."

"When he spoke," I asked, "this Mer Chief, this one you call Lord Sydin, what was his voice?"

"The Mer speak in the local tongue of the humans. Here, in the Caribbean, there are many languages, hence, the Merfolk understand them all. As far as Lord Sydin is concerned, well, he speaks all tongues with ease. The Mer that dwell in the Caribbean are the most intelligent. In my opinion, they are also the most beautiful."

"I see. I understand that the ocean is their home, but surely they cannot swim all of the time. What of sleep? What of food?"

"The tastes and customs of the Caribbean Mer are simple. They eat meat from birds and fish, as well as many types of seaweed. They are keen marksmen and skilled hunters rarely bested by other ocean beasts. Even sharks are no match for a team of Merlords.

"They need rest, just as we do. For example, a man is able to run, but does he run everywhere he travels? Nay. Such logic applies to the Mer. They swim but they have their places of comfort. There are small islands, uncharted and unknown to seaman, which they guard and protect. As I have already said, the Mer are territorial. They prefer islands that rest in rising waters, islands containing grottos and a portion of sandy beach. They love rock formations because rocks provide places to hide as well as warmth.

"The island dwellings are important to the Mer society for other reasons. Certain islands are reserved for raising the Merchildren, sanctuaries of learning and growth. Other islands are cache islands used to store collected valuables and food."

"Valuables?" I asked sharply. "Like what?"

"Rope, wood, metal, bone, rock, coral, and shell. They are skilled in working these materials into items that help them survive. They create arrows, swords, and spears of bone and shields of wood and stone. They use these hidden islands to store what they recover from sunken ships as well."

"You've captured my interest," I said rather smugly. "Is it safe to assume these Merfolk would gather lost gold and silver from a shipwreck, then?"

"Of course. Metals such as gold and silver can be re-forged to make great armor, weapons and even jewelry. I forgot to mention how much the Mermaidens love jewelry!"

Upon hearing the old Darien say this, I nearly leapt to my feet with excitement. To think, the Merfolk gathered Jean L'Ollon's gold! That must have been why Captain Shanley couldn't find it.

I asked as calmly as I could, "Do you know the location of any of these Mer Islands? Have the Merlords privileged you with such knowledge?"

He stared at me for a moment. The orange glow of the firelight illuminated his omniscient eyes. He was studying me as if trying to read my thoughts. I smiled to conceal my eagerness.

"I know of one. It is the largest and most sacred of the Merfolk Islands. Though let it be known, I have sworn an oath of secrecy."

"Oh, come now, your secrets are safe with me," I assured him.

"I can say no more. Ask me anything else, please."

"Where is the island?" I nearly shouted. My lover, who up until this moment hadremained calm, turned and glared disapprovingly at me. I released her hand and asked again, "Where is it?"

"What need to know have you, seaman? Do you now show your true heart? Does the thought of an island of treasure stir your greed?"

While the Darien Chief glared at me, I slowly reached for my knife. The hard handle met my fingertips without anyone knowing. With immeasurable quickness, I drew it from the sheath, snatched my beautiful lover and pressed the steel to her throat. There was a small trickle of blood; she was squirming, and I was holding her too hard.

"Answer me or she dies! Where is the island? What is it called?"

The tired and worn old man seemed to crumble with defeat.

"Forgive me, Sydin, forgive me," he whispered. He looked into my eyes. I could see the regret, the fear, and the betrayal in his stare.

I was not swayed.

"It is called Cerulean Isle. The island is northeast of Puerto Bello, west of Aruba. It is southeast of Old Providence. It is not easy to find and the rocks and coral are treacherous when the water is low. Please, lower your blade!"

It was at this moment that an incredible splash erupted from the dark shore. It sounded like cannon fire blasting into the water. I shoved the girl away, snatched a burning branch from the fire and ran for the shore. It was one of them…I was certain. The Mer were listening the whole time and now they had fled!

Once at the water's edge, I waved my makeshift torch, casting its yellow light onto the wet sand. The black waves lapped over my feet. I noticed something odd. A cluster of shiny black seashells was piled neatly on a patch of dry sand as if waiting to be found. I approached the pile of perfectly stacked shells and knelt close to examine it. Each one was smooth and clean. The old man's voice startled me.

"Look at what you have done."

I turned to him and saw my lover cowering behind him. The chief fell to his knees in the sand.

"What is this? Who put this here?" I shouted.

"You know who put it there. It is a warning. It means this tribe has been shunned. We are no longer their allies. I have betrayed them. Leave us! Go and never return."

I left the Dariens. I was fueled with more greedy desires but I decided, first, that Captain Shanley would pay for what he did to me. We had an agreement, after all.

I journeyed south along the coast of Honduras and down to Panama.

It took me two years to get back to Curacao. When I arrived in Willemstad, I was shocked at what had transpired in such a short time.

I learned that Captain Shanley, after abandoning me, retraced L'Ollon's route but took a more southern course to work around the winds. He combed the sea floor and found the wreck of Jean L'Ollon's galleon, the Hydra. He sent divers to pilfer the wreckage and to his good fortune, he recovered four crates of gold, silver, and jewels. Shanley quickly became one of the wealthiest pirates the Caribbean had ever known. He bought several ships and a lavish estate, of which I wasted no time in discovering the whereabouts. It was time for my revenge.

I stole a broadsword and waited outside his estate. When night fell over Curacao, I broke into the mansion. Two bumbling guards challenged me, but they knew naught of my skill and murderous nature. I was a deadly man. After all, the wicked Jean L'Ollon thought me worthy amongst his crew. Ha! I made quick work of the guards. They were dead in mere seconds. It wasn't long before I drove my boot through the door of James Shanley's private quarters. I found the captain sitting behind a desk pouring over old sea charts. He looked up at me with terror in his eyes. He knew who I was. I was the crazy man who raved of Merfolk. I was the pirate he thought he left for dead on Darien sand. I stood in front of him with my bloody sword and grinned.

"We had a deal, James, and you reneged. You owe me money, and it seems you've gathered plenty in the last two years to pay in full."

"Get out of here! Have you gone mad?"

"I suppose at long last I have."

I lunged for him, sword aloft, but my attack was folly. He drew his pistol and shot me…again.

I landed hard on the floor. His shot had made its home in my right thigh. Everything went dark. When I awoke, I found myself bandaged and restrained. I was in the office of the Dutch Navy. They read a list of charges. Trespassing. Assault. Thievery. Professional piracy. Murder. The officers forced me to stand before the judge. I was sentenced to death by the noose. I asked to speak to the judge privately and that was when I bribed him to spare me the deadly rope of the gallows.

Alas, here I am. I have cheated death four times. Poison, two shots, and a noose. Ha! It is simple famine that will kill this great pirate.

I wish I could find the strength to escape this cursed cell. I wish others would have believed me years ago. I wish I had a ship, one that is small and fast. If I had such a ship, I would sail for the Mer Island at once. Now I am dying slowly. No one would sail with me anyway.

This is my great tale. This is my final work. Whoever is reading this, please know that I speak truthfully. At the time of this writing, Jean L'Ollon captains the great *Obsidian* once more. Captain James Shanley remains wealthy, living gloriously off of Jean's lost gold. However, there is more of it out there, much more, and I believe the Merfolk have it.

Cerulean Isle

There are things in this world that others claim to be pure fantasy. To this I yell, nay! The greatest fiction is always rooted in fact. All stories, no matter how unbelievable, have a point of origin. I wish for this, my last work, to be the origin of a great adventure. There is a place out there named Cerulean Isle, the greatest of all Mer Islands. Seek it. Seek it for you and for me…

In Death's Company,
Owen.

Chapter 18

The Burden of Gold

I reached for the dim lantern and put out its tiny flame. Lying in bed, I felt the sway of the sloop and heard soft creaks from the hull. The breathing of the sea was a lullaby. Sleep came quickly and brought with it a dream of her.

The Mermaiden from the tapestry came to life, her suntanned body drying in the tropical heat, and her silky rainbow-hued hair dangling over her shoulders. I imagined her silver eyes looking at me with the same wonder that I held for her. My Mermaiden was waiting on the smooth slab of stone and smiling brightly, her face lovely. Her slender waist curved and beads of saltwater rolled over her hips; it was in this region of her body that her flawless skin began to change color. The rose-gold tint of her female flesh brightened to a gentle shade of purple. This creamy pastel darkened along the contour of her lower half and spread into slight swirling patterns of deep lavender, brilliant blue, tropical teal, and milky pearl until all of the glorious streaming colors tapered down her length, blending and blooming to become a great fanning fin. This otherworldly part of her crested out of the sea and unfurled, like a translucent sail, over her head. Crystal water cascaded from the dazzling fin and spilled over her face and neck. Sparkling ocean water pattered on her delicate hands and slender fingers—fingers adorned with rings of pearl with nails that shimmered like diamonds.

"Wake up, Jacob." Grant shook my shoulder. He looked refreshed from a deep night's sleep.

"Why do you always wake me like that?"

"I don't know how to wake you otherwise."

"Just call my name or something." I sat up and felt Owen's journal slide from my chest and flop onto my lap.

"Did you read the entire book last night?"

"Yes. You must read it. It's fascinating."

"Perhaps I will once we are settled on land. For now, you had best put it away. Waylin has ordered us to prepare for departing the ship."

"What of the chart? You've put it someplace safe, haven't you?"

"Of course. It's folded and tucked tightly in my shirt."

The crew focused on sailing cautiously over the coral reefs that plagued the shallow green water. Grant and I stood at the bow looking out at the island. Dense fog covered the peaks of the great mountains that ruled the land. Clusters of houses dotted the waterfront, interspersed with patches of sandy beaches. Large black rocks fortified the shores of Grenada, and as our agile sloop swam closer, a thin layer of morning fog fell over us.

"Welcome to Grenada," Waylin spoke from behind us. "We are now entering St. George's Harbor. Grenada is an interesting place; it's always been one of my favorite islands."

"Why is that?" I asked.

"Well, St. George's has the safest natural harbor in the entire Caribbean. The coral we just passed protects it from larger ships. We'll dock in a few minutes. Forgive me, but I must leave you now to take the helm. We'll talk more soon."

Waylin left us, and we watched anxiously as St. George's Harbor embraced our ship. The waterfront was crowded with ships similar to ours. We could see lush green hillsides where farms had been carved out of the tropical forest.

I was nervous about venturing onto a strange island amid strange people. The uncertainty of my future scared me the most. What would become of me? What of Waylin and Christoff? Would the rest of their lives be spent constantly eluding L'Ollon's crew? Would I hear in a year's time that their bones washed up on a distant shore?

"We should help them," I said to Grant.

"Help who?"

"Christoff and Waylin. We should help them as they have helped us. It's only a matter of time before L'Ollon's crew finds them."

"What do you propose?" asked Grant.

"To send them off with their own fortune. A portion of our gold should go to them. What say you?"

"Jacob, listen. You are intelligent and brave, but sometimes you must think of *your* future before the future of others. Only days ago, we were in the bowels of a foul barque, cold and hungry. The tables turned for us when we found the gold in Shanley's storeroom. That is *our* money. We risked our lives for it, and it should stay with us."

"Christoff risked his life to save ours. We owe him something for that."

"What about the deaf boy, Sebastian? Christoff let him die. He stood there while L'Ollon pulled the trigger. He let Shanley die, too. Before all of that, Christoff led us to the lion's den and left us to skulk about on our own. We could have been killed any moment in that villa. He had his own agenda, and we watched it unfold in the foyer. We watched him buy the sloop and pay for the crew. If he cared a pretty shilling for us, he would have privileged us with knowing his intentions the moment we set foot in Willemstad. Here we are, on the edge of a wealthy new life, and you want to give it away?"

"Every reale is stained with the blood of murder," I said.

"Because it was acquired through piracy."

"What is it about the pirate's life that keeps you so enchanted?"

"Pirates are free. What's wrong with wanting freedom?"

"There is nothing wrong with freedom. That's what I want too. But I will have it by making decisions that separate me from people like Jean L'Ollon and James Shanley. There may come a day when you have one chance to choose either right or wrong, a final decision that makes the difference between becoming the person you've dreamt of being, or becoming the person you've feared. What will you choose?"

"I guess…I guess I don't know," he answered.

I turned from him and walked away.

"Where are you going?" asked Grant.

"To tell Christoff about the gold and that he may keep my share. I don't want it. I don't need it."

"Wait," he shouted after me. "I'm coming with you. I don't need it either."

Chapter 19
Sharing the Wealth

We found Christoff standing beside Waylin at the bridge of the sloop. Waylin clutched the helm with both hands and turned the large wheel. The graceful sloop responded and drifted smoothly into the wharf. The deckhands tossed line to the dockworkers, and together they eased the ship close to the wooden walks and moored it tightly to the pilings. The crew prepared the gangway for us to disembark. Once all was secure, Christoff gave us his attention and we revealed our cache of gold and silver.

"This sack contains a fortune, lads!" Christoff exclaimed. "You say you stole this from Shanley?" He handed the wealth to Waylin, who poured out a handful.

"Do you know what kind of a coin this is?" Waylin asked, holding the large gold coin under the sunlight. It gleamed as if on fire.

"It's a doubloon," I said.

"You are familiar with currency, Jacob?"

"A little. My village in Cuba was a trade post settlement. My father was a great…" I stopped my ramble. "Go on."

"Allow me to explain what you've got here. Obviously, gold is worth more than silver. To be quite accurate, an ounce of silver is worth one-sixteenth the value of an ounce of gold. All of the common silver coins that you see glimmering in the palms of merchants and smiths are called reales." He picked a silver coin from his palm and tossed it to me. "That is a reale; its value is one."

I had seen many like it throughout my short life.

"Here," he tossed me another silver coin, much larger. "That is called a piece of eight. It is worth eight reales, making those two silver coins worth what?"

"Nine reales," I answered.

"Correct. Now, here is a medium-sized silver coin. This one is worth four reales. It is called a half piece of eight. On to the gold," said Waylin. "This large doubloon is one ounce of gold, worth sixteen pieces of eight."

"Sixteen of these?" Grant held up the large silver coin.

"Indeed, lad. And equally so, this doubloon is worth one hundred and twenty eight reales. That's right, one hundred and twenty eight of the small silver coins that you see everyday. Every single gold coin you stole is a doubloon and nearly every silver coin among them is a full piece of eight. You have made yourselves quite rich."

Christoff stepped toward the bow and gazed out at the rolling water. He stood for several minutes with his hands clasped behind his back. He took a deep breath and let it out slowly as if finishing a thought. His attention returned to us.

"I must ask you lads if you were successful in carrying out Jean L'Ollon's orders. Did you recover his sea chart and the leather book as he instructed?"

I did not know what to say. I did not want to reveal the book to anyone.

"Yes," Grant answered. "We stole the sea chart and found

the book, but both items were lost during our escape. I'm sorry."

"Then it be just as well," declared Christoff. "Things of such controversy are better lost."

Waylin poured the coins back into the bag and handed it to me. I gave the pouch to Christoff. "We wish to repay you for saving our lives."

Christoff stared at the pouch. "I...I cannot accept this. It belongs to you and Grant."

"It is not my wish to keep it," I replied.

"Indeed, Christoff," Grant concurred. "There is enough to share. It's the pirate way. The captain's articles guarantee a share of all loot. For example, the great Bartholomew Roberts' articles forty years ago said, 'The captain and the quartermaster shall each receive two shares of a prize.' Are there not articles governing this sloop that should be enforced in this matter? Let us do what is right."

Christoff looked over at Waylin, who shrugged. Christoff said, "I face two worthy seamen, two fair pirates. If this is your solemn pledge, then the bounty shall be divided equally amongst us or not at all. Good lads, thank you."

Waylin shook our hands. "From this day forth, I will be at your service," he vowed. "Wherever life takes you, should you need me, I will come. This, I regret, is all I can offer in gratitude."

Chapter 20

A Real Scoundrel

Waylin led us off the ship. My legs trembled and my stomach began to turn as my body acclimated to the unmoving land. I breathed slowly until my stomach settled.

The people of Grenada welcomed us. Women batted their eyes at Waylin and fellow seafarers shouted 'aye' as we made our way along the harbor.

"Follow me," said Waylin. "We'll surely find Raphael at Cod Fish."

"Who is Raphael?" I asked.

"And what is Cod Fish?" Grant added.

"Raphael Renard," answered Waylin, "is a man who knows how to make people disappear. He'll make sure L'Ollon's men can't track you down. Cod Fish Tavern is the busiest watering hole in St. George's."

A short walk along a stony road led us into the capital of St. George's. To the east I could see the ominous peaks of Grenada's two mountains, the smaller St. David and the larger

St. Catherine, rising above the dark green hillsides. Set against the bright blue sky, they wore thick shadows. The mountains were grand but silent, like two fallen giants kneeling in defeat. St. George's was bustling and boasted a large marketplace where farmers, merchants, and traders networked, and common folk spent their money. Once outside Cod Fish Tavern, Waylin stopped to warn us.

"This place is always full of seamen from all over the world. Sometimes, there are rival pirates. Keep your mouths closed and stay by my side. A place like this can be dangerous. We'll find Raphael and go from there."

The sounds of clanking mugs and the smell of rum filled the air inside the tavern. Barmaids brought foaming carafes to tables of boisterous men. Some of the patrons played games with dice, others arm wrestled, all of them laughed at those who lost. I heard many different languages, but each one was slurred from too much drink. We snaked through the crowd and met a man seated at the bar. He was a wiry man, sunburned with short sandy hair. He and Waylin shook hands.

"Raphael Renard, this is Jacob and Grant. They have need of your talents."

"Aye, Waylin. Let us be off to my shack on the edge of town. We'll talk in detail there."

We left Cod Fish Tavern, and at a nearby stable Waylin paid for the use of two brown horses and purchased two more. I was given a white horse and Grant took the reins of a black one. We mounted up and rode across town to Raphael's residence.

He had called it a shack, and rightly so. The structure was made from scrap wood, planks and thatch. It was large enough for a table, chest, and bed. We sat around the table and formed a plan.

"I can help, but it'll cost yah. I don't work for free," said Raphael.

Waylin put four pieces of eight on the table. Raphael leaned back in his chair and crossed his arms. Waylin put down two more silver coins. "Take it or we go elsewhere."

"Where else you gonna go, Waylin? I don't work for silver."

"You're a damn crook, a real scoundrel!"

"Of course," Raphael replied with a grin, his remaining teeth brown and broken.

Waylin collected the silver coins and put down a gold doubloon. Raphael's eyes widened. He snatched up the coin and stuffed it in his pocket. "I'll take care of these boys, Waylin. They can stay with me for a few nights. I'll put them aboard a merchant ship next week that'll take them north, out of the Caribbean entirely, to the colonies. Sound good, boys?"

We nodded, and Waylin stood up from the table. "Then it's settled. I shall leave you in the care of Raphael. Christoff and I set sail in a few hours. The day is young and we can catch the winds north west. Good luck to you, lads. Be well always." We shook Waylin's hand and watched him leave the shack.

~~~~~~

We passed the day listening to Raphael tell stories about the various vagrants and pirates that he helped evade capture. His primary connection was with traders and other mercantile companies. His business was simple: a criminal would pay him to book passage aboard a merchant ship sailing out of the Caribbean. To maintain the connections with the merchant captains, Raphael sabotaged the affairs of other merchants by stealing cargo, damaging rival ships, or poisoning crew members to delay scheduled departures. For him it was easy work, but he often gambled away his income, forcing himself to live in poverty.

We had decided on riding into town for a meal before nightfall when a man with a thick French accent called from outside the shack. "Raphael Renard! This is Commandant Leopold. Surrender or be taken by force!"

"Blasted French Navy! They've been trying to bring me in for weeks, but I've been hiding here." Raphael pulled a small knife from his belt and hid behind the edge of the doorway.

"Ceci est votre derniere chance," shouted the commandant. "This is your last chance. Come out now or we'll send someone in to get you."

"Go ahead, Leopold, but I know the truth. You want to put me away because you're as corrupt as I am." Raphael pointed to the wooden table we had been sitting at. "Topple that table, boys, and stay behind it. They're likely to start shooting."

We overturned the table and crouched behind it. I peered through the cracks in the boards. A naval officer entered the shack. When he passed through the doorway, Raphael lunged for him, wrapping his arms around his shoulders and slicing the man's throat. The officer fell dead in the doorway.

Raphael stepped out from hiding. "His blood is on your hands, Leopold. You sent him in here to die." Shots rang out. Raphael was filled with holes as he stood over the dead officer. We watched him fall, lifeless and bloody.

Chapter 21

The Commandant

Commandant Leopold entered the room. He wore a wide black hat and dark blue overcoat with shining gold buttons. His scarlet vest was tight around his torso and a polished silver cutlass gleamed as it hung from his white belt. He kicked away the table and glared as he spoke. *"Qui êtes vous?"*

Neither Grant nor I understood French. The commandant's brow dipped. "Who are you?" he asked sharply.

"My name is Grant and this is Jacob."

"Since you were in the company of that swine, I can only assume that you are criminals." More naval officers entered the shack. The commandant gave them an order. *"Emmenez les avec vous."*

The officers bound our wrists and forced us from the shack. We walked as the officers rode atop their horses. They pulled our black and white horses behind them. We ventured through town and came to St. George's jail, a gray stone building with small barred windows. The commandant led us down a narrow hall and forced us into a small cell with cold iron bars. A mound of straw in the corner was the only means of comfort. An older man with curling grey hair looked on from the cell across the hallway.

Commandant Leopold untied our wrists. "You two will remain here until I decide what is best for you. Now give me your possessions, the pouches on your belts."

"I'm not giving you anything!" shouted Grant.

Leopold struck him with the back of his hand, then shoved him to the ground. A stream of blood ran from his nose. Grant wiped at it, his hands balled to fists. I felt anger swelling inside of me. I leapt for the sword hanging from Leopold's belt. My hand closed around the handle, and I drew it from the scabbard. The blade rang as I readied it, just as Beelo had shown me. Grant scrambled to his feet.

"Stand aside, Commandant," I ordered. "We will have our freedom."

He stood motionless, staring. I ordered him again. "Move away from the cell door, or I will run you through."

He reached behind the tails of his blue overcoat to produce a pistol and aimed the barrel at me. "Hand over your belongings and live or come at me and die. Choose."

"Here," said Grant. He tossed his pouch, and it landed at the commandant's feet. "Just take it. We'll cooperate henceforth. Lower the blade, Jacob."

I relinquished my sword and pouch. When the commandant opened our pouches and saw the silver eights and gold doubloons, he smiled wide, slammed our cell door closed, and secured the heavy lock.

"You've made me a rich man, young pirates. Enjoy your new home." As he turned to walk away, the man in the cell across the hall stopped him.

"Leopold, you're a rotten thief. It is you who belongs in that cell. Not them."

"Silence, Martin, or I'll see to it that the three of you are hanged at sunset."

Martin pressed his round face against the bars. "You're the biggest criminal in Grenada. Someday I swear you'll—" the commandant punched him square in the face. Martin fell backward with a groan. Commandant Leopold left. I could hear our fortune chiming in his palms.

The cell was cold when night eclipsed Grenada. We sat on the mound of straw, frustrated and angry over the loss of our fortune. A guard delivered our dinner—grits and mugs of water.

Martin called out to us from his cell. "Are you boys well enough?"

Grant swirled his grits with his spoon. "Yes. We'll be fine. Thanks for trying to help."

"Wish I could've done more. Say." He looked at me. "You've got some courage, don't you? That was a bold move you made. I would've loved to see you cut Leopold down, but a sword is no match against a pistol."

Grant swallowed a mouthful of the pale paste. "So what did you do to end up here?"

"Three months ago, Leopold and his men came to my farm and forced my son to join the French Navy. I knew I couldn't possibly work the farm alone, and besides, I love my son. I didn't want him to go."

"So you tried to stop them from taking him?" I asked.

"That's right. I did all I could, but I am just a farmer. My wife and I watched them take our only boy away, and with him went our chances for making ends meet. I was jailed for interfering in official matters. My wife, Anna, came to see me a week ago and told me that she'll have to sell our farm soon."

"I'm sorry for your troubles, Martin," offered Grant. "When will you be released?"

"I won't be, as long as Commandant Leopold is in charge.

When it comes to fighting the French Navy, I am outnumbered."

"We'll just have to even the odds, then."

"How can we possibly do that from behind bars?" Martin asked.

"No worries." Grant took his spoon and snapped off the thin metal handle. "I have an idea."

Chapter 22

In Leopold's Pocket

Grant jammed the spoon handle into the large iron lock. He had to reach around the bars to get to it, and in that position he was forced to pick the lock backward. The guards had begun patrolling the grounds, giving us a small window of time to escape. The lock popped.

Grant said, "Head for the doorway and watch for the guards. I'll work Martin's lock. Tap the floor if anyone approaches."

I crept to the front door of the jail and peered into the night. The guards were gone, likely patrolling the rear of the building. After only a minute, Grant and Martin joined me.

We were free, running as fast as we could to our horses. I mounted my white horse and Grant saddled up the black one. Martin stole one of the guard's horses and we rode down the shadowy road.

Martin laughed and inhaled the cool night air. "It feels great to be free, boys. Wondrous and rejuvenating! Hang on, dear Anna, I'm coming home."

"Not yet, Martin," Grant shouted over the hammering of the horses' hooves. "Escaping was the first part of my plan."

"What's next?" I asked.

"Get the gold and put an end to Leopold."

"We don't know where he is."

"I do. He's celebrating his wealth. That's what any man would do. What's the busiest watering hole in St. George's?" Grant asked.

"Cod Fish Tavern," I answered, remembering Waylin's earlier words.

"And that's likely where he'll be. Come on." He cracked his reins. "Let's get our gold."

~~~~~~

Cod Fish was brimming with drunkards, sailors, and commoners. In the far corner of the room, pirates played cards beside a large open window.

"It's a betting game, now," shouted one to another. "Let's up the stakes like men should."

"Aye. Name your price for the next hand, and I'll see me way in."

"I've fancied that shiny gold ring you've got on that necklace since Bonaire. Buy in with that and we'll have a game."

"And what of you, mate? What are you offering?"

"Me dagger will pay me way in." He pulled a long clean knife from his belt and put it on the table. "Me own mum used this blade on me pappy when I was boy. It's been cutting down men since." The pirates broke into a roar of laughter.

"Aye, a worthy prize to gamble for. Deal the cards."

Commandant Leopold sat at the bar. He was out of uniform and wore a clean white blouse with brown pants and black shoes.

"Look," said Grant. "Our pouches hang from his belt. I'm going to steal them back in a moment, but we must get ready." The pirates roared again as the card game commenced. "Jacob, go outside and hide on the other side of the open window near the pirates' card game. Once I've picked the gold off Leopold, I will pass it to you there."

Martin interrupted. "I don't like this plan of yours. Listen, boys, we're free. Let's just go home to Anna. We can relax and have a nice meal."

I stood up, ready to do as Grant asked.

"You're going through with this?" Martin asked. "You're likely to get killed."

"I've learned to trust Grant. Besides, that gold belongs to us, and I will fight for it however I can. We need it more than you know."

Martin let out a defeated sigh. "What can I do to help?"

"Ready our horses and wait outside with Jacob," ordered Grant.

Martin and I went outside the tavern and slipped around to the side window. From there, we could see the entire room.

"Ahoy! The prize is all mine," shouted one of the pirates. After revealing his winning hand, he tossed the cards into the air. He scooped up the necklace bearing the gold ring and held it up proudly. The others cheered. He returned his dagger to its sheath.

"Be it well," said the defeated man. "Lady Luck will be me whore before we set sail, you'll see." He leaned back in his chair and drank from his mug.

The winner kissed the ring and tucked it in his pocket. It was then I saw Grant creeping up behind him. Martin saw him, too. "What is he doing?"

Grant's eyes were fixed on the pocket containing the gold ring. He snaked toward the men, stepping in and out of view, ducking behind patrons, vanishing briefly among the shuffle of the crowd.

"They don't see him," Martin exclaimed. "I don't believe it."

"It's his good fortune they're all drunk," I remarked.

Soon, Grant was stooped behind the victorious pirate. He did not linger. He made one ghostly movement with his hand, and slipped back into the crowd. I lost sight of him for several minutes. I fixed my gaze across the room; Commandant Leopold called for another drink. He brought the mug to his lips, leaned back, and drank. Grant, the red-haired phantom, appeared behind him and in two moves had reclaimed our pouches. He slipped away.

Leopold reached for the pouch of coins to pay for the drink. He found only an empty belt and noticed Grant dashing across the tavern. "Stop that boy," he shouted.

Grant ran toward the window. Leopold chased after him, knocking down patrons and stumbling over chairs. Grant reached the window and threw the pouches of gold and silver to me. Leopold grabbed him. "I've got you now, you little bastard!"

Grant shouted, "This man stole your ring, I saw him do it!"

The pirate sprang from his chair and checked the pocket where his prize had been. His face reddened, and his eyes became angry slits.

"That's absurd," argued Leopold. The men circled him. "Do you know who I am? I am Commandant Leopold of the French Navy. Stand down, all of you."

"He's lying to you," Grant insisted. "He's Grenada's finest thief. He's been at the bar all night waiting to pilfer your winnings."

"Aye, that's right," said the pirate. He pulled his long dagger from the sheath and grabbed Leopold by the front of his white blouse. "You have been at the bar all night. I've seen ya there."

"Check his pocket," coaxed Grant. "You'll find the necklace and ring there."

"Silence, you foul little vermin," ordered Leopold. He wrenched Grant closer to him. *"Vous n'avez pas raison!"* There is no reason for that; there is nothing in my pocket. I can assure you."

Cerulean Isle

Grant's hand moved behind Leopold.

"Then you won't be minding if I have me a look. If I find me prize, you're dead." The pirate pulled Grant away from Leopold's grip. "You've done well by me, lad." Grant stepped away from the circle and made for the window.

The pirate checked Leopold's pockets and found the necklace and ring. He dangled it in front of his face. "You lying, bloody thief. No one steals from a pirate and lives."

"This is an outrage. I did not steal your—" Commandant Leopold's words were broken as a dagger slammed into his stomach. A sickening scream echoed through the tavern as the pirate turned and twisted his blade. The commandant fell over, his face smacking against the wood floor. Blood pooled around him. The pirate held the necklace over his head; the others cheered and began dealing cards.

Chapter 23

Rosewing Farm

Martin led us up the hillside to his farm. The restless ocean shimmered through breaks in the tree line. The night was clear; the bright moon was high, and its reflection danced on the black, starlit sea.

"Keep riding, boys," Martin called. "Rosewing is just ahead."

"Your farm is called Rosewing?" asked Grant.

"Yes. All good farms are named; it's a way of distinguishing the property and product. It creates pride and identity. My family has owned it for many generations. Rosewing was carved out of the fertile hillside by my forefathers. Up until recently, it was one of the finest farms in Grenada."

We came to a two-story white house with many windows and a large porch. We dismounted and hitched our horses.

"Anna," called Martin, racing up the short staircase to the front door. "I'm free!"

The door opened and there, holding a candle, stood Anna.

Her face, confused at first, brightened in joy. Tears streamed down her face as she put aside the candle and threw her arms around her husband. They held one another tightly for several minutes under the light of the Caribbean moon. He whispered things to her, words I could not hear from the base of the stairs. She laughed and cried at the same time and pulled away from him to clasp his face in her hands.

Martin remembered us and quickly turned to make a proper introduction. "Anna, I'd like you to meet Jacob and Grant. They're the reason I'm with you now."

Anna came down the stairs and hugged us firmly. "I've been praying for God to save Martin; it seems He heard my prayers and sent two angels. Welcome to Rosewing. Please, won't you come in? Let me make you something to eat." We accepted her offer and followed her inside.

Lanterns warmed each room with a soft yellow light. The farm house was clean and larger than the ones I recalled from my village. The wooden floors creaked as we followed Anna through the halls to the dining room.

Anna served a hot meal of chicken, vegetables, and mugs of goat's milk. She buttered warm rolls set atop small bowls of honeyed rice. As we dined, Martin told her all about the events leading up to our freedom. His account was animated; he impersonated me leaping for Leopold's sword, then Grant crouching to pick the cell locks. Martin even did his best to mimic the pirates in the tavern. When he told the moment of Leopold falling to the floor, Anna smiled and clapped in delight of our victory.

"How can I ever repay you boys?" she asked.

Grant finished his rice and pushed aside his bowl. "In all honesty, we have nowhere to go. If you could show us around the island and help us find a place to live, I'd be willing to call us even."

Martin refilled our mugs, then sat back in his chair. "Why not stay here with Anna and me? I don't know how much longer we'll have this place, but you're welcome to—"

"You're still going to sell the farm?" I asked.

"I've been in jail for too long. The crop has suffered, and we don't have the help to work the fields. My land has died. We have no choice but to sell."

Anna gathered our empty bowls and plates. "You see, a farm is a living thing. The soil must be nurtured and the crop meticulously cared for and harvested. A farmer needs to become a part of his land. Only then will the farm be fruitful."

Grant leaned back and folded his arms behind his head. "It sounds like a lot of work."

"True," replied Martin. "But it's the most important work there is."

"Why do you say that?"

"We're talking about food. Saloons open and close, peddlers offer odds and ends, but it's food that *always* sells. Who is more valuable, more necessary than a farmer?"

Grant looked deep in thought. "A farmer can offer his produce to everyone, but he sets the price."

"Correct," replied Martin. "The many farms throughout the islands of the Caribbean keep the seamen alive at sea. When a ship returns to the harbor, the captain's first priority is restocking. There is money to be made."

"And deals, too. Tell me, Martin, what if a farm becomes known for supplying the best quality food throughout the Caribbean? What then?"

"Then that farmer becomes a rich man, noble and respected for his work."

Grant looked at me. "Supply the best to become the best. Sounds easy enough."

"What are you suggesting?" I asked.

"Martin wants to sell the farm, I suggest we buy it!"

I nodded my agreement. Grant opened his pouch and poured a fistful of gold and silver on the table. "Martin, Anna, we wish to buy Rosewing, the land, the home, all of it." Martin's eyes widened, and Anna gasped in disbelief.

I added, "And you will stay here. This will always be your home."

"Besides," Grant said with a smile, "I don't know the first thing about farming."

"Yes," I agreed. "We need your help. Teach us to farm; teach us how to make Rosewing better than the rest."

...Part Two...

Grenada, Ten Years Later

Chapter 24

Trouble in the Tavern

From the farm on the mountainside, we could see the lively town of St. George's, and behind it, the never-ending Caribbean Sea. The sky and ocean mirrored each other; the burning sun teased its trembling reflection with splashes of orange, pink, and yellow. Far off, the edges of blue touched to create the horizon's seam. As the western ocean swallowed the daylight, we finished our labor and spoke of evening plans.

Grant told me he was going to Cod Fish Tavern after working the fields. Cod Fish had become his favorite establishment. It was the largest of all the pubs in St. George's, owned and operated by an old fisherman from the north. For a mere half piece of eight, a patron could rent a room for the night. When Grant asked if I wanted to join him, I declined.

"Why not?" he asked, following me into the barn.

"I just don't feel like the company of drunkards tonight." I began hanging the tools while Grant unrolled the tethers and reins for tomorrow's trip to the market. The black horse, named

Teach, and the white one, Morgan, neighed and snorted in their stalls.

"Come now, Jacob. It's been a long time since I've seen you enjoy yourself. You aren't happy."

My anger had grown with each passing year. Many things reminded me of my early life: the farms, the market, and the jostling crowds. The customs of the Grenadine people were very much like my trading village in Cuba. Whenever a mother and child passed me, I would feel an old pain flutter within me. Hearing the slur of drunken beggars or the cackling laugh of ill-mannered seamen made me recall the sounds of L'Ollon's men reveling on the deck.

"It's the dreams, isn't it?" he asked. "You're dreaming of your father again."

I nodded. The long and restless nights were awful for me, and my fatigue and anger made my imaginings darken. My hands never forgot the feeling of stabbing Jean L'Ollon. In my remembrance of that day, my mind replaced L'Ollon with my father. Yes, I imagined killing my father. I imagined this more and more, and when I did, I felt satisfied; only then could I sleep. "I don't mean to burden you."

"No worries. You've got to fight it. The best way to overcome the darkest of nights is to have the brightest of days. You have to do things that make you happy and when you lay your head to rest, you'll do so smiling and then, my friend, you'll sleep peacefully."

"Perhaps you're right."

"Of course I'm right." He smiled playfully. "Come to the Cod Fish. I'll buy you a drink and we'll see if there are any lonely barmaids interested in the company of two seafaring nobles."

The sailors enjoyed talking with him in the pubs, and the ladies gathered around to hear his tales of thieving as a youth.

"Still living in a fantasy, I see."

"Just having the brightest of days."

In a decade's time, we had grown to become strong men. My arms were solid with lean muscle, and my hands had become tough and leathery from farming. My skin was bronzed and my short brown hair bleached with swirls of gold from the merciless Grenadine sun. My face wore constant brown stubble; I was not very good at shaving. Having agreed to accompany Grant to the tavern, I changed into a clean white shirt that laced below the collar with long sleeves. With this I wore a black belt, loose brown pants, and pigskin shoes.

Grant was a few inches taller than me. He had let his red hair grow to become a fiery, curly mane which he seldom tied back. He loved to stand out in a crowd, and I was not surprised when he chose to wear his favorite scarlet blouse. It had gold embroidery along the blooming cuffs and wavy hem. His brown belt tapered the red garment around his waist, and his tight black pants tucked into his floppy brown boots. The sunlight gleamed off an oversized, brass belt buckle, and he carried a short sword on his hip. He looked like the grandest of pirates.

After changing into clean clothes, we saddled our horses and rode to town. Only a sliver of the sun remained above the horizon. One by one, the stars ignited and glimmered softly over the island. St. George's refused to rest. Lanterns burned and the orange light dispelled the thickening shadows. Candles lit in windows and the bright glow from household hearths made every home look warm and inviting.

Grenada was peaceful. The French were kind and intelligent. Many spoke fragments of English, enough for use in commerce. Each year, more and more English settlers inhabited the island. People came from all corners of the world to make Grenada their home, and with them came stories of far away lands. In the pubs I met folks from Portugal, Spain, Great Britain, Africa, South America, and even the Colonies.

A light burned outside Cod Fish Tavern, a beacon to the wayward or weary. We secured Teach and Morgan and stepped inside. Not much had changed in the establishment over the years.

Grant led me to the bar where two stools waited for us. He motioned for the barkeep. "Rum please, my good man!"

"Aye!" roared the barkeeper. "Anything for the Lords of Rosewing…as long as you've brought some of your wealth to spend."

With Martin and Anna's help, Rosewing was renowned for producing the finest produce and spices on the entire island. Our prices were fair, our goods fresh, and we paid our workers well. At the markets, the people hurried to our stand.

Though we had become skilled farmers and successful businessmen, Grant never stopped fancying life at sea, and this passion won us many contracts with local seamen. Grant offered discounts to seafarers if they signed with Rosewing as their sole supplier. His knowledge of sailing and his cunning personality made him a talented businessman along the wharf.

~~~~~

The barkeep set a carafe and two mugs in front of us. Grant poured my drink. I lifted the mug and took a few gulps of the harsh rum.

"This is awful," I said. "I think I'll ask for some wine."

"Wine?" asked Grant disapprovingly. "You don't go to a pub to sip wine." He swallowed down the drink. "Rum is the only thing that'll put wind in your sails."

After two more drinks, he wobbled on his stool. "See, the ship's swaying already." He lifted his empty tankard.

"That's enough for tonight, friend," said the bartender. "Time to pay up."

Grant wore a pouch of coins next to the short sword on his belt. He removed the pouch and dumped the contents. Silver reales and eights gleamed and every patron seemed to hear the chiming coins fall. The barkeep gathered up what was due and I gathered the rest.

Cerulean Isle

"Put these away, you fool," I snapped. "You know better than to flash around money like this."

"No worries, it's my money to flash. Bartender, give Jacob some wine, he's a man of refined tastes."

"Forget the wine. I think I should get this lout home." I took Grant by the underarms and helped him off the stool. His legs were shaky and he leaned his weight on me for stability.

The sailors at the table to our left jeered. Grant heard their taunts and staggered to their table. He stood over the leader of the group. "You got something to say, rabble-rouser?"

"Get out o' me face. I'll send your floggin' ass about the gravel in two shakes, rat!" yelled the seaman.

When I heard the man speak, I knew what he was. It became clear just how serious the situation could get.

"Two shakes? It's going to take more than that to best me," Grant slurred.

The men laughed. The leader stood up, a large man. I made my way to Grant's side. The pirates saw my approach and glared at me. I stepped in front of Grant and faced the leader.

"Come to save the rat, have you?" asked the leader.

"Like many in this place, he's had too much to drink. Pardon his remarks and we shall pardon yours," I said calmly. The entire room gathered around. The leader stepped closer to me, his dirty, sunburned face a mere inch from mine.

"Best do what he says," Grant said. "'Cause Jacob's killed far worse than you."

"Grant," I muttered through gritted teeth. "Silence."

"That so?" hissed the pirate. "No one is worse than me."

He shoved me hard. I stumbled backward and knocked into Grant. He fell, collapsing a table. Broken boards were strewn about the room. I staggered but remained on my feet. I turned to my attacker. His fist struck my face hard. A brilliant flash exploded behind my eyes as I fell.

Blood trickled over my lips, and when I tasted it, my anger inflamed. Though I was in the tavern, the scene changed in my mind. The crowded barroom melted, revealing a back alley and rocky dirt road. The man standing over me became Jean L'Ollon. I stood up, and he swung at me. I ducked and slammed my fist into his stomach. The barroom returned. The dirt road darkened to become the wooden planks of the tavern floor.

The leader recovered quickly from my punch. He rushed for me. The crowd was enjoying the brawl. I had nowhere to run and little space to move. Men gathered in a tight circle to watch the fight. A table was behind me, atop of which were some empty bottles. I grabbed one and gripped the neck tightly. He lunged forward; I sidestepped and smashed the bottle over his head. Glass shattered and filled the air. A shard tore the top of his head open and blood poured. He was dazed. I punched his face as hard as I could. Thick globs of blood sprayed into the crowd. My enemy fell, clutching his wounded head. There was a tremendous cheer from the crowd, but among their hollers of admiration, I heard Grant groaning as he struggled to get up. I lifted him out of the rubble.

"Sorry about all this," he said wearily. Suddenly, he paled, his eyes fixed on something behind me. A strange silence filled the room.

I could smell the powder and felt the hard barrel jab into my back. The pirate spoke slow and clear. "The red-haired rat has a lot o' money in that pouch o' his. Give it to me and I might save me shot."

I looked down at Grant's belt. The pouch dangled next to his short sword. *The sword!*

"You try me patience. Give me the pouch."

I took hold of the pouch.

"Hey! That's mine," Grant slurred drunkenly, about to pass out. His knees buckled.

As Grant collapsed, my hand shifted from the pouch to the hilt of his sword. I drew the blade from the scabbard and swung it fiercely behind me. The sword flashed yellow from the lantern light and a metallic chime rang out as the perfect edge sliced the air in a deadly whirl. The blade cut deeply into the pirate's shoulder. He screamed in agony. The pistol fell and exploded. The shot blasted a hole in the wall behind us.

The feeling of the sword in my hand was empowering. An old remembrance swept over me. It had been many years since I had used a sword, but there was no awkwardness in me. The sword was my guide, a friend forged for protection.

My bloody enemy stood alone, defeated, his friends gone. Such is the way of pirates.

I moved forward, the sword driving me on. The pirate saw my advance and staggered backward, his face a crimson mask. He fell to his knees and cringed in terror as I held the sword aloft. *What was I doing?* An overwhelming fear seized my heart. I froze. I stood over my adversary as he clutched his awful wound. Blood pooled around us.

Noticing my apprehension, the others seized their mate and pulled him out of the tavern. I dropped the sword and walked away.

Chapter 25

The Old Man

I helped Grant mount my white horse, Morgan. I secured Teach's reins to my saddle. The ride home was slow. The hour was late. Rain clouds had come and swept over the moon and stars, making the road dark. I held tightly to Grant and pulled Teach close behind. My drunken friend was beginning to fall asleep and it became difficult to ride and hold his weight in the saddle.

Once back at Rosewing, I let the horses roam and hoisted Grant over my shoulder. As I carried him to the front door, I heard a crackle in the surrounding forest. I stopped and peered into the dark. I heard the sound again. Someone, or something, was lurking in the forests of Rosewing. Our farm was a favorite target for all kinds of creatures, and over the years it was a constant battle to keep our crop safe. The noise was likely an animal.

I locked the doors and half-carried Grant to his bedroom. He collapsed on the bed muttering, "The cooper's nail is never dull, ahoy." I retired to my suite.

For an hour or so, I stared at my collection of paintings and let my thoughts trail. Living among the rich culture of Grenada, I had developed a profound interest in art. I often scoured the marketplace for new paintings, primarily interested in renderings of sea life. I had exquisite likenesses of sea turtles floating within rippling blue worlds and silver-gray dolphins cresting from serrated waves. I adored the paintings of tropical fish schooling around castles of coral. Yet my collection was not complete. I had canvases of nearly every creature dwelling in the sea, except for my Mermaiden.

I blamed myself for this evening's events. How could I have let something like this happen? Our success as suppliers was contingent on our reputation. Grant and I must maintain our professionalism and keep the respect of the island. No seafarer or trading company would do business with ruffians or criminals. Grant's careless drinking and constant reveling needed to cease. Had I not accompanied him, he might have been killed for a mere pouch of eights.

My comfortable bed eased my body. My eyelids grew heavy as the gentle pull of sleep began.

~~~~~~

The next morning, I found Grant standing on the front porch with a mug. The sun climbed over the fields and the dewy green land sparkled. The radiant ocean far below sent its salty aroma on the wind. Anna came out to greet us, carrying a tray. "Good morning, Jacob. I've brought you some hot tea."

I thanked her as she poured me a cup. "How is Martin feeling today?"

"Oh, he is well enough. He always gets a cough this time of year. 'Something in the air,' he says, stubborn old goat."

"He needs to rest," I said firmly. "Make sure he relaxes today. I don't want to see him in the fields. The help will arrive in an hour. There is no need for a man his age to be laboring the way he does."

"You're very kind, Jacob. But you know Martin. The work makes him happy. It's just who he is." She gathered the tea. "Let me worry about him. Breakfast will be ready soon." Anna gave us a bright smile and went back inside.

I turned my attention to Grant. "And how are you feeling?"

"I feel like I got trampled by a horse. Other than that…"

"You must be careful, Grant. No one can know the truth, that we knew Jean L'Ollon. Don't you understand what might happen to us if Grenada found out? We'd be cast away. We'd lose everything."

"I understand."

"Do you? Because you almost spoke of it last night."

He offered no response, looking away in shame.

"Promise you'll go easy with the rum."

"I promise."

"What's in that mug?" I asked.

He looked into it and quickly emptied it over the side of the porch. "Nothing."

We laughed and went in for breakfast.

~~~~~

The Grenadine sun was hot over the farm. Grant set out to harvest the herb gardens. Around midday, I heard him call with urgency in his voice.

"Look there." He pointed to footprints that trailed into the forest. "Did you walk this way last night?"

"No." I bent down to study the tracks. "These were made by bare feet. I wore shoes." I remembered the crackle from the shadows.

We decided to finish our work and forget about the mysterious footprints. Grant said it could have been a harmless thief picking our fields. He admitted to robbing farmers in his youth and claimed it was a common practice.

We loaded our market wagon and harnessed Teach and Morgan. It was off to St. George's square, where the Lords of

Rosewing were expected to bring the finest spices and produce.

Grant looked flamboyant in his scarlet garb; I remained comfortable in my plain white shirt. As we guided the horse-drawn wagon down the winding mountain road, we talked about business. Grant spoke of a prospective deal with a new company that had just arrived.

"They sailed into the harbor three days ago. Their company is called A.B.C. Trade Co."

"That's a rather unusual name."

"It stands for Aruba, Bonaire, and Curacao."

Hearing the name of the small island of Curacao made my heart skip. I pushed back the memories of Shanley's estate, the battle aboard the *Obsidian,* and the death of a father and son. "Curacao is an appalling place. I don't want to do business with that island. We've had enough association with it."

"I feel the same. However, they intend to sign with a Grenadine supplier before they set sail in four days. The contract is for one stop every three months. The pay is well worth our consideration. We can easily accommodate them. After they restock in Grenada, their trade route brings them west to Puerto Cabello, then of course, to Bonaire, Curacao, and lastly Aruba. The A.B.C. Trade Co diplomat said we could label our crates and barrels with the name J.G. Rosewing of Grenada, putting our name all over the Caribbean. This could mean big business for us, Jacob. At least consider it."

He was right. It would be a successful deal and it warranted further consideration. "How long did you say they are in town?"

"Four days," he replied. "The other farmers are fighting for the deal, but it is Rosewing that has the company intrigued."

~~~~~~

At the base of the mountain trail, where the main road to town intersects, rested a worn and dirty man. Sitting on a stone, he clutched a knotted walking stick and lifted his head as our wagon approached. He had a rough face with deep brown eyes, eyes that were alert and calculating. He looked right at me. Though he looked to be in his late fifties, his forearms were solid and defined. His nose was twisted and bent, indicating that it had been broken several times. Our wagon was full of food and I thought of stopping to share some with him, but I hesitated, unsure of his intent.

As we rode by, he did not stare at the produce as a beggar would. He stared at me. His gaze was chilling.

I turned to Grant. "Have you seen that man before?"

"No. But look at his feet." He was barefoot. "I think we found our thief. Throw him a loaf of bread or something."

"Are you sure?"

"Yes. I know what that life is like."

I reached into a basket, withdrew a large golden loaf, and tossed it to the old man. The loaf landed in the dirt and rolled off the road. He made no motion to get it. He just stared back at me.

"That's odd," said Grant. "Maybe he's of ill mind. Let's forget him. If I catch him around the farm tonight, he'll be in for some trouble."

As we passed, he stood up and watched us ride down the main road.

~~~~~~

The market was crowded as usual. It did not take long for the eager crowd to gather around to obtain our goods. The people were glad to see us and exchange the usual pleasantries with Grant.

White clouds glided across the blue sky. The wind was steady and cool. The day was prosperous from the start and I was pleased. Among the merchants and patrons I spotted a few official-looking men. They looked like members of a royal fleet in their dark blue uniforms. They approached eagerly. Grant stood up and shook their hands; I did the same.

"Pleasure to meet you, Jacob of Rosewing. My name is

Robert of the A.B.C. Trade Company. Allow me to introduce my partner, Davis."

"Nice to meet you both," I assured.

The men could have been brothers. They each had short, sandy hair and wore curling mustaches. Davis seemed troubled. His eyes scanned the townsfolk as if looking for someone.

"Fine day for making money, eh?" asked Robert.

"Indeed. Today has been good," replied Grant.

"Forgive my haste," said Robert, "but Grant expressed an interest in supplying our company. Do you share this desire?"

"I believe it is your company that is interested in Rosewing." I did not like his arrogant tone. Merchants from all corners of the Caribbean would quickly sign with us if given the chance. These men were not exceptional by any means.

"It goes both ways, sir," he answered.

"I disagree."

Grant nudged me as if to tell me to relax.

"Be that as it may," continued Robert, "we need our vessel restocked. Our journey westward must commence soon."

Grant noticed Davis's increasing anxiety. "What's wrong with your partner?"

Robert hesitated, then said, "After docking, we checked our ship's stock and noticed several barrels of smoked fish, nuts, limes, and bread had been opened. A bottle of wine had been consumed as well. The crew is convinced that we had a stowaway. But I assure you that—"

"Stowaway?" I interrupted. "Is your company that vulnerable?"

"The entire matter is absurd," insisted Robert. "We've had trouble with an old sea-scab from Curacao, a thief who insists on stealing from our stock. I personally inspect the cargo hold prior to each voyage, and I am certain that no one has stolen passage aboard my ship." He withdrew a handkerchief and wiped the sweat from his brow. "The sun here is fierce, isn't it?" He folded the handkerchief and then turned to Davis. "Hand our business proposal to Master Jacob. I'm sure he'll agree that it—"

"I'm not interested in your company."

"Is that so?" Robert scoffed incredulously.

"Yes. Your professionalism is lacking. You've chosen a marketplace to talk business, your stock has been compromised, and yet you approach us with arrogance in your tone."

"If you don't desire to sign with the most respected trading company in the Caribbean, that is your choice. Perhaps we've wasted our time on your little farm."

"Do not speak down to me," I shouted. Grant put his hand on my shoulder to calm me.

"For all we know," added Grant, "you might be in the practice of sailing with beggars to rid your homelands of them. Yes, that must be it. Leave now or I will tell the island that transients hoist your mainsail."

Robert and Davis expediently took their leave. Grant sat and laughed.

~~~~~~

As night fell, Grant and I packed our wares and set the wagon on the road. As we rode toward Rosewing, something caught our eyes. In the shadows, seated under a tree, was the old man staring at us as we passed.

"That's the same man we passed this morning," I said. "We must confront him and find out who he is and what his interest is in Rosewing."

"Would you like to challenge him now?"

"No. It's getting dark. Tomorrow we'll find him."

Chapter 26

Unexpected Guest

The next morning I woke to the rumble of thunder. The rain was heavy. The dark green jungle swayed in the reckless wind. I dressed and met Grant, Anna, and Martin in the dining room. Anna had prepared a simple breakfast of eggs, warm bread, and milk.

"Top of the morning to you," greeted Martin. "Grant told me all about the strange man. What are you going to do?"

"We'll find him and question him about his interest in our farm," I answered.

"Perhaps he's just looking for work," Martin suggested.

"The way he stared at us was odd. And, if he wanted a job, he could have met us at the market."

Grant stood up and went to the window. "It seems that the rainy months are upon us. It's going to be a tough time for the homeless. That wind is getting worse, and I am sure that you'll find an angry sea. No ships will be coming in or going out until this storm passes. That old man, if he is a stowaway, won't be leaving the island for a while. I'll take Teach into town and look around the market and the wharf. What about you, Jacob?"

"I'll take Morgan and ride along the trails and back roads. I'll also check the beaches. At days end, say five o'clock, we'll meet at the Cod Fish Tavern."

Our faithful horses didn't seem to mind the rain. I could see the harbor in the distance as we rode down the sloping road to town. The masts of the ships swayed, and the ocean smashed against the piers. All ships were battened down and moored securely to the docks. A few workers scrambled to secure lines. Soaked from the rain, I rode on.

The ocean was loud and violent. Formidable waves crested and slammed over the shoreline. The rain hammered on my shoulders. I found no one along the stretch of beach, so I raced over the stony sand and back onto the road. I knew of several old vendor huts that drifters often used as shelter. Perhaps I'd find our man there.

I came to a hut and approached it cautiously. It was small and made of thin planks. The thatch roof provided minimal protection from the relentless rain. I dismounted and went to the door.

"Hello," I called out over the pounding rain.

Thunder rumbled overhead. No reply.

"Is anyone in here?" I shouted. I could taste the rain dripping into my mouth. The door opened without resistance. I peered inside. Empty.

I checked every hut. It seemed that I was the only one mad enough to be out in the terrible weather. I wondered how Grant was doing. After several hours, I had covered the entire length of the main beach, traveled the road three times, and checked every shack and lean-to in the area. I had begun to shiver as a harsh cough brewed in my chest. My search was over.

~~~~~~

The town square and marketplace was barren. Morgan's

shoes shattered the large puddles. My cough was becoming painful. I rode through the square but did not find Grant. I decided to get out of the rain.

I tied Morgan under the covered corral and went into Cod Fish Tavern. There was a different barkeep, a woman this time. She saw me enter and rushed to my side.

"You look dreadful." She wrapped her arms around my soaked shoulders and led me to a table by the fireplace. I sat down and coughed. "Stay right here until you're dry. I'm going to get you something hot to drink."

"Thank you, miss." I shivered. My hair clung to my face and my pants dripped, making puddles on the floor. Some of the seamen in the crowded tavern looked at me and laughed. I ignored them and enjoyed the comforting warmth of the fire. The woman returned and handed me a dry towel and a steaming cup of tea.

"May I ask you a question?" I asked.

"Of course."

"Have you seen anyone unusual pass through here? Anyone who you've never seen before?"

"There were two men from a trade company here not long ago."

"I've met them. Tell me, what did you find unusual about them?"

Worry formed on the barmaid's face. "I'm not comfortable saying so, really."

I reached into my pocket and took out ten reales. I placed them in her hand. "Tell me. It's important."

"I overheard one of them talking business. I hear all sorts of conversations, you know. Well, this man was telling a horrible story. He spoke of Curacao and said it has become a dangerous place over the last ten years. He mentioned something about an old pirate leader named Shivley, Shortley…no that's not it…"

"Shanley?"

"That's right. Shanley."

The image of Captain James Shanley's dead body dangling off the starboard bow of the *Obsidian* flashed in my mind.

She looked over her shoulder to be sure no one was listening to our conversation. "He said some terrible men murdered Shanley and his son ten years ago. Everyone in Curacao prospered from Shanley's fortune in those days…at least, so said the trader."

"What else did he say?"

"That the death of Shanley started a decline in their society. They had no leader and no protection. Crime fell upon Curacao as swiftly as a September hurricane. Raiders came often to sack what remained of Shanley's empire. Curacao did its best to fight back, but they were no match for the pirates. The fighting and pillaging eventually ceased, but the chaos had repercussions."

"What kind of repercussions?"

"Criminals escaped. During the largest of the raids roughly eight years ago, Curacao's main prison was ambushed and blown open. The worst criminals to ever plague the Caribbean were set free. Thieves, pirates, assassins, and arsonists fled the island. These prisoners were all supposed to be executed in due time, but the government of Curacao is notoriously slow in this matter.

"The man from the trade company said that he hated stopping in Curacao. The harbor of Willemstad is full of beggars and thieves. He said that one thief routinely targeted their ship. They did nothing to stop him for one reason."

"What reason is that?" I coughed and sipped my tea.

"The thief matches the description of a madman who escaped the prison. He is a criminal so cunning and ruthless that they decided to let him steal from their stock for fear that he would kill them."

"Let me guess," I insisted. "This madman stowed away on their ship and is now in Grenada?"

"Yes! How did you know?"

I coughed again and replied, "Their representatives blurted something about their problems with stowaways." I sipped my tea. "One last question, miss. Have you seen a red-haired man tonight, probably as wet as I am?"

As I finished the question, the door to the tavern swung open, and Grant hurried in and rushed over with a look of concern.

"Did you find him?" I asked just above a whisper.

"I searched the town high and low, before I realized our folly. He's not in the town or the harbor. He's not in the market or pubs, neither hiding along the roads, or in a hovel on the beach. The jungle is not safe in a storm like this, so what is the one place that we didn't look?"

"I don't know," I admitted.

"Rosewing."

I almost spat up my tea.

"I rode back to our farm as quickly as I could," Grant continued. "Let me ask you, did you leave a lantern burning in your room?"

"No."

"I didn't think so. We found him. Now let's go get him."

~~~~~~

Grant was right. A yellow light burned from my window. We paused on the front porch to form a plan.

"Where are Martin and Anna?" I asked.

"They should be asleep. It's about the time when they turn in. Look there." Grant pointed. "Their room is dark and the curtains are drawn."

"I hope no harm has come to them."

"Don't think that way, Jacob. So how do you want to handle this?"

"I'll go in, grab a sword from the wall in the parlor, and corner him in my room. You'll wait under the window in case he decides to jump."

Grant slipped through the shadows with the finesse of the finest thief. I entered the manor with tender footfalls. I went to the parlor and took a long, sharp cutlass off the wall.

I came to Martin and Anna's room and quietly opened the door. They were safe and asleep in their bed. I moved on through the hall. Outside the door to my room, I heard the shifting of feet on the floorboards. With my sword readied, I kicked open the door. "Stop where you stand, vagabond!" I commanded with my blade's tip pointed at him.

He stood behind my desk in tattered, gray clothing. His stabbing brown eyes lifted slowly and met mine. He was not scared of me and didn't even acknowledge the sword in my hand. He stood like a man who had ventured to the farthest regions of hell and back, a man of cunning and control.

The nostrils under his crooked nose flared and a strange smile began to form. I could count the remaining teeth with one hand and have fingers left over. The lines on his face were deep and shadowy in the lantern light.

"Come away from the desk," I ordered.

"First it is 'stop where I stand,' and now you order me to move? Which will it be?" His voice was dry and his words were well pronounced. He seemed entertained by me.

"Do not mock me. Do as I say."

"Mockery is such a motivating thing. Don't you think?"

I did not reply. He stepped away from the desk.

"I was getting worried about you, good Lord of Rosewing." He stood in front of my desk, caring naught for the deadly steel in my hand. "That storm was merciless, as they all tend to be in their own way. Just like men."

"If you desire mercy from me, stranger, you'll be silent and make your way downstairs. There, you will answer my questions."

"Good. And you shall answer mine." His eyes glanced at my cutlass. "You can lower your blade. As you can see, I am unarmed and outnumbered. You can order the other Lord of

Rosewing to come back inside now. I yield, Jacob."

"How do you know my name?"

His strange smile widened. "I know *everything* about you. And you know *everything* about me."

"I don't understand. Who are you?"

"I guess you could say I am a writer. You have my masterwork among your books." He held out his hand for me to shake. "My name is Owen. It is an honor to meet the man who bested Jean L'Ollon."

Chapter 27
An Important Message

Grant and I escorted our intruder to the parlor. I kept my sword readied. Our unwanted guest looked around the room. His eyes touched the rows of books, the vases of flowers, the blazing fireplace and shelf of wine, ale, and rum.

I lifted the tip of my cutlass to enforce my words. "You say your name is Owen, that you are the author of that old journal. How will you prove this?"

"Proof? Aye." He began to disrobe. He tore off his stained shirt and then his ragged pants. "Here." He pointed to his left arm, revealing a deep scar just above his bicep. "And here." A similar scar was in the middle of his left thigh. "Permanent remembrances of Shanley's pistol. One shot bested me while on Darien soil, the other in Shanley's private quarters."

I lowered my sword and held out my hand. "Welcome to Rosewing."

~~~~~~

We presented our guest with a small feast: a steaming bowl

of potatoes, carrots, and chicken with another dish of fruit, golden rolls, and a tall mug of fresh milk. Owen ate slowly and savored every bite.

"You have truly strengthened me. I am in your debt."

"You can repay me," I replied, "by telling me why you've come here."

"You are as impatient and as passionate as they told me you would be."

"They? Who are *they?*"

"Christoff and Waylin."

I sat up at once. "Christoff and Waylin, you say?"

"Indeed, Master Jacob. It is under their order that I have come to Grenada. I have come to deliver an important message."

Grant and I stared at him.

"L'Ollon's men, the pirates of the *Obsidian,* are coming." Owen's eyes burned with urgency. "It is time for you to leave, and you must do so immediately."

I stood up. "That is preposterous! It's been ten years. Surely, L'Ollon's men have been locked up by now."

"Nay," Owen said. "They're already here."

"What?" Grant asked.

"Who do you think it was that you fought with in the Cod Fish? That was one of them. They are trickling in slowly, Lords of Rosewing. They do this to avoid suspicion. Their numbers are great, and I am certain that on the morrow they will begin their search for the two lads who killed their captain, the two lads who are now two men."

There was a moment of thoughtful silence. My mind drifted to memories of the long ago days of hardship.

"Past and present clashing like great battleships," shouted Owen. "Ahoy! And now the adventure goes on. Oh at last, at last!" He laughed and spun around the room. A madman, indeed.

"Enough," I yelled. Owen stopped dancing and sat at the table. "Tell me, Owen, how did you survive your prison? How did you get free and then come to know Christoff and Waylin?"

"As you know, I was jailed in Curacao after attacking Shanley. One day, while weak from hunger and curled up on the cell floor, Shanley entered and pulled my journal from my feeble arms. I could not fight him. He sifted through the pages, and then took it with him. I imagined he would toss it into a fire and the thought sickened me. I feared that the truth would not survive after I died. I took to eating insects and drinking rain water that dripped into my cell.

"Weeks later, I heard that L'Ollon's cunning pirates had lured Captain James Shanley from his estate. That Shanley was captured and forced aboard the *Obsidian,* and under its furled sails he and his son were killed. Curacao's naval fleet tried to overtake the *Obsidian.* They were not fast enough. L'Ollon's ship sailed away."

The storm raged over Rosewing. The wind howled, and I could hear the rain beating on the roof. I recalled the barrel room of the *Obsidian* sounding like this at night.

Owen continued. "You can imagine my elation upon learning of Shanley's ruin. It did not take long for chaos to ensue. Without a leader, Shanley's precious island became a battlefield. Pirate clans fought over his gold. For two long years, I clung to life in my cell. I watched from my barred window as Willemstad soured.

"One night, a massive fleet raided the island and opened fire on the town. I could see the flashing of distant cannon; the earth quaked as their shots landed. The screaming was endless. The sound of homes being blasted apart still echoes in my ears today. Aye, blasted apart is right, friends. As my luck would have it, a cannonball tore through the wall of my prison. A portion of my cell crumbled, and I was able to squeeze through the crack.

"I hid in the jungle and waited out the merciless raid. The jungle was better for survival than the cell. I found plenty to eat: plants, fruits, and once strong enough, small animals. I built a lean-to in the depths of the jungle and lived there in secret for five more years, free to steal all I wanted from a ruined town."

Grant interrupted. "I understand your means of survival. Tell us how you came to know Christoff."

Owen scratched at the stubble covering his cheeks, then leaned back in his seat and stretched his arms. He let out an exaggerated yawn. "All this talk and a stomach full of food have made me tired. Let me rest here, and in the morning I'll share all the details. I've delivered the message, the rest can wait."

Chapter 28

A Letter and a Plan

The aroma of hot spices woke me. I entered the dining room to find Grant, Martin, and Anna sitting at the table while Owen poured bowls of steaming soup.

Anna sipped from her bowl. "Tastes wonderful, Owen. Well done!"

Owen greeted me. "Morning, Master Jacob. Stew?"

"You've prepared breakfast? Why?" I asked.

Anna came to my side and pulled me toward the table. "Oh, Jacob. Sit and be kind. We woke this morning to our guest working hard on this meal. Join us, please."

"Yes," added Martin. "Owen's been pleasant company. You should've waked us last night to meet him. I feel terrible about sleeping while you and Grant made proper introductions."

Grant smiled. "I wouldn't say *proper*."

Owen poured a ladle of soup into a clay bowl and handed it to me. "A gesture in hopes that you'll trust me." I accepted and sat across from Grant.

The sunlight streamed in through the wide windows. The storm had long since passed and a warm breeze swept in, rustling the curtains. In the distance, I could hear the horses neighing in the barn, anxious to be out in the sunshine. I was eager to know more about Owen. There was still reason for caution. I drank the stew, pushed my empty bowl away, and looked him square in the eyes.

"Continue, Owen. Tell us of your dealings with Christoff and Waylin."

Owen cleared his throat and began. "There came an evening when a sloop with white sails and blue boot-top docked. This ship caught my eye since it had some unique alterations to its quarterdeck. I decided it was worth taking a closer look. I crept aboard, but I was caught, a cold steel blade pressed against my throat. Under the light of a lantern, I saw that a golden-haired gent held me. His captain, a gray-haired salt, stood scowling at me.

"'What business do you have aboard my ship?' asked the gray captain.

"'The truth it shall be if your mate stays his blade,' I answered boldly, as always. The captain acquiesced, and the steel came away from my throat. 'My name, good fellows, is Owen. I am a man of the sea. I escaped from prison five years ago. I make my thieving rounds along the harbor weekly. It is not an honest life, but I have not harmed anyone, at least not for a very long time. Forgive this old beggar's intrusion.'

"The captain's brow lifted with intrigue. 'A former seaman named Owen, once a prisoner and now dwelling in Curacao—tell me, Owen, have you ever written any books?'

"I was taken aback by his question. How could he know of my journal? I did not respond. He nodded as if my silence was all the answer he needed.

"'Though I have not read your book,' said Christoff, 'I know what fills its pages. Your stories of the Merfolk drove L'Ollon to madness.'

"'They are not *stories,*' I yelled.

"'You are a passionate man,' he said. 'My name is Christoff. I was once Jean L'Ollon's quartermaster. And you, beggar, thief, *pirate*...you sailed aboard the *Obsidian* too. I am in need of assistance and could use a seaman of your experience. Come, join me for a drink.'

"I joined Christoff and Waylin for a drink at the harbor-side saloon. The two men wore hooded cloaks into town to conceal their identity. I didn't care who saw me. The hour was late and most of the town slept. Once in the saloon, we sat and talked over foaming mugs.

"'I have little desire to sail over troubled waters,' I said to them.

"'On the contrary,' replied Christoff, 'I think you miss the ocean. Life on land is beginning to cloud your judgment. You have skills that are fading. I am offering you one last mission. There are people dear to me who need our help. At this time, I cannot go to them. You are the only man who can get to them and convince them to follow you.'

"'You would have me be a messenger?' I scoffed.

"'It is critical,' added Waylin. 'We would go to them now if we were not being followed. The *Obsidian* still sails. L'Ollon's men are tireless and thirst for our blood. Their only desire is to find us and the two lads, and hang us from the very bow where they hung Shanley.'

"'The *Obsidian* is two days behind us.' Christoff reached into a pouch and produced three pieces of eight. 'Payment for your time thus far.' I took the coins eagerly and accepted the job."

"I can't believe the *Obsidian* sails," I said.

"And all for us, it seems," said Grant.

"They instructed me to hand you this." Owen reached into his shirt and pulled out a weathered parchment.

I took the letter and broke the wax seal that kept it closed. Unfolding its delicate edges, I held it before me and began reading.

Cerulean Isle

Dear Friends,

If you are reading this letter, ill times have befallen us all. My friends, they have found us. I suppose it was inevitable and that I was a fool for underestimating them. What troubles me is that I do not know how they have managed to operate so effectively without L'Ollon.

I have known that you were successful in obtaining the journal and sea chart from Shanley's estate. It was wise of you to hide these items. Grant, you are a man of the sea. Use the chart. Unlock its secrets. Jacob, you must believe once more in the Water People. My boy, they are as real as you and I. As for Owen's role in this...he will guide you to the eastern shore where you will board the sloop. You should know, lads, I am dying while I write this. I have become quite ill as of late and nothing can cure what ails me.

There is a battle to be fought and a war to be won. Stay and defend Rosewing or follow Owen. The choice is yours. My journey is over at last. Goodbye, Jacob. Goodbye, Grant.

C.

"There is little time, Lords of Rosewing," said Owen. "A decision must be made. The pirates of the *Obsidian* will discover this haven and they will attack without warning."

"Tell me, Owen," I snapped. Thoughts of the past ignited my anger. I drew my sword and pressed the tip against his chest. My sudden fit of rage surprised him. "Are they real? Are they?"

"You ask me of the Merfolk?" His eyes were locked on mine.

"Answer me, you crazy old fool!"

Anna let out a frightened scream and Martin hurried her out of the room.

"Yes. The Merlords and Mermaidens are real, damn you! I refuse to be challenged on this anymore." Owen forced the blade away, snatched the hilt, and tore it from my hand. He struck me hard in the face. I fell backward, my head slamming against the floor. Owen leapt on top of me. My blade was readied in his grip and the cold point was pressed against my throat. He glared at me, the corners of his mouth wet with spit. His dark brown eyes burned into me. His free hand pulled my hair, forcing my chin upward, exposing my neck.

"Look at you, Jacob," he snarled, "your anger is your weakness. You are not in control. I am. And so is the enemy. Destruction, cruelty, and death will march for Rosewing. The pirates of the *Obsidian* will force their way inside. They will tear down the doors to get you. Then with blades sharper than this, they will pin you to the wall. They will slay Anna first, then Martin, then Grant. *You* are the one they want the most. *You* killed their captain. When the room is red with the blood of your friends, they will set fire to everything. They will leave you then. You will be alone in the smoke and heat with a sword in your belly and your dead friends at your feet. The entire island of Grenada will be under attack. And you show *me* anger? After being truthful, you lift a sword against *me?* Tell me why I should not cut you down right here."

I did not know what to say. He was right. I had no authority to challenge him.

"Tell me," hollered Owen. "Tell me why I shouldn't kill you."

"Because *I* will kill *you* and you'll never see your Mermaidens again," said Grant from behind. He was holding a loaded pistol. He pressed the broad barrel against Owen's head. Owen dropped the sword, and I moved away.

"Aye! I am pleased beyond measure," the old man exclaimed. His face brightened and he began a queer dance. "Jacob is reckless and Grant is a fool but together they are unconquerable, ahoy!"

"What is wrong with you?" asked Grant.

"Many things, Grant." Owen then turned to me, saying, "Let us be affable, Jacob, and forget our quarrel. Grant, save your shot for those more deserving." Owen and I shook hands. "We have preparations to make regardless of what you decide to do."

"What should we decide, Jacob?" asked Grant.

I looked sharply at him and said, "Get the sea chart."

~~~~~~

We assembled in Grant's suite, and he unrolled the old blue chart. The edges of the parchment spilled over his desk. Grant smoothed out the document, then reached into his desk and produced another chart. This one was white, crisp, and clean. He untied the ribbon and let it unfurl over the other.

"This is my copy," Grant said. "Over the years I've worked to reproduce L'Ollon's. The original is stained and weathered, and I feared that it would be ruined from time's uncaring touch. In all modesty, my duplicate is perfect."

Owen studied the new chart. "Perfect indeed, Grant. Fine work!" His fingers slid over the lines and traced the measurements that Grant had reproduced. "This is where it happened. This is where L'Ollon's fleet was bested." Owen's finger followed a series of dashes that began at Curacao, trailed northwest, and stopped in the middle of the Caribbean Sea.

"Is this where L'Ollon lost his gold?" asked Grant.

"Aye."

I said, "And that is also where you, Owen, saw the Merfolk for the first time."

"Indeed it is. Fired me shot at them, I did!"

I placed a finger on the island of Grenada. "We begin here," I said. "Though I am uncertain of where to go, we must get as much distance between us and L'Ollon's men as possible."

"West is our only choice," said Grant.

"Why not north?" I asked. "We can leave the Caribbean entirely."

"With the trade winds filling our sails, we will cover a

great distance in little time; the quickness of the sloop will be unmatchable. It is safer for us to plot a westward course, since there is land only a few days north or south."

"Then it is decided," I said. "Tomorrow we shall prepare for our departure. By the evening we will say goodbye to Rosewing."

Chapter 29

Restless

Owen bid us a good night and went down stairs to sleep in the parlor. I stayed awake, unable to find peace, my mind as restless as the sea. Hours passed. The stars wheeled slowly over the island. I decided on a drink and left my room.

I found Owen awake in the sitting room. Seated by the fireplace with a stack of books at his feet, he heard my entrance and motioned for me to join him. "I was wondering which of the lords was the restless one."

"To be honest," I admitted, "I don't sleep well."

"Another thing we have in common, Master Jacob. The old salts say captains do not sleep; they rest but they do not sleep."

"Are you likening me to a captain?"

"Aye. Why shouldn't I?"

"I'm not much of a seafarer. Grant would be a fine captain."

"Then what are you?"

I did not answer.

He continued, "A captain is a leader. A captain plans and

thinks ahead. Grant may be capable of sailing a fleet of brigantines, but can he motivate a listless crew? Can he show the others what it means to be fearless? Can he acknowledge the strengths and weaknesses of everyone on board, including his own?"

"And you think I can?"

"Of course. Listen here; I am a man with many flaws. Knowing this makes me strong. I am greedy. I am impatient. I know naught of remorse, and I do not believe in forgiveness. Look into your heart and understand your flaws."

"Well, I am angry, stubborn, and I guess I am too protective."

"What makes you so angry?"

"My father. Everything in my life makes me remember him and how he betrayed me. I am stubborn because I will not let this go, and I am protective of the things I love because I do not want them to be taken from me. Yet, that is exactly what is happening, isn't it? I am losing everything—Rosewing, Grenada, my home. Once again I will be without a place of solace." I paced the floor. "Curse those pirates. For ten long years I have fought with my memories and worked hard to build a new life. Now it is all threatened. I thought about staying and defending my keep, but I know we will lose and bring doom upon the island. It's better if we go."

"There! You speak like a captain. You know your flaws and why you have them. You assessed the danger and considered the alternatives. You have formed a battle plan and have centered it on the welfare of the innocent. Good, good, good!"

"And what of this battle? In Christoff's letter, he wrote, 'there is a battle to be fought and war to be won.' What did he mean by this?"

"Aye. It is the battle for your freedom and the war against L'Ollon's men."

"How are we supposed to defeat them? The sloop is no match for the barque. Their numbers triple ours."

Cerulean Isle

"That is correct. At this time they are stronger. However, we will get help, Jacob."

"Who will help us? No one in the Caribbean would do battle against the pirates of the *Obsidian*."

"Those who I mean to align with have already bested them once." A thoughtful distance filled his eyes and a grin spread over his face.

"What?"

"You hear me well. It is to Cerulean Isle that we will sail. We will find the Merfolk, and they will aid us in destroying what is left of L'Ollon's forces."

I looked around for empty wine bottles. I found nothing. He had not been drinking.

"Owen," I began as delicately as possible, "I believe in Merlords and Mermaidens, but why would they want to help us?"

Owen rubbed the inner corners of his eyes. "While in my cage I had time to think on many things. The most dominating of my thoughts was the terrible night aboard the *Obsidian*. I remembered it clearly: the black raging waves slamming against the hull, the storm tossing us about. Then there was the light in the water. It was like starlight, only it wavered and shimmered through the depths. When I saw the Merlord staring at me, I panicked. Alas, I was young and foolish. In my superstition, I assumed they meant us harm. The Merlord in the water looked at me in kindness while I responded with fear and aggression.

"They are a peaceful race. They came to help the most ruthless fleet on the Caribbean. They will help us, I am sure of it."

"Owen, that sounds wondrous, but what if the Mer remember you and your pistol shot? What if they remember when you turned on the Darien chief to obtain their secrets? If they recognize you, they will not have dealings with us. They will kill us."

"Aye! Thinking like a captain again!"

The morning brought a gray mist over the island. As we settled in for breakfast, Grant and I spoke of the previous night's happenings.

"Your quarrel with Owen was risky, Jacob. We hardly know the man. He might have ended you had I not been there. You must be cautious around him. He is a madman, after all."

"He and I had words late last night. I don't think he is as mad as we initially thought. Or, perhaps I am beginning to understand him."

"I will keep one eye on him, one on you, and the other on my rapier, should things get out of hand again."

"That would mean that you have three eyes."

Our laughter quieted when we heard approaching footfalls. We turned to see a strange man enter the dining room.

Having spent nearly an hour in the washroom, Owen hardly resembled the beggar we had befriended. His face was smooth from the caress of the razor; his skin was clean and appeared two shades lighter. Without the grime and tattered garments, Owen looked five years younger. His brown eyes were bold, alert, and eager. He had helped himself to a set of my clothes; a sleeveless brown tunic, dark brown belt, and black pants. His feet were bare.

"Good morning, Owen," I said as I pulled a chair from the table.

"Aye. Thank you both for your hospitality. The clothes make me feel like my old self, and it is truly grand to be clean again." Owen bowed.

"No worries, friend," said Grant.

We enjoyed a hearty breakfast of boiled potatoes seasoned with the finest spices from Rosewing farm, buttery rolls, wedges of imported cheese, and a bowl of mixed fruit and nuts. After breakfast, we began with our preparations.

"Grant, you and Owen load the wagon with as much food

and supplies as possible. The sloop's stores are sure to be low. I will pack clothing, weapons, books, charts, and anything of great value that we might trade later. I want our wagon stocked and ready before the evening."

"We must traverse about ten miles to the eastern shore," said Owen. "Christoff's sloop will meet us in two days. The plan is to depart at night and sail around the southern coast, then westward, passing our pursuers unseen. The sooner we start, the better."

Chapter 30

Leaving Home

"Do you think we will ever come back?" Grant asked.

He and I were tending to Teach and Morgan in the stable. It was late in the afternoon when we finished loading the wagon.

"Perhaps once we are rid of L'Ollon's men. Rosewing is our home, and I've come to love this island. But we must consider Martin and Anna. If we stay, we'll bring danger to them. They are safe here. I must admit, a large part of me wants to stay and fight."

"We'd lose," said Grant.

"I know that."

Anna and Martin came into the stables. Martin put his hand on my shoulder. "You haven't told us much about what's going on."

I could see the worry brewing in Anna's eyes. She clung tightly to her husband. I said, "We tried to start a new life, we tried to hide, but some things are too big to hide from and we—"

"Listen, boys," Martin interrupted. "I've never asked for an explanation about your gold, your troubles, or your past. Something tells me that it's better if I don't know."

Anna took my hand and one of Grant's. "Just promise you'll be coming home."

Grant kissed the back of her hand. "We'll be back, Anna. I promise."

"Very well," said Martin. "We'll look after the farm while you're away."

We shook hands with Martin, and Anna wiped the small tears from her cheeks. The two left the stables. Grant went back to brushing Teach's mane. "So it is to the ocean that we return, to uncertainty. We've come full circle."

"Full circle, indeed," I replied.

~~~~~

The sky darkened fast as the sun fell behind the clouded horizon. It was time to leave. Grant and I did a final sweep through the farm house. We looked for any last minute necessities but found nothing worth taking. We had both copies of the chart, Owen's old journal, a bundle of weaponry, and barrels of food for the sloop.

We gathered at the edge of the farm where the road down the hillside began. I went to the front of the wagon where the weapons were wrapped in linen and selected the arms for our party.

"My good man, this is yours." I handed Owen the cutlass that I wielded against him when we met.

"She's a fine blade, Master Jacob." He twirled it around with finesse and slipped it into his belt. "I'll spill blood in your honor!"

Grant had a bejeweled rapier hanging from his belt and a gold-hilted dagger sheathed in his boot. I handed him a loaded pistol. He took it and secured it on the other side of his belt. "What about you?"

I had one last bundle of linen tucked under my arm. I pulled back the wrapping to reveal a gleaming broadsword. Its mirror-finished blade was flawless with a perfect cutting edge. The handle was tightly wrapped in brown leather and boasted a dark round sapphire. Like all ornate swords, the hilt was the most eye-catching. Forged from solid gold and meticulously crafted, the sword's guard was a Mermaiden, her fish-like body coiled around the handle in a horizontal figure eight. Her glorious fin fanned out over the blade. It was an intricate, beautiful weapon.

"Where did you get this?" Grant asked.

"At the market last month. The merchant said he found it on the beach, but I think he stole it. I bought it and I've kept it secret should it come up as stolen property. I figured I'd wait a few months before wearing it around."

"Why didn't you show it to me?"

"As I said, I thought it might be stolen. You would have blurted something about it at the tavern and I'd get in trouble."

"True. It's a wondrous weapon."

"Yes. And it is unusually light for steel and gold. Also, I haven't had to clean it since I bought it."

"No oil on the blade?"

"Nothing. The finish remains no matter how often I handle it."

"Aye," interrupted Owen. "We'll see if that holds true when it runs a man through. Enough talk. We must be moving; the day is fading, and with it, our chances of escape."

Chapter 31

Lights in the Forest

After a few hours of travel, the forest wall on the right side of the road began to fracture. Through the gaps in the knotted vegetation, I could see the brilliant glimmer of the blue ocean.

"Men, we should be arriving at the coast any moment and with time to spare. The beach that Waylin commanded I bring you to is roughly a mile ahead," said Owen.

Soon our path broke from the forest and a small golden beach opened in front of us. The crystal clear surf swayed over the sand. The sound of the rolling water and rustling breeze eased my tension. We stopped the wagon at the edge of the small cove and stared out to the endless azure sea. The fiery glow of the falling sun cast hues of orange, red, and purple into the darkening blue sky. There were no homes, shacks, or lean-tos on this pristine bend of beach. The white-gold sand was fine and speckled with bits of shells and edgeless stones. The shoreline was smooth with no trace of habitation. It seemed that the settlers of Grenada had forgotten this cove.

"This beach is magnificent. I didn't know it was here," Grant said. "How is it that no one lives here?"

Owen replied, "The water is too shallow and hides deadly coral. Large ships can't get close. Waylin and Christoff were wise in choosing this cove."

"Did they specify their time of arrival?" Grant asked.

"Nay. The plan was to leave under the cover of night. I can only assume we'll see the sloop come into view just after the setting of the sun."

~~~~~~

As night fell over the island we prepared for the sloop's arrival. Owen said that they would anchor as close as possible and send lifeboats to the shore. We stacked our barrels close to the water's edge and unloaded our trunks and crates. When the wagon was emptied, we released Teach and Morgan from their harness and let them wander the beach.

The stars were distant torches. The sky had turned to black and the water was ghostly and restless. The moon was full, but wispy gray clouds sailed by it as if intentionally diminishing its light. We sat atop our crates and stared out at the dark horizon, hoping for any sign of the sloop.

"What was that noise?" Grant leapt up and took a few cautious steps toward the forest.

We heard a short series of cracks, followed by what sounded like rolling rocks.

I began to see shapes moving. As I focused, I made out the shapes of men. Friend or foe, I could not tell.

"Ahoy!" Owen pointed to the ocean. "Look yonder, there be a light floating on the water. The sloop, my good men, has arrived."

I turned my attention from the shadows lurking in the black jungle to the soft orange glow of a lantern rocking on the waves.

"We must signal them so they know we are here," said Grant. He pulled out his pistol, loaded a shot and held it aloft. A loud explosion and a blinding yellow flash erupted from the pistol. The sound echoed across the ocean and through the dark forest.

The shadowy human shapes scurried about but did not emerge from the tree line. I expected a succession of fire to blast from the woodland in response to Grant's shot, but none came.

If pirates lurked in the jungle, they would have taken the shot as a call to war. Whoever was in the forest was as cautious as we were. I looked out at the approaching ship, with its starboard bow facing us. It had set three more lanterns alight. Two more lanterns, then four, illuminated the ship. The ten fires burned and reflected in the water. The single mast loomed toward the stars. The bundles of heavy white sail were furled on the crosstrees. The lines and rigging looked like fine spider wire. Faintly, I made out the blue striping along the hull.

After the sloop lit its lanterns, ten ghostly lights appeared from the boundaries of the forest, moving toward us. I heard Owen draw his blade and the metallic chime of Grant's rapier. I rolled the handle of my broadsword in my palm. The figures from the jungle drew near, large men wearing white tunics and gray pants. The flickering light illuminated their serious faces and shadowy eyes.

"Ten men are a laughable challenge," boasted Owen. He stood ready, poised with a bare blade and clenched fist.

Grant was silent as he held his jewel-encrusted rapier outward. The fatal tip gleamed in the forthcoming light. I took my position next to him.

"Do me a favor," he said.

"And that is?"

"Pretend these men are Beelo."

They had formed a tight circle around us. We stood back to back. They remained motionless, lanterns in one hand, cutlasses in the other. The leader of their group came forward.

He was bald, muscular and seemingly unimpressed with what he saw.

"Are you Jacob of Rosewing?" asked the bald man in a deep, flat voice.

"Indeed. My name is Jacob."

"Are you the same Jacob that escaped the *Obsidian* and Jean L'Ollon ten years ago? Answer me truthfully." The encircling group remained silent.

I thought about his question, hesitant to admit my past, when Grant stepped in front of me. His blade touched the man's chest.

"He is the same Jacob, and I am the same Grant. We bested L'Ollon and his vile crew and did so with ease. Be forewarned, a ship waits yonder with cannon readied against you. If you value your life, you will yield and call away your band."

"Aye!" Owen hollered.

The leader lifted his sword. *The battle for freedom is at hand*, I thought. His long blade sliced the air and, to my complete surprise, jabbed into the sand. He released the handle. The sword wobbled and stood on its own.

"The ship that you say is readied against me," the leader said with a smirk, "is ours. Turn down your arms, men," he called to the group, "it seems we've found them." The men sheathed their swords and came away from us. His attention returned to me. "My name is Bartholomew. Call me Bart. I am currently serving as quartermaster under Captain Waylin." He put out his hand, and I accepted. "It is a pleasure to meet you both."

"Allow me to introduce Owen. He has been our guide."

"Pleasure to meet you, Owen. Waylin told me to be careful around you."

"His judgment is uncanny," snarled Owen. He brushed away Bart's hand. "Heed his warning."

Bart waved his lantern to signal the sloop. On board the distant ship, a light waved in response. "I've just indicated that we have met you. They will be sending the rowboats." He withdrew his sword from the sand and moved toward the shore.

"Just a moment," I snapped. Grant, Owen, and I still held bare blades. "Why were you skulking about in the forest? Why didn't you make yourself known?"

"We had to be sure that you were the party we were sent to meet. We heard the shot ring out and we held back."

"Understood." I returned my sword to its scabbard. The others did the same.

Bart pointed to our provisions. "I see you've come prepared. I was told there was a battle plan of some sort, and that you'd provide the details."

Owen interrupted. "You'll know when the time comes."

"Correction," piped Bart, "as quartermaster I must be informed of all plans to ensure the welfare of the crew. I will know when I ask to know."

"Let me correct *you*. I am a seasoned pirate. And if you speak to me again as though I have never hoisted a rigging, I will cut out your cursed tongue and wear it on my belt."

"Owen," I said, "calm yourself. These men are not enemies, and I would have it remain that way."

Owen snarled at Bart and pushed passed him. He stood alone on the shore looking out toward the drifting sloop.

Chapter 32

Destiny

We sat in a wide rowboat. Bart took the oars at the bow, Grant and I sat on the middle bench, and behind us two crewmen worked the oars at the stern. They refused our help. Owen was in the rowboat behind us; he wanted to guard our provisions. Four men managed the craft while he sat and glared at them.

"You knew Christoff?" Grant asked Bart.

"Yes. I met him in his later years. He was ill when I signed his articles. A fair captain. He worked hard with us and did so until the end."

"Did he die in peace?"

"As peaceful as any man could. After spending a few days on the lawless island of Curacao, Christoff asked the crew to elect a new captain. The consensus was for Waylin. Then Waylin asked the crew to elect a new quartermaster. I was voted in. The crew signed new shipboard articles.

"Come nightfall we gathered to dine, but Christoff's chair

was empty. Waylin went to check on him and found the old man cold in his bed. The next morning, we set sail and once on calm waters, gave our old captain to the sea."

After a moment of silence, Grant said, "Christoff, may the warm winds fill your sails and guide you to the seas of heaven."

"Tell me, Bart," I said, "what do you know of us and of what is to come?"

"Two days after Christoff's passing, Waylin told me of the mission to find you. He said two men on the island of Grenada were in trouble and that he promised these men that should they need him, he would come. When you, Jacob, plunged a sword through the chest of the infamous Jean L'Ollon, you started a war. L'Ollon's men sailed for years searching for you."

~~~~~~

The rowboats drifted along the hull of the sloop. Seeing its massive body looming over us made me feel like a child again. This was the second time that the nameless ship would be our savior.

We climbed the rope ladder and stood on the clean deck for the first time in ten years. A man with long blonde hair stepped from the midst of the crowd. As he drew near I saw streaks of white in his gold locks. His lengthy blue coat flapped around his waist.

"Waylin!"

We gathered and shook hands.

"Look at you, lads. You are strong and well. Christoff would be pleased."

Grant, Waylin, and I walked to the bow of the ship. The sloop began to pull away from the cove. Waylin gave a few short orders to the crew, then spoke to us. "We are about to embark on a quest with only two possible outcomes: our death or the death of L'Ollon's men. There is one final piece of business." Waylin turned to the crew and yelled, "Pending crew consent, I hereby relinquish authority of this vessel to Jacob and Grant of Rosewing. All in favor, say 'aye.'"

The entire crew hollered the word in unison. The decision had been made.

"Before we depart," added Waylin, "which of you will be captain and which will be quartermaster?"

I placed a hand on Grant's shoulder. "What is your first command, Captain?"

He smiled wide and hollered, "Man the helm! The swift sloop *Destiny* sails west. Ahoy!"

~~~~~~

The five of us gathered in a small office built beneath the raised quarterdeck. It was a new day and we had slowed the sloop *Destiny* to a drift about five miles off the western coast of Grenada. It was morning and the winds were steady.

"I propose two courses," began Waylin. He unfurled two large sea charts. "The first is a westward route. We sail until we pass Aruba. At which point, we cut southwest and make for Puerto Bello. They are strong and their garrison will fend off the *Obsidian* with ease. I doubt L'Ollon's men will dare sail in the waters of Puerto Bello."

"What is your second course, Waylin?" Grant asked.

"This one, if agreed to, would need to be implemented soon. We turn our bow ninety degrees and sail north, to slip through the islands of Hispaniola and Puerto Rico and into the Atlantic Ocean."

"I think the westward course would be the easiest and fastest," stated Grant. "There is nothing in the western waters of the Caribbean Sea that would slow us. The water gets shallow, but *Destiny* will sail unrestrained. The *Obsidian,* if it follows, will be forced into deeper waters and around the coral reefs. I am in favor of this route."

"We will not make it through the Caribbean as easily as you predict, Captain Grant," said Owen. "This course will take us into Lord Sydin's waters."

"Lord Sydin?" Waylin asked.

Owen said, "With Master Jacob's permission, I will explain." I nodded and he continued. "An island blocks our passage. It is not on your chart. It is Cerulean Isle and it rests in the waters of Sydin, Lord of the Caribbean Merfolk. You will find the Mer to be a greater force than the pirates of the *Obsidian*. With their aid, we can defeat our pursuers. With that said, yes, I am in favor of this route."

Waylin chuckled. "You propose we should ask a school of mermaids for help?"

"Not a *school,* a tribe. And not just the Mermaidens but the Merlords as well. If I do not have the support from my crewmates, then I have nothing."

"I believe him," I said sharply. "I always have."

Waylin sighed, and Grant stared at the chart.

"What will you do, Master Jacob?" said Bart. "Will you walk onto the main deck and inform the crew that we sail for a mythical island? Will you have the navigator holler when he spots a mermaid?"

"Mermaid-*en,*" corrected Owen.

Grant explained, "The answer is simple. We will inform the crew that we will be sailing west to Puerto Bello. If Owen's claims are accurate and we find Cerulean Isle, so be it."

"Do not humor me," snapped Owen.

"I am not humoring you," said Grant. "If Jacob tells me he believes in the Merfolk, I believe too.

"Understand, Owen, that the rest of the crew will not be so quick to accept the possibility of Mermaidens and Merlords. They're seasoned sailors. For them, the Water People make good yarns and shanties; that's all. Without actual proof, the truth of the Mer-island will have to remain a myth."

"Aye. The proof you desire is in this room." Owen pointed his twisted finger at my broadsword. "There be your proof, Captain."

"How much madness do you wish to listen to on this day?"

questioned Bart. "The man's mind is troubled. Keeping secrets from the crew is a violation of the shipboard articles."

"Do not insult me, Bart," Waylin growled. "I am not in command of this ship. Jacob is quartermaster and Grant is captain."

"And that is another issue! What qualifies them to command this vessel and its crew?"

"Ten years ago, they gave Christoff and I equal shares of a large bounty and asked nothing in return. With that gold… with *their* gold…we maintained the ship. By rights, this sloop belongs to them."

"I see your judgment has become clouded as well," remarked Bart. He faced Grant and I. "I refuse to be a keeper of secrets and pursue childish ideals. I am off to inform the crew of the lunacy that plagues this ship."

As the bald pirate moved for the doorway, Owen pulled the broadsword from my belt. He stepped in front of Bart, blade drawn and held mere inches from his throat. "This blade can be two things: proof of the Mer or the cause of your death. Decide!"

"Damned fool," yelled Waylin. "Release him, at once!"

Owen forced the blade closer to Bart's neck. The flawless edge touched his skin.

"Jacob," whispered Grant, "you'd better do something about your madman."

"Owen," I said. "Lower the sword."

"Nay!" he hissed. "Everyone onto the main deck."

Owen forced Bart through the cabin door, into the bright Grenadine sun. The crew gathered around. None dared to defy the old pirate. We massed in a tight circle at the port bow. Owen kept my ornate sword pressed against Bart's throat.

"The Merfolk are a wondrous people, skilled in many things. The forging of weapons is one of them. This," Owen shouted as he shoved Bart away and held aloft my sword, "is proof. Behold!"

He threw the broadsword overboard. The silver blade

flashed as it fell to the sea. Waylin rushed to Owen and seized him, slamming the old pirate to the deck. Owen's face hit the wood with a thud.

"You will be restrained until we reach port," said Waylin angrily. "Someone fetch some rope."

Grant grabbed my arm and turned me around to face to the water. My eyes fell to the rolling sea. Floating on the waves, as if made of mere driftwood, was my sword. Every man on deck looked on in wonder as the silver and gold sword rose and fell in cadence with the waves.

"It's a Mersword," Owen shouted. "Gold and silver forged with a special ore from the sea. Aye! Proof!"

"Where did this weapon come from?" Waylin asked me.

"I bought it at a market, from a peddler who claimed he found it on the beach."

Waylin nodded, then ordered a team to take a rowboat out to retrieve the floating blade.

"It is proof, Waylin," shouted Owen. "The sword will never sink; the metal of the Mer is buoyant. It will not rust or corrode. It is as hard as diamond and as light as a fistful of sand. The Merfolk are out there, and that sword is but a taste of the wonders that await us at Cerulean Isle. We must find Lord Sydin and ask for his help. We must bargain with them. Barter, trade, or pay them. I don't know what they will ask of us in return. I will offer my very life, if need be."

Waylin ran his hand through his gold and white hair, then panned the faces of his crewmates. He produced a small knife and cut Owen's restraints. Owen rolled over and sat up.

"The next time you draw arms against any of this crew, you will be killed," said Waylin gravely.

"Aye. You believe me, then?" Owen wiped the blood from his nose.

Waylin helped the old pirate to his feet. "For now, yes."

"We seek the Merfolk, at last," Owen shouted. "To Cerulean Isle!"

...Part Three...

Facing the Past

Chapter 33

Sea of Fog

The sloop *Destiny* sailed light and fast over the sparkling Caribbean Sea. Two teams of watchmen kept a vigil around the clock. The scouts panned the horizon with a small telescope. They took their positions atop the stern and the bow with specific orders to watch for the *Obsidian* or any ship bearing three masts. A large bell served as an alarm if a threat to the ship appeared. They watched for common obstacles like coral reefs, rock formations, sudden shallows, or fierce tides. The greatest threats, of course, being other ships. On the open water, there was no trust among seamen.

Our most clever devise was our trunk of flags. When sailing in waters claimed by other countries, we would hoist their banner above our mainsail. Waylin had collected banners from every country in the Caribbean, including flags of royalty and religion.

On the fourth evening, we sailed into a thick fog. We hung lanterns over the starboard and port bows. The yellow glow did little to open our view. Grant ordered the crew to slow the ship and bring her to a drift. With such poor visibility, caution became our priority. The last hues of daylight fell under the western edge of the sea. The curtain of fog grew under the starless sky, as our sloop cut through the black water. Before long, I could no longer see across the deck.

"We are getting closer, Master Jacob," said Owen. At the stern, he and I struggled to see through the fog. "This fog is a warning. We have entered Lord Sydin's domain. He does not want us to come any closer."

I saw fear in his eyes. "Be at ease, friend. If we are in the domain of the Mer, an ambassador of their race will make himself known, and together we can form a plan against the *Obsidian*."

"The Mer are not in the custom of welcoming ships and those who sail them."

"Then we must hold a crew meeting at once. Help me to gather the men around the main mast."

Destiny's crew was uneasy. I motioned for Owen to stand beside me as I addressed the crew.

"Good evening, men. Until now our westward voyage has been swift. This fog has slowed our travel for the time being. Fog such as this is an indicator that a landmass is near. How large of a mass or how far out, I cannot say. We may have sailed into claimed water. Owen, share your knowledge, please."

Owen stepped forward and panned the crew. His chest puffed as he stood with his hands behind his back.

"Worthy seamen, welcome to the waters of the Mer. Every yarn and shanty will now become real. Be watchful of the water. Do not lean too far over the bow. If you hear anything, speak of it at once. If you see anything, call out for others to come. This is the domain of Lord Sydin. He is their general, their leader. If we are to be met by any of the Water People, it will be him. If you see a man in the waves, stay your pistols and blades or you will cause our ruin."

"Thank you, Owen," Grant said. "My friends, we shall keep a slow drift until this dreadful veil lifts. Take rest. Eat. Drink. I would, however, like two men to serve as additional watchmen for the starboard and port bows. Any volunteers?"

Two mates volunteered and took positions as instructed.

"Owen, you are head of the watch team. Make rounds to all points of the ship. Relieve any of the scouts as needed. Report to Waylin, Jacob, or me if the Mer come."

"Understood, Captain Grant." Owen, eager and proud, went to work at once.

~~~~~~

"Do you really believe the Merfolk are out there?" Grant asked me.

"It doesn't matter. If we find them, and they help us, then I will be ever grateful and indebted. If not, then we will continue for Puerto Bello and with their help, meet L'Ollon's men head on. Either way, we fight.

The watchman's warning bell rang out over the deck. Grant and I ran toward the bow as the entire ship lurched forward. The mainmast rocked and the crosstrees swayed violently. Lines broke and floorboards snapped. The entire hull whined under the sound of iron trusses buckling. It was a direct collision. Grant and I were tossed forward from the sudden momentum shift. Our bodies flew and we landed hard on the deck and rolled before scrambling to our knees. Grant groaned and clutched his arm. Some of the crew were knocked unconscious and others were entangled in line or struggling to emerge from broken crates and toppled barrels.

As my vision cleared, I fought to see through the fog. Whatever we hit held *Destiny* in place.

As I made my way to Grant, floorboards cracked and splintered. The deck creaked. The bow of the sloop was tilted down, the stern angled upright, and I imagined the rudder was nearly out of the water. The tall mainmast leaned dangerously forward, with the sails as disheveled as an unmade bed.

"Come, let's brace and sling your arm." I broke a floorboard in half over my knee and cut a rag to make a crude sling. With some strips of fabric, I tied the boards to his broken arm, a makeshift splint. He groaned and cursed as I pulled the strapping tight. I tucked his arm in the sling and wrapped it around his neck and shoulder.

I ordered men to look after the injured and commanded the rest to begin repairs wherever they could.

"I don't understand," said Grant. "What could we have hit? Waylin and I plotted a clear route. There are no rock or coral masses marked on the sea chart. Mainland is still several days out. What if this is…?" Grant paused. The color in his face faded.

"Say no more. Let's find Owen and Waylin."

~~~~~~

We found Waylin peering down the hatch that led below deck to the storerooms. "Have a look, lads. Ill times are at hand."

The entire bilge had flooded. Ocean water filled our storeroom, ruining our supplies of food.

Grant said, "Have a few men go down there and recover whatever they can. Tell them to salvage fruit, water barrels, and the extra weapons. Whoever goes down must wear a rope around his waist with someone above holding the other end. No one enters the saltwater unless a lifeline is tied and manned."

~~~~~~

Owen stood at the bow with a lantern burning in his hand, its yellow light illuminating our ruined ship. The bowsprit had snapped in half and the rails bent around shards of the hull. A massive gnarled rock stretched from the water and pierced our bow; its sharp point loomed over us, stabbing at the sky. The stone had a combination of smooth and rough edges. As I looked upward, I guessed it was taller than our house at

Rosewing Farm and wider at its base than our sloop's main deck. Owen leaned daringly over the edge of the mangled bow and touched the rock. The ship creaked under him as he leaned.

"Owen," hollered Grant, "come away from there."

"On the contrary, my captain. You should come closer and have a look at this stone."

We went to the ruined bow. Under Owen's lantern light, we saw the stone's color—a liquid blue with specks of black and bits of silver.

"Blue…" Owen seemed in a trance. "Azure. Cobalt. Indigo."

"Cerulean," I said.

"Yes," he said. "Welcome to the greatest of all Mer islands. Ahoy!"

"This big blue rock is Cerulean Isle?" Grant remarked.

"Nay. When the fog lifts, you'll see the island. We are in its shallows. I'd guess about three hundred yards from its beach. When the morning sun comes, it will burn away the fog, and then we shall celebrate!"

"Celebrate? Have you seen our ship?" Grant waved his good arm about. "As we stand here in awe over this abomination, the *Obsidian* sails closer and closer with cannon readied. I'll celebrate when we fix the sloop and set sail."

"Master Jacob. Captain Grant." Bart made his way to us as he spoke. "One barrel of water and a crate of bottled ale is all that remains. Our stock of food was lost to the sea."

"What of the extra arms?" I asked.

"There is a crate of pistols, but we've lost the powder. Only the swords remain."

"Prepare the lifeboats for tomorrow," Grant ordered. "If there is land yonder, we'll go to it. Until then, no one is to go into the sea for any reason. Ensure that the crew adheres to this command above all else."

"You have my word, Captain," said Bart.

Chapter 34

Cerulean Isle

I awoke late in the morning. It was unusually quiet, no sounds of a working crew—no hammer falls or chewing of saw blades. I heard only the soft lapping of the ocean against our motionless hull. The crew gathered at the downward tilting bow.

The fog had lifted sometime in the night and now, as the sun broke through the clouds, the body of stone that ensnared our ship seemed to glow as blue as the sky and sparkled like the water that splashed against it. In the distance, beyond the unyielding wall of rock, was a small island lightly blanketed with white mist and surrounded by similar towering stones of silver and blue. The island rested in calm sapphire water and seemed to be made entirely of the mysterious stone. It was jagged and angular and completely guarded by the dangerous, teeth-like rocks. The sunlight played on the blue-stone island and a strange illusion unfolded. The entire landmass appeared to glitter and move, the colossal stones glowed, and soon I could hardly differentiate the island from the sea and sky. It was hidden in the endless blue. It sparkled like the ocean, yet remained as still as the cloud-dressed canvas of the heavens. The threatening forest of stone teeth standing around us was all that could be seen. I squinted through the blazing sunlight; the island was still there.

"Where did it go?" asked a mate in disbelief.

"It turned blue!" exclaimed another.

"It was a mirage. The sea is playing tricks on us."

"Nay, you bloomin' cleats," Owen shouted. "It's reflecting! The island is made of rock that shines like the sky and water. That be why seamen don't see it as they pass. Besides, most won't sail in shallows like this, and you can see why not." He stomped his foot on the splintered deck to make his point clear.

"Bart, let the boats down. It's time we explore that island," Grant said.

"Wait," Owen yelled. "This is Lord Sydin's realm. We must not enter his water without invite."

Waylin came forward. "Our enemy sails in our wake and we are crippled. We must go aground and take what will help us."

"Nothing there is free for the taking," said Owen.

"Ha! A notorious pirate speaks of ethics."

"I am warning you," growled Owen. "Do not go on that island. They will not be pleased."

"Who? Your Mermaidens and Merlords? If this is the 'greatest of Mer islands' as you say, where are the Water People?"

Owen's eyes darted across the sea. He panned the horizon for anything that would prove his claims. "I don't know," he finally said.

Waylin said nothing more. He walked away from Owen and the crew followed. I felt sorry for the old pirate, but there was nothing I could say or do.

~~~~~~

Grant elected to stay onboard, to remain with the ship and crew. I selected a team of five to join me for the first expedition of Cerulean Isle. We set out in two rowboats, three men in each. Waylin, Bart, and I took the oars in one, while Owen followed with two mates, Hammock and Konopo.

Hammock, a heavy man, was not one for climbing rigging or running about the deck. His shaggy hair was the color of mud. His uncanny strength made him an invaluable member of the crew despite his laziness. His arms were massive; no one onboard the sloop could best him in games of might. He arm wrestled for money when in port and he was often the first choice for protection. That is what earned him a seat in the rowboat. He worked the oars with ease and precision.

Konopo was a tribal seafarer. His name meant 'rain.' The islanders of the Caribbean valued rainfall and thought it a great blessing. He was one of the few remaining Carib tribesman and knew the ways of many natives that still dwelled in the ungoverned lands. Waylin had rescued him from slavery and offered him a job aboard the sloop, valuing his combat skill and knowledge of the old native customs.

Soft-spoken Konopo never wore anything more than pigskin drapery around his waist. His skin was like black leather and his head bald, save for a long black braid that sprouted from the back of this head. He kept a dagger tied to his right calf.

We rowed steadily toward the glowing, blue island, carefully maneuvering around the foreboding stones. Owen rambled on about his dislike for Waylin while Waylin ignored him.

As we drifted closer to Cerulean Isle, I noticed a small cove void of vegetation. Only the dazzling blue rock and pearly sand embraced us. Our boats crunched over the sparkling shore and came to a halt. We climbed out and stepped into powdery sand. I knelt down and scooped up a handful. The granules were bits of the reflective silver rock mixed with pristine white sand. Where the powder touched my fingers, the skin shimmered in the sunlight. All around us loomed sharp and towering slabs of crystalline rock. Some of the stone figures were so smooth that I saw my reflection staring back at me as if trapped in a strange world.

We pulled the boats away from the water. I looked back over the waves and saw the wrecked sloop in the distance. *Destiny's* entire front had crumbled beyond repair. The sloop would never sail again.

"Don't linger, Jacob," said Waylin. "Dwelling over our misfortune will not better the situation."

We walked away from the shore and toward the dense wild of the island, a forest of stone. Giant shards of blue and silver stretched from the ground and twisted to create arching passages and ominous caves. A low and resonating howl filled the air as the steady breeze blew through the gaps in the blue rock forest. Brilliant beams of reflected sunlight were colored in many hues of purple, indigo, and soft green. These ethereal rays bounced off the shiny walls and brightened when the clouds moved from the sun. We ventured through the crystal passages, but dared not go in places where there was no light. The scent of the sea remained strong. As we passed the mouths of dark caverns, we could hear water echoing from within.

"Grottos," said Konopo. He stood close to one of the lightless caves and listened. A cool breeze came from the dark entrance. "These are not normal caves. These are waterways. The sea flows under this island."

Owen rushed over to the mouth of the grotto and took a step inside.

"Owen, get out of there!" I ordered.

The old pirate looked back at me, then walked into the dark entrance and disappeared. We heard a splash.

Waylin shouted into the grotto, "Owen, can you hear me?"

There was no reply, not even the splashing of Owen treading water or swimming to get out. Only a soft dripping and gentle lapping echoed from the dark.

"Make way. I'm going after him." I stepped into the dark, feeling the cool water on my toes. I jumped forward into a deep pool of salt water.

Smooth rounded walls of cold stone surrounded me. I let my body sink and fanned my arms over my head to speed my descent through the blackness. As I ventured deeper, the walls around me widened and brightened, signifying light. My feet appeared as black silhouettes against a pale whitish-green light. As the round walls opened away from me, I found myself within a large chamber. Sharp crystals grew from the ceiling, and from another opening streamed a ray of sunlight. The beam of light cut through the water and was absorbed by a multi-sided green crystal. This crystal bent the sunlight and shot it out in all directions, bathing the entire room in a pale emerald glow. My mind struggled to comprehend such a place of beauty. If not for the burning in my eyes and the growing pressure in my lungs, I would have remained in that chamber for hours.

The increasing need for air forced me to think fast. I scanned the emerald room for Owen, and then swam for the center of the chamber and into the beam of white sunlight. I kicked and clawed through the water, rushing for the surface. The sunlight grew brighter as I swam. With a forceful kick, I erupted through the waterline and nearly choked as I drew in the warm air. I floated for a moment, savoring every breath. I rubbed my eyes and surveyed my surrounding. I had come into a circular pool wrapped in the same powdery-white sand. Owen, on his hands and knees, crawled around in the sand.

I swam to the edge of the pool and climbed out of the water onto the hot sand.

"Ah, Master Jacob. My apologies for going ahead of the group."

"You jumped into an unknown grotto!"

"As did you."

"I came to help you."

"But I'm well."

"We thought you'd drown."

"Who would have cared if I did, eh?"

"I would have, you old fool."

"Look what I found." In his palm he held a smooth red clamshell fashioned from a crimson stone. A thin gold chain was attached to it. A closer inspection revealed an engraving on the other side. Four looping letters formed the word *CORA*.

"Where did you find this?"

"There," he pointed. "It was half in the sand, the chain glinting in the sun. It would be wise to leave it here."

I held it up to the sun and marveled at the beauty of the shell. "It looks tribal. We should take it to Konopo and see if he can tell us anything about it. Take a deep breath, Owen, it is back through the grotto for us."

Chapter 35
Something in the Water

When Owen and I emerged, I put on my dry shirt and shoes and summoned the group to gather around and see the shell necklace.

"You say you found this beyond the waterway?" asked Waylin.

"Yes. This grotto descends roughly twenty feet and opens to a crystal cavern filled with green light. In the center of the ceiling is an opening to another waterway that leads up to a small pool and beach."

I went to Konopo and handed him the crimson shell. "What people would make jewelry like this?"

Konopo handled the necklace delicately, holding it up to the sun and turning it around. He read the inscription, and then he brought it to his nose and sniffed it. His dark fingers caressed the gold links and the curves and ridges of the clamshell. His black eyes met ours and he said, "Woryi…my tongue for your word 'woman.' It belongs to woryi. Though it looks like the armor of a clam, it is not."

"What is it, then?" asked Hammock.

Konopo handed me the necklace. "Tapire topu," he said in his strange language. "Red stone. Ruby. Many tribes shape jewels into relics or charms. They are often sacred totems. This bears a word I do not know. Cora."

"No doubt worth a fortune," guessed Owen, his eyes fixed on the necklace.

I put the gold chain around my neck and tucked its ruby pendant into my shirt. "Let's get moving. We can examine it more on the ship. There is much ground to cover and we should be very careful about where we wander." I looked squarely at Owen as I said this. He nodded and the party set out through the mysterious forest of rock.

As we wove our way through the labyrinth of stone passages, I tried to form a mental map so that later I could draw it out. We made deep marks in the ground every few paces, as guides to follow out. We found some large leafy plants and networks of vines growing around the looming stone structures, but no trees.

We heard the babbling of a stream and followed the sound until we came upon a small rushing brook that bubbled up from a cluster of stones. Konopo dipped a finger in the water, tasted it, and nodded. We all knelt by the edge of the stream and drank.

Following the water, we found that it emptied into a large reflective pool. Within it rested six wide chairs, each rounded on the edges and forged from the island's dominating azure ore. The chairs were partially submerged in the clear water and ornately decorated with shells of various shapes and colors.

Around the edges of the clearing stood beautiful sculptures made from smooth, white clay. There was a sculpture of a cresting white dolphin, a detailed shark, and a graceful sea turtle.

The sky opened above the clearing and reflected off the

water to create dancing rays of light that made the surrounding walls of cerulean stone sparkle and shimmer. We walked along the edges of the bottomless pool.

"Master Jacob," called Hammock in his low and rumbling voice. "Look in the sand. Jewels!"

There were diamonds, gold nuggets, shards of sapphire, bits of emerald, and whole pearls among the broken pieces of the cerulean rock. I sifted the fine sand with my toes and uncovered even more jewels. Konopo stood beside the sculpture of the fearsome shark. He touched the art softly as if it would help him unlock the artist's secrets of creation.

"This is a courtyard," said Owen, "and those small pools are the openings to more underwater tunnels. I'm sure of it! Look at the lovely statues and there, in the center pool, the thrones of the Mer that protect this sacred place. We've just entered the heart of Cerulean Isle."

Konopo spoke in a serious tone. "This island is inhabited. We stand in a hallowed place. We should not linger here."

Waylin said, "I think this island *was* inhabited but is now forgotten."

"No," the Carib seaman replied. "These are not ruins."

"Konopo is right," added Bart. "Look around, Waylin. If the island were abandoned, this courtyard would be a mess. The sand would surely be windswept and the pools would be sullied. Those thrones are un-weathered and the sculptures are pristine. This place has been maintained."

"I see no footprints from the caretakers," added Waylin. "No signs indicating man's inhabitance."

Owen chimed in, "That's because men do not live here and the caretakers do not have feet."

I motioned for Owen to be silent, then addressed the crew.

"I agree with Konopo. This place is not abandoned. They must be a seafaring people. How else could they settle an island? They may return. We should make for the sloop and inform the others. Leave the jewels and gold where they are. We take only the necklace."

~~~~~~

I spoke to Grant in the privacy of our quarters. We sat at a short wooden table with a bottle of ale opened in front of us. "Here, look at this." I pulled the ruby clamshell from my shirt, took it off my neck, and handed it to him. "Owen found this in the sand. There is a word on the back."

He turned it around. "Cora must be the woman who owns this. So, what's the next part of our plan?"

"I was hoping you might have an idea or two."

"We need to fix the bow. We'll tear apart these quarters and use the wood from the raised quarterdeck. There's enough wood here to get the ship seaworthy, at least enough to get us to the mainland."

"From the island, I saw the extent of the damage. It's much worse than you think."

Grant drank from the bottle of ale. "In the morning, we'll send down our most skilled swimmers for a thorough examination of the bow and keel."

~~~~~~

Two of our men, Miley and Smirks, offered to dive under the ship. They tied ropes around their waists and entrusted the opposite ends to our mighty friend, Hammock. He stood near the rails, ready to haul them in if they tugged the line.

Not long after the two entered the water, Hammock's line pulled. Hand over hand, Hammock lifted the divers from the ocean. The men pulled themselves aboard.

"What's wrong, mates?" asked Hammock.

"We saw something down there." Smirks wiped the saltwater from his eyes with trembling hands. He stared at the lapping ocean. "It was a monster of some sort."

Miley said, "It looked like a dolphin but with a man's face. It had long hair and a beard that looked like seaweed. It came for us fast and when it got close, two enormous arms came out from its sides. Thank God you pulled us up, or we'd surely be dead."

"Did you get a look at the bow as instructed?" asked Grant.

"Yes. I can make a drawing in a few minutes."

Grant dismissed the crewmates. He and I stood near the bow, looking over the edge and into the choppy waves. "What do you think?" I asked him.

"The crew is tired. The last several days have not been easy. Hard times such as this affect people in different ways. The most important issue at hand is the bow and how we will repair it. Let's concentrate on fixing this ship and setting sail."

Chapter 36

A Call for Help

The sun and moon wheeled overhead, and it felt as though the days were getting longer. We were running out of water and bottled ale. Hunger gripped the crew. I wished for rain, but the sky remained cloudless. In the nights, no one told stories or played games. The men struggled to sleep with groaning bellies. Repairs on the ship had stopped. Without wood or the means to dry dock, the bow could not be fixed.

On the morning of the tenth day, Grant and I discussed plans for another expedition to the island. This time, we intended to barrel and bottle fresh water from the stream we had found. The watchmen's bell sounded, and we hurried to the man positioned at the stern.

"What is it?" asked Grant.

"Look yonder," said the watchman. He pointed to the sea and handed Grant a long telescope. "There is a large family of dolphins coming this way. I have never seen so many."

Grant put the scope to his eye and looked out. "There are

nearly fifty dolphins heading in our direction. That's quite the sight." He handed me the telescope.

The dolphins crested from the water and fluttered above the waves like gray feathers tumbling in the wind. As they drew near, we could hear the cackling laughter that pierced the air. *Destiny's* crew heard the approaching commotion and gathered around the edge of the ship.

Owen danced like a madman. "They're here," he cried. "They've come back at last! Now you'll see. The keepers of the isle, the Merfolk have come!"

The dolphins raced by the sloop, missing the hull by mere inches and swerving around the stone pillars. The ocean whirled as their powerful fins fanned the water. They leapt from the waves as if to show off, and we felt the cool spray hit our faces. The dolphins paid us little mind. They tore through the sea effortlessly, their bottlenoses parting the water better than the bow of any ship. It wasn't long before the last dolphin swam by. Soon, the commotion was over and the sea returned to it normal cadence. The dolphins were gone, undoubtedly swimming within the warm shallows of the blue crystalline island. Owen's shouts and ridiculous dancing soon got everyone's attention.

"In case you didn't notice," said Waylin, "those were dolphins. Not mermaids."

"For the last time, they are called Mermaid*ens*. And anyone could plainly see those be dolphins."

Waylin kept on, "Then why do you now sing that the Merfolk have arrived?"

"Are you that blind? You call yourself a man of the sea?" challenged Owen.

"Jacob," yelled Waylin, "you talk to him. You seem to understand this lunatic better than all of us. I'm ready to maroon him!"

Grant and I motioned for Owen to follow us to our office.

"Explain your outburst about the Merfolk," ordered Grant.

"The dolphins serve two primary purposes for the Mer," he said. "They are cover."

"What do you mean?" I asked.

"Just as zebra group together to appear as one. Just as the cunning tiger lays within grass the same color as her face, the Mer travel with the dolphins. That way, they are safe. Did you see the beautiful Mermaiden as she passed?"

"No," I replied.

"Ahoy! Then it worked. Didn't it? Ha!"

"What is the other purpose?" asked Grant.

"Dolphins are fierce warriors. If one dolphin can kill a shark, imagine what a group can defeat. The dolphin is sacred to the Mer. They value them as much as they value their own kin."

"Can the Merfolk talk to dolphins?" asked Grant.

"Of course they can, like you can talk to a dog. It doesn't mean the dolphins truly understand them. They may obey simple commands like a dog, but that is all."

"Owen," I started, "in the strange courtyard there were sculptures—a dolphin, a shark, and a sea turtle. What does this mean? Are these animals special to them also?"

"The dolphin represents family and wisdom. The shark is for strength and pride. The sea turtle is the totem for balance and peace. These six virtues are the core of their culture."

I thought on this for a moment. I recalled the center pool. There were six thrones in the water. Six places for six people… one for each virtue. Owen's claims were holding true.

"Lord Sydin and his tribe of five are the keepers of Cerulean Isle," said Owen. "There are many Mer who dwell in these waters, but the six of them are the leaders. These things I know from my journeys. The Dariens alone told me a great deal about the ways of the Mer. More than I could ever write in that old journal."

~~~~~~

The rest of the day was uneventful. As the sun fell away, I sat alone on the bow near the great cerulean rock that clutched *Destiny*. I held my fancy broadsword and thumbed the blade. The golden Mermaiden on the hilt stared at me, and the tight leather wrapping on the handle was still soft and clean. The mirror-finished blade reflected the colorful western sky. I saw blues, pinks, and shades of orange flash from the sword. I forced away my sadness. What was it my mother promised long ago on her deathbed? I recalled holding her frail hand. I heard her in my mind. *You will have my love so that you may overcome even the hardest of times. I promise to protect you from harm and Death itself.*

I sheathed the Mersword and wrung the rails of the broken bow in my hands. I looked out to the darkening sky; the mysterious island turned to a shimmering shadow in the distance. I spoke to the black waves. "You promised to protect me, Mother. Where are you now? My crew is weak and each day death draws nearer. We will die. Can you hear me out there? Help us…please help." I fell to my knees and leaned against the rails. There, alone at the bow, I fell asleep.

~~~~~

I woke to loud cheers and laughter. I wiped the sleep from my eyes and saw one of the crewmates stuff a large chunk of smoked meat in his mouth. *Where did he get it?* I soon noticed strange wooden crates piled about the deck. The men hauled more of them from the sea.

"Where did these provisions come from? Did a ship come?"

"We don't know," said Grant. "This morning, at first light, the watchmen noticed dozens of crates floating around our ship."

"And they heard and saw nothing during the night?"

"Nothing, but we can trouble ourselves over it later. Come, eat. You must regain your strength. Waylin is controlling the distribution and noting everything. Konopo and Bart are inspecting the food, water, and wine before anyone consumes it."

~~~~~~

The food was as fresh as if packed only hours ago. The water was crisp and cold. I enjoyed several cuts of smoked fish and savored the sharp cheese and earthy nuts. The ship's cook had taken a bundle of potatoes and prepared a spicy stew. I drank two bowls and took some wine. When all had bested their hunger, I ordered the men to rest under the shade of the sails. Slowly, morale returned as vigor was restored. As the evening fell around us, Bart led a team in stacking and labeling the containers.

The canopy of stars took light above our wrecked ship, and the men talked long and loud through the night. I joined them in card games and listened to Owen tell one of his adventure stories. Grant practiced a few rounds of swordplay with his good arm and we cheered when Konopo bested him. Eventually, the crew gave in to the pull of sleep. I walked about the deck, careful not to disturb anyone, and found myself at the broken bow.

The moon was full and high. Its silver light made the distant island quiver and shine. The starlight gleamed from the tips of the colorless waves. A breeze stirred the waves, and I thought of my mother. A dark cloud moved over the moon.

"Thank you for your help," I said to the endless sea. Two pale lights glowed in the blackness near the hull. I focused my eyes and looked through the rippling waves. The lights were like two little stars, and as I stared in disbelief the stars came up to the surface and faded away, like candle flames suddenly extinguished. The moonlight returned and in its luminance, I saw a face in the water, a woman's face looking at me.

I gasped and fell away from the edge, tripping and landing on my backside. There was a splash from below the bow, then silence. I shook my head, took a breath, and forced myself back to the rails. With a pounding heart, I looked into the water. The woman was gone. *Too much wine, Jacob,* I thought.

My eyes lifted to the island. I saw her again, fifty feet from the ship, a shimmering wet silhouette against the moonlight. Her hair was long and clung to her face and shoulders. She drifted effortlessly in the sea and remained out there, staring at me with an expression of wonder. I raised my hand and reached for her. In one graceful movement, she slipped soundlessly into the water. What I saw next, I'll never forget. A majestic fin emerged from where she had been. It crested high above the waterline and opened in the moonlight. Seawater rained as it fanned to reflect the light of the stars. Even in the night, I could see its dazzling lavender hue. The fin fluttered and sank into the ocean.

Chapter 37

Cora Star

Grant, asleep in a hammock, smelled of rum.

"I saw her! The Mermaiden from the tapestry is out there, and we must go to her."

Grant stared at me, and then rolled out of the hammock, still careful of his broken arm. "Let's get a rowboat ready, but you'll have to do all the rowing."

We informed the night watchmen of our departure, telling them we wanted to fish the surrounding waters and that we would return late in the morning. We lowered a lifeboat as quietly as possible. I thought about waking Owen, but he was too unpredictable, and an expedition such as this was no place for a mad old pirate. Grant brought a lantern and his rapier. I brought my broadsword.

"We'll head to the spot where I last saw her." I turned down the lantern, allowing only a faint glow. "In the meantime, look for lights."

"Lights?"

"Yes. Before I saw her face, I saw two small white lights burning in the ocean. I think it was her eyes glowing. It sounds odd, but that's what I saw. This is it," I said, pointing to the side. "This is where her fin crested from the water. Right here."

We peered into the ocean for several long minutes. The waves lifted and lowered our boat rhythmically. The breeze was cool and salty and we could hear the distant creaking of our trapped ship as the waves beat against its hull.

"I don't see anything," said Grant.

"What are you looking for?" asked a gentle female voice, followed by a soft splash.

Startled, we looked in every direction, seeing nothing.

"What…who was that?" asked Grant in near panic.

"Turn up the lantern," I said. "It seems she's been watching us."

Grant turned up the lantern's wick and shined the yellow light over the black water. The ocean sparkled from our flame. "Where is she?"

"Under water, no doubt. We must let her know we're harmless." I drew my broadsword and placed it on the seat nearest the stern. "Take the rapier from your belt and place it with my blade."

"Are you mad? We have no idea who or what is out there. I've heard my fair share of Merfolk yarns, too. The Greeks called them Sirens, beautiful women with beautiful voices that lured seamen to their deaths."

"If that were true, we'd already be dead."

"Perhaps you're right."

Now fully disarmed, Grant and I sat on the middle bench. We kept our light on the water and panned the surrounding sea. Toward the bow, we heard another splash. Grant aimed the lantern at the front of the boat. There was nothing out there. We sat with the lantern glowing between us. I looked toward the stern and noticed something strange.

"Our weapons are gone."

"My rapier? I love that sword! Where is it?"

"She took it. The splash ahead was a diversion."

"Wonderful for us that we deal with thieving Merfolk," muttered Grant. He leaned over the boat and stared into the waves. "You said to look for two little lights, right?"

"Yes."

"Good. Because they are right there and getting closer."

I peered into the waves. The glowing lights shone from two fathoms below, flickering on and off as they rose slowly to the surface. In the soft white glow I saw faint shimmers of purple, pink, and gold. The lights faded and disappeared.

A lovely young woman emerged from the dark ocean, seawater streaming over her face, neck, shoulders, and chest. Her hair, smooth and wet, rippled behind her in the water. She had flawless, suntanned skin that gleamed in our lantern light and eyes like shimmering wet amethysts. Her ivory smile was bright and nearly reflective. She remained afloat two feet from the edge of our rowboat.

I struggled to form words. "Hello," I managed.

"Hello," she replied. It was hard to tell if her response was true or if she was mimicking me. Her voice was melodic and breathy. She kept her large purple eyes on mine. They were rimmed with a silver hue, unlike any eyes I had ever seen. The ocean trickled from her hair and streamed down her face. Salty water rolled into her eyes but she hardly seemed to notice. She did not blink as most people would.

"My name is Jacob of Rosewing, Grenada."

She looked at me as if taking time to absorb my voice. The sweet smile remained on her face.

"This is my friend, Grant of Rosewing."

"Hello," said Grant. He held out his hand. She looked into his green eyes and she studied his thick red hair. She did not take his outstretched hand. He pulled it away. "It's nice to meet you."

There was a long moment of silence.

"Do you have a name?" I asked.

"Yes."

"What is it? What may we call you?"

"Cora," she answered, "Cora Star. It is nice to meet you, too."

"Well, Cora," Grant began, "do you have my rapier? Because it doesn't float like Jacob's sword and if it sank—"

"Grant. Enough," I said sternly.

Cora laughed. It was like music. "You have something of mine." Her silver rimmed eyes turned to me.

I couldn't help but admire her pure and perfect beauty. So the ruby shell was hers. I reached into my shirt and pulled it off my neck. Dangling from my fingers, it sparkled in the glow of the lantern. Cora came closer. Her arm broke from the surface of the water, and dripped as she reached for the red shell. Her fingers were smooth, slender, and adorned with the most ornate and unusual rings I had ever seen.

She held her cupped palm under the dangling ruby shell. I lowered the necklace into her hand, and as she took it, our fingers touched. She was warm, slick, and wet. As she took the ruby shell, her hand closed around mine. She came to the edge of the boat. Grant looked on as the maiden from the sea examined my hand. Her smooth fingers delicately rubbed my knuckles and slid into the grooves of my palm. She turned my wrist around and opened my fingers. My skin was dry and cracked. She studied my scars, cuts, and splintered nails. As if satisfied that she knew me better, she released my hand and looped the necklace over her head. The scarlet shell rested just below her collarbone.

"Thank you, Jacob." Cora's hand caressed the red jewel, then slipped back into the water. Hearing my name come from her lips was dreamlike. "Please do not be afraid. I tell you this on behalf of my people. Will you tell me the same?"

"Of course. You have nothing to fear. My crew is good at heart," I said.

"We have met fewer and fewer men and women who live peacefully. It is our wish to know you and for you to know us. I shall let our lord speak his desires. I have completed my task."

"What was your task?" Grant slid closer to the bow, the rowboat dipping from the sudden imbalance. Water spilled in. Quickly, Grant returned to the middle of the boat.

Cora laughed softly. "To learn if you will be friend or foe."

"Please, Cora Star, tell your people we wish to be friends."

"I will." Her smile lit up her face. "I have a better idea. You two shall tell them."

With incredible grace, she slid through the water toward the front of the boat, reached in and took hold of our mooring line. "I will bring you."

Soundlessly she vanished below the surface and a second later her extraordinary fin emerged mere feet from the boat. Astonished, we looked on as the fin unfurled like a small sail, its center becoming rigid like a mighty oar. The fin glistened violet, silver, and creamy pink in the lantern light. I guessed its span was six feet from edge to edge, not counting the added length of its rippling, banner-like hem. I imagined that Cora could wrap herself in it once around and still have length to spare. The great fin forced its way through the waves with a tremendous splash. Saltwater rained down upon Grant and me. With incredible power, the boat jerked forward, and soon we were racing across the sea. Cora Star was somewhere under the waves ahead of us with our line in her grasp as she pulled our rowboat fast toward Cerulean Isle.

We watched as the dark island grew. Soon our boat slowed and made a smooth slide into the sandy cove. We got out and stood on the beach, peering out at the waves. Cora emerged and swam toward the shore.

"Can she leave the water?" asked Grant.

"I don't know."

She slipped out of the water and glided, almost serpent like, over the smooth wet sand. I saw her body clearly under the lantern and moonlight. It was the tapestry in reality. She was a fit woman from the pelvis up. Her hips were curved and her waist defined and smooth. Her long wet hair hung below the line of her elbows, shining with striped hues of blue, green, lavender, and red.

The lower half of her, the dolphin-like body, began below the pelvis, as the flesh of her waist darkened to become a pink and purple skin that appeared leathery and smooth. The purple trailed down and darkened to blue, blue blended to purple again and as such, the color scheme repeated until the purple met the start of the great fin.

The fin was translucent and rippled as the surf rushed over it. It looked as though she had wrapped her feet in a silken sheet that swayed in the stirring sea. Cora's Mer-half was intricately striped with fine patterns of silver and gold. The erratic markings created an enchanting mosaic of swirling shapes along her body and stopped at her navel. She was a gorgeous creature, and somewhere in the deepest chambers of my heart I vowed to protect her against all harm.

The Mermaiden giggled. "The first time I saw a human, I wore the same expression that you wear now."

I felt ashamed for staring at her. Where had my manners gone? "Forgive our ignorance. We don't wish to offend you."

She nodded her acceptance. "Though you have been here once already, allow me to welcome you to Cerulean Isle."

"Thank you, Cora Star. It's an honor." Grant gave a noble bow.

I took her hand in mine. Our eyes locked. "Thank you."

Cora led us to the far right of the cove. "Around those rocks," she pointed, "you will find a pool. This is but one of our gathering places. Go there, and I will summon the others."

Cora embraced the rolling waves and vanished back into the ocean. We made for the rocks and climbed around them. A massive tide pool gleamed in the moonlight. Its water was calm and mirror-like. Grant and I sat in the sand beside the pool and waited.

"Let's be gracious guests this night and if things go well, we'll find an opportunity to ask for their help," I said.

"I wonder what Cora meant when she said, 'let our lord speak his desires.'"

"If I had to guess, I'd say he has some kind of business he wishes to talk to us about." I took a deep breath and exhaled. "I'm nervous."

"I wish I had my rapier."

"Enough about the rapier!"

Chapter 38

Keepers of the Isle

The water in the pool began to tremble. A light shone from its depths. Soon the water was blue and bubbling, like a mystical oceanic cauldron in the middle of a white-sand cove. The pool erupted into a geyser of cold seawater, drenching us. We rubbed the water from our eyes and beheld five stunning Merfolk, each one stunning and unique. The water beneath the five Mer began to effervesce once more. The surface broke, and we saw Cora emerge to join the group. They smiled at her but remained quiet. I thought of Owen's description regarding their system of beliefs and hierarchy. The dolphin: family, wisdom; the shark: strength, pride; and the sea turtle: balance, peace. Six virtues for six Mer, and the six now drifted in a spacious pool in front of us.

They studied us with thoughtful, silver-rimmed eyes. One of them, a sapphire-eyed male, floated in the middle of the group. He had lengthy black hair that hung in braids adorned with shells. His face was aged more than the others, though it was smooth, sunburned, and composed. He looked weathered and worn but strong. He wore bands of gold around his arms and a gleaming gold breastplate on his chest. The craftsmanship of the armor would have captivated the finest of blacksmiths. Pressed within the metal was the symbol of a leaping dolphin. I could see the beginnings of his lower half and noticed it was black and silver

He spoke in a strange tongue. "New'atta lee may, Sydin. Anu-yah, Jacob of Rosewing."

Guessing it was an introduction, I smiled and bowed. He came forward and lifted his chin. It was clear that the black-haired Mer was the leader. The other Mer watched in anticipation.

"Lah o'na," he growled. I did not understand. I dared a glance at Cora.

"My Lord Sydin wishes you to kneel," she said in a whisper.

I obeyed. Now I knelt in the sand before him. He cupped the water from the pool in his hands and held it over my head. His fingers parted and I felt the cool saltwater rush over my hair and into my face. The Merlord smiled and held out his hands for me to take. I accepted, and he helped me stand once more.

"Woh n'ay mu'ama Azu Terra," said Lord Sydin.

Cora interrupted softly, "They have English tongues, my lord."

"Yes, of course," he said with a smile. "Welcome to Cerulean Isle, home of the Caribbean Mer." He lifted his hands, his palms opened toward the sky. The others cheered the strange word "woh n'ay," and they all came to the edge of the pool to greet us. I wished then that I had brought Owen to see the realization of his life's quest.

A massive green Mer approached. His long, matted green hair sat atop his wide shoulders like clumped seaweed. His face was hidden in a thick mossy green beard that hung to the center of his chest. His coal-like eyes looked back at me with curiosity. His powerful body had what looked like barnacles all over his shoulders and around his chest. On his left shoulder was a scar, like a branding, in the shape of a writhing shark. He wore a thick gold chain around his waist and on his hands, and covering the knuckles were bands of metal. The edges of his hips, where his Mer-half began, darkened to a forest green.

Effortlessly he flipped his body out of the water and onto the sand beside me. He put his huge, wet arm around my shoulders. "My name is Manta," said the brawny Mer in a low and rumbling voice. Beads of water trickled from his beard. His incredible green fin swayed in the shallow of the pool.

I said, "It's nice to meet you, Manta. Lord Sydin seems like a very nice man."

"He is not a man."

"Right. Sorry. He seems like a nice Mer…"

"Merlord is the correct word in your English voice. All male Mer are called Merlords. The females, Mermaidens."

Owen was right again, I thought.

"Our people have been called many things by many races of man. You have heard stories, I am sure."

"Yes. I have."

Manta laughed. It was loud and resonated through the sand.

"Tell me, Manta," I began, "what is your role among your people?"

"I am a wrecker."

"A wrecker?"

"Yes. When the need arises, I go beneath ships and punch holes in the hull. Depending on the ship, of course."

"I see. How many ships have you wrecked?"

"I do not waste my time remembering such things." He looked around as if to confirm that no one would hear his next few words. He leaned closer and whispered, "Probably twenty-five or so." He let out a rumbling laugh.

"I notice your arm is branded. The scar looks like a shark. What honor does it hold?"

Manta's wide fingers gently touched the branding on his left arm. "I am a Keeper of the Shark. It is my totem. I was chosen by Lord Sydin to embody the sacred attribute of strength. The others here tonight are Keepers as well."

"There are three animals that you 'keep,' as you say?"

"That is correct. Shark, sea turtle, and dolphin."

"Two qualities exist within each of the creatures that your people identify with?"

"The Mer need these icons to inspire and guide them. Do the men of the land have totems?"

"Not in the way that you do."

"Then how do you stay together as a common race?"

"We do not think of ourselves as common. Humans flourish when divided. We live among those who speak the same language or happen to live in neighboring countries."

"I do not understand your word 'countries.'"

At this time, Cora returned to my side and pulled her lovely body from the pool. She sat in the sand, her sparkling fin fanned in the water. "Hello, Manta. Hello, Jacob."

"Greetings, Cora," he said. "Jacob was explaining the human concept of 'countries' and how man lives better divided. Strange."

Cora said, "Land and ocean are not so different. Countries are territories. Just like the many seas. Our home is in the Caribbean. You are a native of the northern coast. You see?"

"Ah, yes. I understand now. Thank you."

"You came from the north?" I asked the large green Merlord.

"The Atlantic was once my home. That is why I am much larger than the others, and that is also why my color is green. The Atlantic Merfolk are bigger and stronger. They must be if they wish to survive the icy water. My old tribe parted ways many years ago, after our lord was killed. I swam for warmer waters and was welcomed by Lord Sydin. I am happy here. These are good Mer, and the Mermaidens are the most beautiful, as you can clearly see."

"Thank you, Manta." Cora smiled. "Come, Jacob, the others are anxious to speak with you." She took my hand and led me away from Manta.

"It was a pleasure talking with you, Manta," I said.

"We will speak again." The massive Merlord slipped quietly into the pool, hardly disturbing the water. After a small ripple and chorus of bubbles, he was gone.

Grant sat at the edge of the pool with his feet dangling in the water. A Mermaiden with frothy pink hair drifted in the water beside him, caressing his curly red hair. Her eyes were piercing emeralds, her skin peach-colored and fair. She wore strings of pearls around her body. The pearls snaked around her arms and wrapped about her waist like sparkling, beady vines. She had rosy lips and wore heavily jeweled bracelets and rings. Her lower half was slender, silver, and white.

"Jacob, I'd like to introduce Pearl. Pearl, please meet my good friend, Jacob."

She held out her hand in a pretentious manner as if she were royalty. "Cora, you've brought such handsome walkers." I took her fingers and lightly kissed the back of her hand.

"They are men," Cora said sternly. "Do not call them 'walkers.'"

"Jacob," said Grant, "Pearl was telling me that she's able to grant wishes."

Cora interrupted, "That is not true!" She swam between Grant and Pearl and forced the jewel-covered Mermaiden aside. "Why would you tell our guests such a thing, Pearl?"

"But I *can* make wishes come true, Cora." She looked at Grant with lusty emerald eyes. "It depends on the wish, doesn't it?"

"It sure does," said Grant.

"It seems the fun is over for now," said Pearl. Her wet hands slid through Grant's hair. "I will see you later, Grant. Here." She took a string of pearls off her wrist and slid it over his hand. "A welcome gift blessed with virtues of pride." She slid into the water and was gone.

Chapter 39

Enemy in Common

The sound of our laughter caught the attention of a Merlord with blue and gold striped hair. He smiled at us, his silver-brown eyes filled with wonder. On his chest dangled a pendant in the shape of a sea turtle. His skin was bronzed from the sun. This Mer wore bracers on his forearms made from turtle shells. There was something overwhelmingly pleasant and calm about him. From what I could see, his lower half was bright blue and gold.

Cora greeted him in a warm embrace, took his hand, and led him closer. I felt a sting of jealousy when she wrapped her arms around him. Pushing aside the foolishness, I smiled at the Merlord.

"Jacob, Grant, I would like you to meet my older brother, Driften."

The jealousy dissolved. The suntanned Merlord extended his hand. His smile was kind and bright. "It is a pleasure to meet you, Grant and Jacob."

Cerulean Isle

"Likewise, Driften." Before letting the Mer's hand go, Grant turned Driften's wrist around to better examine the shell bracers. "Does this truly make effective armor?"

Driften grinned. "Has the turtle ever asked for anything more?"

Cora wrapped her arms around her brother's neck playfully. "Driften is a Keeper of the Sea Turtle, like me. He is the fastest Mer in our tribe."

"Are you trying to embarrass me in front of our guests?" He slipped away from Cora's grasp and splashed her.

"Keeper of the Sea Turtle…what does that mean?" asked Grant.

Driften caressed his turtle-shaped pendent. "In our tribe, the sea turtle embodies balance and peace. I am the Keeper of Balance and Cora Star is the Keeper of Peace."

"And Manta and Pearl are Keepers of the Shark," I added to show my understanding. "Pearl holds the virtue of pride and Manta holds strength."

"That is correct, Jacob," confirmed Driften. "Our Lord Sydin and his son, Brine, the young Mer, are the Keepers of the Dolphin. Sydin holds true to the virtue of wisdom while his son values family. The three totems are sacred and can be seen in many seas. They remind the Merfolk and serve as guides by which one may live his life."

"Your culture is pure and fair," I said. "I admire it and a part of me wishes that I lived as you do."

Driften smiled, and Cora came near me again.

"From what I have heard about you, Jacob of Rosewing, your way of life is not so different. You value the same things. Asking for help for your crewmates proved it to us," said Driften.

"It was your people who supplied us with the provisions?"

"Of course," he chuckled. "Cora Star is the head scout of Azu Terra, Cerulean Isle by English name. She watches the fringe of our territory. Since your ship wrecked, she has watched and listened."

"Thank you. If not for the compassion of your people, we would have perished."

"And Jacob really enjoyed the wine," added Grant. "He has refined tastes."

"Well, I must be going. I believe Lord Sydin awaits you both. My sister will remain with you and be your guide. Until next we meet." Driften nodded and sank slowly into the water. His striped hair flowed and waved. In a flash of blue and silver, he was gone.

I stared into the water. Its center was dark and bottomless. Then the mirrored surface began to tremble. I looked up and saw the Lord of the Merfolk before me.

"I would like to introduce my son, Brine." Sydin motioned for a young Mer to come closer. The youth swam to his side.

The Merchild had short, muddy-brown hair. His face was freckled from the sun, and he wore a band of leather around his forehead bearing a bone-carved dolphin similar to the one embossed on the gold plate of Lord Sydin. At the tops of his arms, he wore bands of leather, and around his waist was a belt of pouches. This one had the look of a young adventurer, and his colors were right for it. I imagined his brown and gray lower half would allow him to blend with many surroundings.

Their eyes were the same dark blue, a definitive confirmation of lineage. Lord Sydin turned to his son and spoke strange words. "Du kanna ah'lo tay."

Brine nodded his understanding and reached behind his back to produce two gleaming swords. He handed the weapons to his father. I recognized them as my broadsword and Grant's bejeweled rapier. The Merlord offered the hilts to us.

"My people are not thieves," said Lord Sydin, "but we take precautions when appropriate. The Keepers have welcomed you. The need for precautions has passed."

We took back our weapons with a respectful bow.

"Though you have regained your strength," Sydin continued, "it seems your troubles are far from over. Tell me,

Jacob and Grant, what led you to these waters? What would force skilled seamen to sail so recklessly?"

I did not know if speaking of L'Ollon or the *Obsidian* would be wise, but the fact remained that we shared the same enemy. As Sydin had said, the need for precautions had passed. "We are being pursued by murderous pirates. Their numbers are great and they will not be satisfied until we are all killed."

Sydin's brow lifted with intrigue. "What have you done to render such a bounty?"

"Ten years ago I killed their captain."

My reply troubled the lord of the Mer. "That is not the way of pirates," professed Sydin. "Normally, the crew elects a new leader or they divide whatever wealth is aboard and go separate ways. I have even heard of pirates aligning with rival bands. If a captain perishes in combat, so be it. Never have I heard of a crew wasting a decade to avenge the death of a captain."

"It is a perplexing situation," said Grant, "but it is happening. The *Obsidian* sails in our wake and it won't be long before they come upon our ruined ship and finish us off."

"The *Obsidian,* you say?"

"Yes, the one and only. According to one of our mates, the Merfolk fought against her years ago, is that true?"

Sydin's piercing blue eyes studied us. The young Mer beside him remained quiet.

"Yes," he answered. "Long ago, a terrible storm jostled a barque with a corpse on the bowsprit into my territory. The storm tossed the ship around as if it were a toy. Two other ships sailed with her, a galleon and a sloop similar to your own. The fleet was doomed. I called for my tribe to assist them. We were not well-received. A pirate opened fire on a Merlord, wounding him. Our only intent was to guide them out of the storm, but their captain was foolish. He ordered his crew to war, and so it was that we defended ourselves. If not for the raging sky and sea, we may have been defeated. The captain, Jean L'Ollon, abandoned his sinking fleet and escaped with his life.

"Fate is the reason for our meeting and for your hardship. Strange that such a terrible man has poisoned both of our pasts. Your situation is unsettling. I do not believe that Jean L'Ollon died. What happened after you stabbed him?" asked the Merlord.

"He sank into the sea, and we rowed away as fast as we could."

"Then you do not know if his men dove in after him. Let us imagine that his crew pulled him from the sea. If your blade went anywhere other than the heart, he could still be alive. Did you stab him in the heart?"

"I...I don't know."

The Merlord fell silent. His face darkened with distant thoughts. "The answer is obvious," he said. "Captain Jean L'Ollon is still alive and commands his crew. He has been commanding them to search for you for ten years."

I was struck by a sudden realization. "We are not all he is searching for, then." I turned to Grant. "Do you remember his plan?"

Grant looked away to recall the days aboard the *Obsidian*. His eyes widened as he remembered. "Yes, He planned to kill Shanley and use the sea chart and Owen's journal to find Cerulean Isle. He wants his gold."

"Lord Sydin, I must ask you; do you have Jean L'Ollon's gold?"

"As I have already stated, we are not thieves. However, what falls to the ocean floor is free for the taking. Yes. I have it. I have gold and jewels from many fallen fleets. We use it to forge azumetalla, the same metal that is folded within your blade. When the rock of this isle is heated and combined with melted gold, it becomes buoyant and resistant to the harshness of the sea. It is harder than any man-forged ore. Azumetalla is the most versatile and most coveted material for all Merfolk. We use it to craft everything from tools to weaponry and armor. We do not value man's gold as currency. We cannot get the precious land metals by any other means. In essence, we are scavengers or collectors, as my son likes to say."

I said, "Then we are as good as dead. Our ship is beyond repair, and even if we hadn't wrecked, they outnumber us in manpower."

"And," added Sydin, "that would also mean that my tribe is in danger. We must work together, your crew and my tribe." Sydin paused to think. "I would like to invite all aboard your ship to meet and discuss this. I ask only that none come bearing weapons. This is a sacred island, and I will not permit tools of violence." He turned to Cora. "Meet the men of the sloop *Destiny* before the noon sun and guide them to the courtyard. The water of the Sacred Lagoon will give us the clarity to choose the right action."

"Yes, my lord."

"Jacob, Grant, this night has been an honor for our tribe. Take my invitation to your men. Share with them all that you have learned. I bid you both a good evening."

Lord Sydin put out his hand and we accepted. His black and silver form disappeared in the crystal water. His brown-finned son gave us a quiet smile and followed after him.

"I will meet you at the rowboat," said Cora.

I watched her slip into the pool. The rippling water lapped over her face and lifted her rainbow-streaked hair. She stared at me as she went below. I saw a white glow take light in her eyes. The luminance banished the remaining shadows in the water.

Chapter 40

Invitation

Cora Star pulled our boat to *Destiny's* hull, swimming out of sight just below the surface so as not to alarm the crew. Grant awkwardly climbed the rope ladder with one arm. Once on the deck, he engaged the watchmen to distract them so I could say goodnight to Cora.

"Thank you for everything. You saved me a lot of rowing," I said, in awe that I spoke to the creature I had dreamt of as a child.

Cora smiled and reached for my hand. Though her fingers were wet, she was still warm. The soft light in her eyes dwindled and went out. Two clear amethysts stared at me. Her skin shimmered in the pallid moon. "Thank you for being kind to my tribe."

"Did you think I wouldn't be?"

"It is hard to guess the true intention of men."

"You have known others, then?"

"No. You are the first man I have ever spoken to," she

admitted with a smile. "As a scout, I have watched many ships pass along the fringe of our territory. I have seen men treat each other in surprising ways. I often find the bones of seamen rolling along the ocean floor, and I wonder how they could let these remains fall away from their world. Humanity is mysterious and unpredictable."

As I listened to her, my mind was filled with images of my mother's flowered coffin drifting out to sea.

"What is wrong, Jacob?" asked the Mermaiden.

"Nothing. You just reminded me of things from long ago. Before I say goodnight, may I ask you something?"

"Yes."

"What is it like down there? Is there another world under the sea?"

"We all live in the same world. Sky touches land, land touches ocean, and ocean touches sky."

"But what is down there?"

"What are you looking for?"

I thought about it. She pulled her hand away from mine. The rolling waves began to swallow her.

"I'm not looking for anything anymore," I said, "now that I've found you."

"Kay lu'ann, Jacob; it means goodnight. I will see you before the noon sun."

"Kay lu'ann, Cora."

~~~~~

I lay awake that night thinking of the rainbow-haired Mermaiden. I wondered where she spent her nights. I watched the sky brighten from the coming sun. The starry blackness overhead turned to gray, then to blue. Soon the first hues of daylight streamed out from behind the horizon, red and orange like a distant fire burning just out of sight.

~~~~~

Just after breakfast, I met with Waylin. We leaned against

the starboard bow.

"The watchmen reported that you and Grant went fishing last night," he said, "I am not a fool. I know you went to the isle."

"We went to the isle, and we met with the inhabitants."

Waylin's eyes widened. "There are people there?"

"Yes. An entire tribe."

"That is wonderful! Perhaps they can help us."

"I am sure they will. They are very kind," I said. "Where is Owen? The news that Grant and I have would be of great interest to him."

I looked out at the island and wondered what the Merfolk were doing on this morning. Did they eat breakfast? Were they speaking of last night's meeting? Perhaps they looked out at our ship and asked these same questions.

Waylin interrupted my thoughts. "Owen is the other matter I wish to speak of. That old salt has been filling our men's heads with wild tales. Merfolk. Those are the only yarns he knows."

"You might want to listen to a few of his stories."

"I am all for a good fable when the time is right, but not all of his are good."

"What do you mean?"

"I have heard him tell that the Merfolk are killers, man-eaters. He has some of the men believing that we are in grave danger. Smirks and Miley, the divers, still claim to have been attacked, and this only validates Owen's ravings. Hammock has come to me and asked if we have taken the necessary precautions against the Water People."

This news was difficult for me to understand. I had never heard Owen say anything ill of the Mer. I wondered why he would make such claims.

Waylin continued, "Owen is the danger. He is poisoning the minds of our already troubled crew. It is all we can do to keep morale high enough so that hope remains. The last thing I need is a lunatic making matters worse. I did what I could to ease Hammock's worry. He's not the only one that Owen has managed to frighten. There are at least six other men who have come to me and asked if Owen's stories are true."

"Have you approached Owen?"

"Of course I have. He tells me there is nothing wrong with sharing yarns and that if the crew is not mature enough to understand that the stories are for enjoyment, they are fools." Waylin sighed and rubbed the corners of his tired eyes. "From the start, I have questioned his intent. He is cunning and intelligent, but so am I."

"What would you have me do?" I ran my hand through my hair and rubbed the back of my neck. I was tired, and it was a struggle for me to focus on Waylin's concern. Images of Cora swept through my mind.

"Order him to cease his mischief. You are the only one he listens to. If it does not stop, I will personally build a new jail cell for him."

"Be at ease, Waylin. I will talk to him."

I left the starboard bow and began my routine main deck walk. The crew greeted me as I passed. The sun was hot, but a frequent breeze blew off the sea, cool and calming. Waylin followed beside me. "Tell me of the people who call that strange land home."

"They are a peaceful tribe."

"Arawaks, possibly."

"No. They are not Arawaks at all. They speak English and have a basic understanding of our customs. Grant and I met with their leader and he wishes for his people and our crew to meet."

"Did they propose a time?"

"Today. We are to venture back to the courtyard with the statues. They call it the Sacred Lagoon. Also, they have asked that we bear no arms while on their land."

Waylin's brow dipped in disapproval. "That request will not sit well with the others."

"I understand, but what choice do we have? Remember that they are the people who saved our lives."

"I have met and befriended tribes from all over the world. This meeting will be no different."

"Well," I began.

"Well, what?"

"Nothing. Come, I must call for a crew meeting and inform our men of what is to come."

I sounded the watchmen's bell, and the crew assembled under the mainmast. Grant stood by me, his left arm in a sling and a smile on his face. Owen stood in front of the crew. The days in the sun had bronzed him and the darkened complexion hid his age even more. Being on the ship and out at sea had rejuvenated him. He looked strong and proud.

I lifted my hand to call for their attention.

"My friends," I began. "Last night, Grant and I met the people of the island." A speculative and excited murmur rustled through the crowd. "The provisions we found floating in the waters around *Destiny* are from them. They have invited us to meet on their land and agreed to help us."

"Who are they?" shouted one of the crewmates.

"They are a peaceful tribe. We must meet with their leader and together we will decide the best way to repair our ship."

Hammock stepped forward. His face was troubled. "What do they want in return? Nothing is free."

"I don't know what they will ask of us in return, but whatever it is would be within our means, I am sure. One would not borrow from a beggar." I turned to the crew again. "The only request they have made is that we leave behind all arms. No one is to carry a weapon while on their land."

This condition upset the men, who broke into a clamor of protest. Owen stared at me strangely.

"Is there a problem, Owen?" I asked.

He smiled slowly. "You tell me, Jacob. I notice that you are not wearing the ruby shell necklace. Did you find the owner?"

"Yes. I met the tribal woman who lost it and gave it back."

"It was no woman you met. Tell me, did you meet the six Keepers? Did you meet the one they call Sydin?"

"We will talk of these matters later."

"Nay!" he yelled. The crew turned their attention on us. "We will talk of it now! You met the Mer of Cerulean Isle. You and Grant went on a private expedition and failed to include me. Damn you."

"Owen, please…"

"I led you to safety and shared my wisdom with you. I bestowed my knowledge of the Mer. I worked for days helping to repair this worthless ship and when the time came to seek out the Water People, you went alone. Why did you leave me out? I'll tell you all why! Because you still, after all I have done for you, believe me to be recklessly mad. Aye!" He turned to the crew and shouted, "Who is reckless after all? Captain Grant and quartermaster Jacob, they are the ones not worthy of trust. They have admitted that last night they abandoned this ship while we slept. They left us. Need I say more?"

Waylin stepped forth and loomed over Owen. "You needn't say more. You need to say less," he growled. "Defame this crew one more time and you will regret it."

Owen spat in Waylin's face.

Waylin hauled back and struck him. Owen stumbled back, then moved toward Waylin who struck him again. This time Owen fell. Blood poured from his mouth. Waylin snatched him by the shirt and lifted him to his feet. Owen was disorientated. The crew looked on as Waylin pinned him against the mainmast.

"You must be proud, Waylin," mocked Owen. "Striking a man many years out of his prime. Aye, proud indeed."

"Silence! You will dishonor us with your madness no longer."

A bloody hiss of laughter came from Owen as the old pirate looked over at me. "Tell him, Jacob. Tell him, Grant. Tell them all that it was Merfolk you met. Do not lead them into danger."

"The Merfolk are *not* dangerous!" yelled Grant.

"Then it is true?" asked Hammock. His sheer size demanded an answer.

A silence fell over the crew. All eyes were on Grant and me. Even Waylin, though he kept Owen pressed against the mast, looked at us, waiting for the truth.

"I said "Last night we met a tribe of people that have made this strange island their home. They are kind, peaceful, and yes…they are Merfolk. The Water People are real and this is one of their territories. They mean us no harm."

"What now, Jacob?" asked Waylin angrily.

"We go to them," I replied.

Grant addressed the crew. "There is nothing to be afraid of. Our enemy is their enemy. They are the ones who brought us the food. They saved our lives. Would a tribe that meant us harm be so generous? Who will go aground on Cerulean Isle without reservation or fear?"

Konopo was the first to raise his hand, intrigue burning in his black eyes. Owen muttered something but raised his hand. I looked over the crew and watched as the hands started to rise.

Chapter 41
Strange Behavior

While Waylin, Bart, and Grant assisted the crew in preparing all seaworthy rowboats, I made my rounds to ensure that everyone adhered to the no weapons agreement. Owen leaned over the port bow with a rag to his nose and mouth. Every now and then he turned it to help cease the bleeding.

"Owen." He did not acknowledge me. "This is the day, Owen, when we meet as allies with the Merfolk of Cerulean Isle. Isn't this what you've desired for so long?"

Owen removed the stained rag from his face. He was no longer bleeding. He threw it into the water and faced me. "You have much to learn, Jacob. There is still time, however. Leave me alone."

He pushed by me and made his way to the rowboats.

The crew of the sloop *Destiny* filled all five rowboats. I shared the lead boat with Grant, Waylin, Bartholomew, and Konopo. Owen, still refusing to be near Waylin, shared a boat with the two divers, Hammock, and one of the watchmen. They spoke softly to each other and from time to time, Owen gave us a cold glance.

Grant stood up and hollered to the rowboats drifting around the hull of the sloop. "We must wait here until our guide arrives. Let this be your last chance to rid yourselves of any arms. If you have so much as a paring knife around your neck, throw it overboard now." Two men from the third boat tossed small knives into the water. "Now, please be patient and await further orders. No one goes ahead."

"Well done," I said. "Now we wait for Cora Star."

"For who?" asked Waylin.

"The Mermaiden, Cora Star, their lead scout. She said she would be here around noon to bring us to the isle."

I felt something wet touch my hand. I turned to find Cora looking back at me. Her shoulders and head dripped with saltwater and her purple eyes sparkled with delight. Her colorful wet hair shone in the sunlight, like the ribbons of a rainbow woven into fine threads. Her skin was lightly bronzed and when her lips formed a smile, my heart melted, and all of the boyhood dreams were rekindled within me.

"Hello again, Jacob," she said, her eyes riveted to mine.

"Good day, Cora."

Her cool hand folded around mine. Her rings of gold and silver glinted almost as bright as her eyes. "Waylin, Bart, Konopo…I'd like to introduce Cora Star."

"It is a wonder to meet you all," she greeted them.

The men gazed at the stunning female drifting in the water beside our boat. Waylin stared. Bart wore a look of fascination. He blinked a few times and then leaned over to shake her hand. "You are every bit as lovely as Grant and Jacob foretold. I am Bartholomew."

Cora heard his name and tried to mouth the word. "Bar…ta'la…mo."

"Just call me Bart, my lady."

Cora giggled. "Bart."

Konopo spoke to Cora. "Awu, Konopo. Amoro Wotoworyi?"

Cora nodded that she understood his Carib tongue. "It is nice to meet you, Konopo, and yes, I am a Mermaiden, a Wotoworyi, as your people say. We have known elders of your tribe. Your people are great warriors."

"Thank you. If I had my urapa, it would be yours to command."

"What is an *urapa?*" asked Grant.

"Bow and arrow," he answered without taking his eyes off the Mermaiden.

Cora drifted back to me. "Are you ready to go?"

"We are ready."

"Then let your mooring line over the bow as you did the night before. Command the other boats to do the same. My friends are all here, waiting under the water. They will take the lines, and we will pull you to the isle."

"No rowing!" cheered Grant. He looked around and asked, "Cora, is Pearl here?"

"Yes, Grant," she replied with a playful smirk. "She is eager to see you again."

Grant sat back and winked at Bart. Bart chuckled but regained his etiquette. Cora slipped quietly under the water. I dropped our mooring line over the bow. From beneath the waves, I saw a glitter of purple and gold, then the line became taut. I stood up to address the crew.

"Let loose your mooring line. Keep one end secured to your bow and toss the other in the water. They have come. They will pull us to the island."

The men leaned over the sides of the boats to peer into the water, and tried to catch a glimpse of a cresting fin. With incredible finesse, the Mer towed our rowboats safely around the dangerous stone pilings. In just under five minutes, our journey was over. The Mer let our lines free and our boats drifted into the bay of white sand.

Destiny's crew took in the fantastical landscape of the island. Some men knelt to touch the powdery sand while others gazed upward at the looming crystal-blue formations. I heard a soft splash and turned to see Cora a few feet from the shore.

"My friends," I called to the remaining crew, "there is someone I would like you to meet."

Cora heard this and instinctively began to fall under the waterline.

"Do not be afraid," I said to her, "please."

The rainbow-haired Mermaiden gave me a cautious smile and remained in view. The other crewmates gathered around.

"Men, I'd like you to have the honor of meeting Cora Star." I pointed to where she drifted.

They greeted her, several dropping to a knee to show respect and amiable intent. Cora was put at ease. I motioned for her to come closer. Slowly, and without taking her eyes off the group, she swam to the shore. I walked into the water to meet her halfway. She came close to me, and I took her hand and looked to the others. Like the previous night, her aquatic lower half slid over the wet sand of the shore. The men saw her body and gasped. Their stares made her uncomfortable.

"Don't worry," I whispered, "they need to see what you are to fully understand. It is better that you be the first Mer they see and not one like Manta."

"Why is that?"

I smiled. "Because you are beautiful, and even I remain enchanted."

Cora squeezed my hand and her face blushed. "I have never had so many humans look at me. I am nervous."

Cora gave the group a shy wave. She was completely out of the ocean with her lower body slightly coiled in the sand. The lapping surf rolled over her rippling violet fin. It swayed and flowed from the water's touch like a shimmering silk garment.

"Hello, everyone," she said softly. "Welcome to Cerulean Isle."

Cerulean Isle

The crew gathered around us. The meeting took an awkward turn when Owen stepped forward. "Greetings, Mer," he said rather smugly.

Cora looked up at the old seaman and recoiled a little. "Hello," she said. Her bright purple eyes fell onto his. He quickly looked away, as if trying to foil her attempts to know him better.

"Cora Star is your name?"

"Yes. What may I call you?"

"My name is Owen. I look forward to meeting the rest of your people."

Cora did not respond. Owen nodded and stepped away, disappearing in the crowd.

She pulled me close and spoke softly in my ear. "That man is not good."

Chapter 42

Men and Mer

"You have been to the Sacred Lagoon once before," Cora said to me. "It is the courtyard with the statues. That is where Lord Sydin waits. Go there. I will be waiting for you as well."

Cora moved back into the rolling surf as the water wrapped around her. She waved to the others before disappearing. Her magnificent fin emerged from the waves, sending glittering beads of water into the sky. There was a splash as the fin shattered the surface of the ocean.

Waylin, Bart, Konopo, and I led the crew into the crystal forest. Grant walked with me and marveled over the blue stone formations and towering reflective crystals. Owen trailed behind.

With the help of Konopo's memory of the terrain, we arrived at the Sacred Lagoon. The statues of the sea turtle, dolphin, and shark stood proud along the far wall. Endless jewels and gold pieces littered the sand. Waylin reminded the crew to leave it alone.

We sat along the edge of the pool. Once all were settled, the water began to tremble. The Mer arrived one by one and took their places in the designated stone thrones that rested in the water. The first to arrive was Cora Star. With a graceful thrust of her lower half, she leapt from the water and into her throne.

Cora's brother, Driften, broke from the water and took the throne beside his sister. Driften studied the crowd of seafarers, adjusted the turtle shell bracers on his arms, and then wrung the water from his gold and blue striped hair.

Grant gasped as though startled by something. Instead of sitting at the edge of the pool, legs folded like everyone else, he had his feet dangling in the water. A flowing mass of pink swirled in the water near his feet. Pearl tugged on Grant's legs playfully and slowly emerged. Her thick pink locks clung to her face and neck. With her hands on his knees, she lifted herself up and out of the water. Grant took hold of her and helped the Mermaiden onto his lap.

She wrapped her arms around his shoulders. "It is so very nice to see you again, Grant of Rosewing."

"And you as well, Pearl of…uh…the ocean." He cleared his throat. "How are you?"

"Lonely," she whispered, her mouth nearly touching his.

"Pearl!" Cora called to her. "Take your place at once."

Pearl slid off Grant's lap. She took her throne but did so with teasing movements. Cora glared at her.

Pearl lost the attention of the group when the water erupted and sprayed us all. The hulking Merlord named Manta hovered in the middle of the pool and studied the surrounding seamen. His muscular barnacle-laden chest heaved as if he had traveled a great distance in little time. Water dripped from his mossy green beard and matted hair. His presence and challenging posture made the men uneasy. Some recoiled from the edge of the pool.

I lifted my hand to greet him. He saw me and nodded. The pool seemed small with him in it. He took his place with the others, sitting beside Pearl.

"Anu-yah, Cora," said Manta. "Anu-yah, Driften."

"Anu-yah, Manta," replied Driften.

Grant nudged me. "I guess that means 'hello.'"

Pearl reached over to Manta and caressed his shoulder. "Anu-yah, Manta. Nee alu-ay. Woe be nah essa oh?"

"What is she saying to him?" whispered Grant.

"I don't know."

Manta responded in English, "Have respect for our guests and use their words. And no, I have not been avoiding you. I have been very busy. That is all, I assure you."

I chuckled. "Looks like you're not the only one Pearl is interested in."

"What's he got that I don't?"

"Do you really want to talk about this?"

"No."

"Good. Now be quiet."

Lord Sydin emerged from the water. His gold breastplate gleamed, and his long wet hair looked like black ink spilling over his shoulders. He regarded Grant and I with a friendly nod and then panned the group of seamen. I looked at the crew and saw Owen standing with Hammock, Smirks, and Miley. The two divers looked anxious, while Owen's face was void of expression. *What is wrong with him?* I wondered.

"My name is Lord Sydin. I would like to extend kind greetings to you all. Welcome to Cerulean Isle." He opened his arms and raised them over his head. The Mer cheered behind him. Sydin lowered his arms and smiled. "This meeting of man and Mer is a great honor for us. Forget your fears and doubts.

"We live by six virtues that are not unknown to mankind. Peace, balance, wisdom, family, strength and pride. Take these now as blessings and understand that we who dwell in the sea are not different than those who dwell on the land, at least not in the heart and mind.

"Your ill fortune has been a challenge for you all. We are

sympathetic to your troubles. However, now you are our guests, and I hope that I may also call you allies."

Waylin stood up. If he was the least bit apprehensive, he did not show it. "Lord Sydin, thank you for the aid that your people so selflessly brought to us."

"You are welcome. Please, you need not address me formally. Sydin will do. I am not a lord among your people."

Waylin nodded.

"What is your name?" asked Sydin.

"I am Waylin."

"You shine with experience, and I feel only goodness coming from your heart. Am I wrong to say this?"

"No, Sydin. I like to think of myself as a man of the sea."

Sydin's presence was powerful and commanding. The other Mer looked at him with respect and devotion. "You are all men of the sea. Not foul thieves and murderous warriors."

I stood up and nudged Grant to do the same. "Anu-yah, Sydin," I said.

"Anu-yah, Jacob. You have learned our customary greeting, I see."

"Sydin, when last we spoke, we agreed to devise a plan. I would like to move this meeting in that direction, if I may be so bold."

"Of course." Sydin raised his voice loud enough for the entire group to hear. "We know of your feud with the pirates of the *Obsidian*. We know that they search for you with cruel intentions. Your presence here places us in danger as well. We must work together in this matter. Join forces, as your people say. We will repair your ship so that you may continue to elude your enemy. It will be stronger and faster; ready for war, should it come to that. After your departure, we will be safe once more. For our services, we must ask you to do something for us, something that has never been done before."

"And that is?" asked Grant.

"Help us relocate our cache of gold and silver. If the *Obsidian* finds this island, the men who sail her will raid it and plunder all that we've accumulated. This island is home to the largest store of man's precious metals. Gold and silver are the only metals that can be forged with cerulean ore. From this comes azumetalla, a metal critical to our survival.

"Once your ship is repaired and afloat, take our gold and jewels aboard. Sail northwest into the Gulf. You will find many deep grottos and caverns along the shores. Find one suitable to hide our cache. Do this and swear to keep its location a secret and you will all be rewarded. Now, what say you to my offer?"

Bart stood up. "At the risk of sounding disrespectful, why are you being so trusting? You seem to have no reservations about filling our cargo hold with your gold."

"I must do what is best for the welfare of my tribe. My personal reservations, if any, must never cloud my judgment. By coming here unarmed, you have proven to me that you are worthy of my trust. You are good seafarers, unlike the lawless pirate clans that sail abroad. Do you understand?"

"I do," answered Bart.

I turned to address the crew. "You've heard the offer made by the lord of the Mer. An 'aye' if you agree to the conditions, a 'nay' if you do not."

A bellow of 'aye' filled the air. The Mer slipped from their thrones and swam to the edge of the pool to speak with the crewmates. Pearl joined Grant once more, and Waylin and Bart shook hands with Sydin.

Cora came to me and wrapped her arms around my neck. "Things will be just fine now, Jacob," she said in my ear. "The Merlords will fix your pretty ship in no time at all."

Her embrace was strong and wet. Her hair was cold and smelled of sea salt.

She pulled away and giggled. "It seems I have got you all wet. I am sorry."

I had often dreamt of what it would feel like to hold a Mermaiden in my arms. At last I knew.

Chapter 43

Betrayed

The lord of the Mer pointed a dripping finger at Owen. "You there. Come closer, please. Do not be afraid."

Owen came to the edge of the pool. "I am not afraid of you. In fact, I've waited many long years to see you."

Sydin drifted closer to Owen, who took a small step back.

"I have spent my life learning all I could about Merfolk," said Owen. "I traveled to distant lands and learned every yarn and shanty there is. I was regarded as a madman for this."

"Belief is something that many give up early in life," said Sydin.

"Not me, Merlord. I believe that even the Merfolk can lie."

Sydin looked confused.

"Ah. No retort, I see. You claim to be a peaceful race, yet your society prospers from gold that is not yours. You are thieves! The strong Mer tear apart ships and the cunning ones wield the bows and whalebone arrows. You kill seamen for sailing in waters that you claim to own. No one owns the sea. No one!"

"Owen, you have gone too far!" I yelled. I needed to silence him. "I thought you would be honored to be here among the Mer, that you wanted to know of their truths. Finding this island has been your passion. What is wrong with you?"

"As I've said before, many things."

"What changed your heart?"

"I keep several hearts. When one sours, I go to the next."

There was a splash in the pool. Brine, the young Mer with the brown hair, swam toward Sydin. "Amu la ee'rah," he said excitedly. "Nay'yoo, es nay'yoo!"

The other Mer heard his words and looked over, alarmed.

"What is he saying?" I asked.

Sydin calmed his son. "He says there is a ship in the distance."

Brine tried his English out of respect for us. "I have saw one boat. Three armed boat that swim far away."

"Three arms?" asked Bart.

"He means masts," replied Grant. "It must be the barque." He turned to Brine. "Is it sailing in our direction?"

"Yes."

"And on schedule, as always," said Owen. He reached into his shirt and pulled out a pistol. Hammock stepped beside him, as did Miley and Smirks, who also drew pistols. Owen aimed the barrel at Sydin.

"Lower the pistols," Waylin commanded.

"Ach! Yours is the last voice I want to hear," said Owen.

"What is happening here?" demanded Grant. "You owe us an explanation."

"Agreed," Owen said. "I am bound by article to inform you of what is to come."

"Whose articles?" Grant demanded.

"Jean L'Ollon's!" Owen broke into a fit of laughter. "You think you're cunning enough to outwit the greatest pirate captain that ever lived? Nay. Let me fill you in on the details, Lords of Rosewing.

"When I arrived in Grenada, I searched for you. During my silent searching, I met up with some of L'Ollon's men at the Cod Fish Tavern. They told me that you, Jacob, stabbed Jean L'Ollon with his own sword and watched him sink to the bottom of the sea. You killed him. At least…you thought you did.

"You left the blade in him. If you had pulled it out, he would have died. His men tended to his wounds. Fools!"

I lunged for him, but Waylin's tight grip on my arm stayed me. "No," he said in a hiss. "They'll open fire. Control yourself."

"Aye, Jacob! Wanting a fight, I see," said Owen. "There'll be time enough. You'll see."

Cora spoke up in a voice calm and sweet. "Please. Do not succumb to such wickedness. I do not believe you are a bad man in your heart. Lower your weapon and we can help you. You are still welcome to be our ally. You must know that Jacob and Grant care about you and have valued your friendship. Look within yourself and find the truth. What is true wealth?" She swam closer to Owen, her purple eyes pleading with him.

"The Keeper of Peace. Your totem should be ignorance! Aye!" Owen turned the barrel of the pistol on her.

"No! Cora!" I yelled. I leapt forward and reached for Owen, shoving his arm as he squeezed the trigger. The explosion was deafening. A terrible yellow flash erupted and black smoke puffed around us. Cora screamed. I heard the ping of a ricocheting round followed by a splash in the water.

I fell to the ground. Owen threw the spent weapon aside and scurried away. Hammock, Miley. and Smirks covered Owen's escape and turned their pistols on us. I rolled over and saw Lord Sydin holding young Brine in his arms. Blood covered the Merchild's chest. Sydin's long black hair fell over the youth. I could hear Brine wheezing and Sydin whispering in their language.

I wanted to run after Owen, but his cohorts protected him. I remembered seeing this all before, only it was James Shanley who cradled his dying son. Blood stained the water of the Sacred Lagoon.

"The gold, Mer!" Owen hollered, running out of the courtyard, toward the beach. "Retrieve your gold and pile it on the shore or Captain L'Ollon and the *Obsidian* will bring more death to this island." Hammock, Miley, and Smirks followed, keeping their pistols on us as they left.

"Go with them, all of you!" Sydin commanded, the young Mer still in his arms. "I said go! You violated the agreement and are no longer welcome here. You are *all* enemies now."

"Sydin, we must not let him get away with this," I said. "Help us fight them."

"Leave us! I do not care about your fate. Fight your battle. Kill each other as men have done for thousands of years." He turned to the others. "Cora, Pearl, Manta, Driften…we go now. Leave these vile humans to their bloody fate."

Manta growled and pounded the water. He dove away, his dark green fin crested and splashed. Pearl looked at Grant and waved farewell.

"Pearl. Wait!" Grant called to her.

Slowly, she sank into the water.

Driften spoke to Cora. "Let us go, sister. You tried all you could." Driften looked at me. "Goodbye, Jacob." He took Cora's hand and pulled her into the water. She tried to resist, but her brother's grip was too strong. She cried and reached for me. I reached back but could not touch her pleading fingers. I watched her sink away.

Sydin cradled his son and went beneath the water's surface. His black hair swirled in the water. We were all alone in the courtyard. I fell to my knees in the white sand and stared at the pool, willing Cora to come back.

Chapter 44

Friend Is Foe

"Listen up, men," ordered Grant. "We are doomed if we give up. I have a plan."

"What is it?" Bart asked.

"We will let the pirates of the *Obsidian* come to us, and we will defend this island. We know the lay of this land, the enemy does not. We can take hidden positions throughout the isle and strike at them unseen. If we hurry, we can retrieve our swords. We will make Cerulean Isle a deadly place to enter. What say all of you?"

Konopo came forward. "I will fight for the Mer!" The Carib let out a tribal call, a proud cry from the heart.

The crew raised their fists and hollered their allegiance to a worthy captain. Grant lifted me to my feet. "It's you and me, friend. Are you well enough?"

"Yes."

"Good. Think of the things that fill your heart with happiness and fight for them. You are my brother. You are the only family I know. Today, I fight for you."

"And I will fight for you."

Grant ordered the waiting crew. "I want a team to make for the sloop and return with swords and daggers. Bring anything that can be used as a weapon. Konopo, Bart, Waylin, round up some men and ascertain the best defensive positions throughout the island."

"Yes, Captain," said Bart and Konopo in unison.

Grant turned to me. "Jacob, go after Owen. You are the only one who can stop him."

~~~~~~

Owen and his men had eluded us through a narrow crystal passage that opened at the far end of the courtyard. I followed Owen's tracks. The sound of hurried footsteps echoed off the sparkling walls and beams of cerulean stone.

The passage made a sharp turn. I waited behind the corner and listened ahead. Hearing nothing I crouched low and peered around the blue stone wall. A small beach surrounded by towering rock ledges opened before me, showing four sets of tracks in the sand. It looked as though one man broke to the right and followed the rock formations to the shore. Whoever went that way must have entered the water to get around the large stone structure, the goal being to get back to the main cove and commandeer one of our lifeboats. The man would have to be strong to accomplish this alone. I guessed the tracks belonged to Hammock.

The other tracks were erratic, trailing in circles and overlapping without reason. Owen was cunning, creating some kind of trap. I had no choice but to walk into it.

I stepped out from the confines of the passage to the middle of the beach. It wasn't long before Smirks made himself known with a pistol shot. The sudden explosion made me crouch and cover. The round found its mark in the sand four feet in front of me.

"Greetings," said Smirks. He loaded another round and came forward.

"Why have you turned on us, Smirks? What wrongs have we committed against you?"

"As Owen said, it all comes down to business in the end. A pocket full of loot from this island is enough to make a man rich. I'm simply earnin' me keep, is all."

"Smirks, listen to me. It's not too late for you to rethink your choice. Help me stop Owen from aiding L'Ollon, and I will forgive your ignorance."

"Do not insult me. I have spent more years on the sea than you could ever endure. I know a prosperous deal when I see one. This is me way out and me chance to be rich beyond measure. But before I can collect a single share, you must die." Smirks aimed his barrel. Without hesitating, I rolled to the right and tossed a handful of sand into his face.

Still crouching, I swung my leg upward and delivered a powerful kick to his midsection. He doubled over. I pounced on him, and we fought for control of the pistol. He smashed his head against mine. I was dazed. He forced his weight on top of me. I held tightly to the pistol's handle. He pulled hard to release the weapon from my grip. Instead of pulling back, I shoved the firearm forward, causing it to slam hard against his mouth.

There was a grotesque crunch as his front teeth broke to shards. Blood spilled from his mouth and pattered on my chest. Smirks fell off me, but I quickly positioned myself on top once more. He spat and choked on globs of blood. I struck his broken mouth and he let out a terrible howl. The pistol fell to the sand. We dove for it. He reached as desperately as I did. I saw his fingers close around the handle. I knew I had little time to react before his next shot. I saw my last opportunity to subdue him and took it.

Knotting my fingers deep into his greasy hair, I pulled back his head and slammed his face hard against the ground.

I heard a muffled crack. He lay still as the white sand turned pink under his head. I took the pistol, now jammed with sand and blood. Useless. I checked his body for any other weapons. A small dagger was hidden in his belt. I concealed it in the side of my boot and scrambled across the sand, hurrying around the adjacent wall of stone.

I came into another pristine cove. The footprints of my enemies were scattered in every direction. The only place for them to go was into the mouth of a small cave that opened in the side of another stone wall, this one twice the height of the other one. I made for the cave and entered as quietly as possible.

The air was salty and moist, and I could smell their lingering body odor. I heard what sounded like the chiming of coins and the gentle clanking of metal. As I drew near, I heard fragments of their conversation.

"This is only a portion of what the island has to offer... Give it here, that's mine... Aye, come on. We must hurry... Be comin' back for the rest of it." The sound of their hurried steps trailed off.

I pressed on after them, but stopped when I entered a round cavern filled with treasure. There were golden vases and silver carafes, piles of doubloons, and mounds of jewels everywhere. My feet crunched on shards of ruby and diamonds. There were trunks marked with crests of distant countries and burlap sacks of old tribal jewelry fashioned from lustrous gems and beads of polished jade. My eyes fell on a long golden rapier with a twisting hand guard and diamond-studded pommel. I picked it up and marveled at its perfect balance and near weightless feel. Satisfied with its deadly edge, I slid it into my belt and continued after Owen and Miley.

The passage was dim, but not dark enough to impede my pursuit. The damp corridor began to incline and spiral upward. Soon, daylight met me as I approached the exit. I listened for them before stepping out of the cave. Hearing nothing, I stepped out onto a narrow path of smooth crystal. I was on the very top of the towering rock wall. The strange terrain stretched out and tapered to become a dangerous cliff.

Owen and Miley stood near the edge looking out at the sea. Beyond them, rising and falling over the radiant water, was the great and dreadful barque of Captain Jean L'Ollon. Its three foreboding masts scraped the sky, and its wide sails sent swaying shadows over the sea. The very sight of the unforgiving vessel after ten long years stirred my fears and forced my heart to remember the old grief. Once again, I felt the sorrows of abandonment smother my heart. I felt the sting of childhood helplessness and tasted the bitterness of rage. I must have gasped because Owen and Miley turned around.

Owen snorted and spat over the edge of the cliff. "It seems ole' Smirks was no match for you, eh?" He stepped forward.

I drew my rapier.

"Nice blade you've got there. Took it from the Mer's cache, didn't you? You know, that sword probably came from a great pirate they killed. Aye! All of that gold down there, it is from men. The Merfolk are nothing but a band of hording scavengers."

"No different from you or the rest of L'Ollon's crew. Tell me, how did you orchestrate such treason?"

"I spent a great deal of time in Cod Fish Tavern and my identity became known," Owen said. "Secrets spill from bottles, after all." Owen's lips curled into a dark smile; his stare was like that of a poisonous snake. "L'Ollon's men reported the news of my existence to their captain and one night, someone handed me a letter from L'Ollon himself. He wrote that if I wanted to return to duty under his articles I would be paid a heavy stipend, a far better deal than Christoff's. I wrote back my acceptance of his offer and told him of the mission I was sent to accomplish. A second letter instructed me to continue with Christoff's plan and to convince you to sail for Cerulean Isle. After all, you have his chart, and he figured you'd use it. All he had to do was follow in our wake."

Owen withdrew a long, curving cutlass. Its edge flashed in the sunlight. As sharp and as deadly as my rapier was, it was not an equal match against his wide blade. Mine was a piercing weapon. His was for slashing. One powerful stroke of his sword would break mine in two. I pushed aside the thought. Miley glared at me with his pistol ready.

"Why don't you think about your position here," said Owen. "You are outnumbered. There is nowhere to run."

I lifted the tip of my sword. "Yield, and the crew of the sloop *Destiny* will show you mercy."

"So you want war?" he replied. "You won't live to see it. The *Obsidian* draws near, Captain L'Ollon approaches. His pirates will raid this island and slaughter everyone on it. They'll take the Mer's gold, then let loose their cannon. There will be nothing left. The Mer that fight will be netted and gutted like the stinking fish they are. But first, you will die. Miley, kill him."

Miley came forward with his pistol aimed at my heart. My rapier was no match for his firearm.

"Drop your weapon and get down on your knees," ordered Miley. "I said drop it."

I dropped the rapier. It chimed as it struck the blue crystal mass beneath us. I went down on one knee. Owen chuckled. "End him, Miley. Ahoy!"

Miley pressed the barrel to my head. "You won't feel a thing, mate."

"No," I replied. "But you will." I pulled the dagger from my boot and plunged it into his chest. My other hand knocked the pistol away. The weapon erupted. Miley groaned in shock as the thin, cold blade entered him. He staggered back and clutched the handle that protruded from his chest, his watery eyes staring in disbelief. He tried to speak, but painful gurgles and desperate draws of breath were all he could manage. His legs trembled and his eyes clouded over. He fell forward,

Cerulean Isle

landing on his chest. The dagger shifted deeper into him. I heard him groan for the last time.

I picked up the rapier and moved toward Owen, who had nowhere to go. He stood dangerously close to the edge of the cliff. I had little time to attack. Owen was an experienced warrior, and while I approached he had probably calculated several moves against me. I relied on the swiftness of the rapier and the fact that he had little room to move. The handle of the golden sword rolled in my palm.

I lunged. The tip of the blade streaked forward at blinding speed. There was a terrible clash of steel on steel. Bright yellow sparks flickered. He had parried my attack with equal quickness. I was off balance. He grabbed the collar of my shirt, sidestepped, and jerked me forward. I stumbled and felt my feet slip. The ledge passed below me. I dropped the rapier and saw it spin as it fell into the swirling ocean. I fell over the edge of the massive stone cliff. In desperation, I reached out and clawed for the stone wall. My hand found and gripped the rock face. My body dangled over the edge. I struggled to hold on and fought to pull myself up. The churning sea clashed and roared under me.

Owen moved out of view for a moment, but when he returned, my heart filled with dread. He was holding a bolder of cerulean rock. He lifted it over his head.

"I've killed many men in my days," he called down to me, "but never like this."

He let the boulder fall. I closed my eyes and tried to move out of its path. It was no use. A tremendous explosion bloomed behind my eyes and blackness filled my mind. The last thing I felt was the rock wall slip out of my grasp.

Chapter 45

Cerulean War

When I opened my eyes, everything was blue. Waving columns of gold sunlight illuminated the strange world. I was underwater. I looked toward the surface; it seemed so far away. I kicked and clawed to lift myself upward, but the swirling ocean pulled me deeper. The pressure within my lungs was unbearable. The harder I tried to swim, the more fatigued I became. *I am going to drown,* I thought.

I watched the sky grow dim as the surface rose. I reached for it desperately. *So far away...* I closed my eyes. I had lost the strength to move.

I looked up at the distant sky one last time. It was as blue as everything else around me, but for a brief moment a shimmering banner of purple passed over it. In my delirium, I opened my mouth as if to say goodbye to the world. When I did, I felt a warm softness close over my lips. A gentle stream of air blew into my mouth. My lungs drew in the dry current. Another steady flow came. I was breathing!

The dreamlike cloudiness faded from my mind. My vision sharpened. I saw Cora's beautiful face pressed against mine, our lips sealed as one. She held me firmly, and her rainbow hair flowed all around us. I held on to her. She kept her lips tightly against mine and continued to breathe into me. I drew in and exhaled through my nose. Bubbles danced up and away. She curled her lower half around me. Her elegant purple fin was like a great sheet of lavender silk wrapped around us. My body began to warm. The soft fin tightened and sealed out the water.

She gave me one last deep breath; it was all she had left within her. She pulled her lips away and looked to the surface, as if asking if I was ready to return. I nodded, though something in my heart wanted to stay down there forever with her.

Her magnificent fin loosened. The cold of the sea enveloped me. Her grip tightened. I held my breath. Her sparkling purple eyes began to glow. The soft white light was enchanting and came from a distant place within her gaze. With a thrust of her hips, a tremendous force propelled us toward the surface.

We broke through the water. I opened my eyes but winced from the bright sun.

"Hold tightly to me," said Cora. "I will take you to the shore of the main cove."

~~~~~~

I crawled from the shore as Cora remained in the shallows.

"Lord Sydin has let his grief cloud his judgment," she said. "He has given up on this sacred island, but I have not, and neither have the others. The *Obsidian* has dropped anchor and the pirates are coming. You and your crew are our only hope. Please, Jacob, find a way to save us."

A tear fell from her purple eye. It was small, but shined brighter than the surrounding waves.

"I will, Cora. I promise."

I heard Owen shouting a command. "Row faster!" I ran

in the direction of his voice. I spotted Owen and Hammock riding the waves. They had commandeered one of our rowboats. Hammock worked the oars. The hulking barque waited patiently in the distance. I could see several rowboats coming toward the isle. I guessed it would take them close to an hour to reach us.

"Owen! Stop," I yelled to him. "Come back and finish what you started."

"It is finished, fool! I will be rich and you will be deceased. Farewell!"

I ran into the water. The ocean rushed over my legs and lapped against my chest. Cora came up suddenly and stopped me.

"No. Let him go," she said. "You cannot catch him. He is too far at sea."

"I have to stop him!"

"Stay with me. Wait and watch if you must." She turned from me and looked out at Owen and Hammock.

Hammock rowed swiftly. Their boat bounced atop the rising waves, yet they appeared to be stuck on something.

Two large hands came from the water and gripped the stern of their boat.

Owen lifted his cutlass to hack at the hands.

The blue water burst at the stern, and through the splash I saw Manta's colossal frame come down upon the boat. The green Merlord used his overpowering might to force the stern into the water. The boat's bow lifted. Owen stumbled and collapsed atop Hammock. Manta growled viciously as he pulled the rowboat into the sea.

Owen and Hammock screamed in terror as they tumbled into the water. There was an enormous splash, and in it I glimpsed a wide green fin thrash and flail. As suddenly as the chaos began, it ended. The boat sank and the water calmed. Owen and Hammock did not emerge.

Cora looked away and sighed. She pressed her head against

Cerulean Isle

my chest. I held her as she whimpered. "Forgive Manta," she said softly.

"He deserves praise, not forgiveness," I replied. I took her face in my hands and looked tenderly into her liquid eyes. "I must find Grant and the others. We will protect Cerulean Isle with our lives. Tell this to Sydin. Tell this to any who will listen. Most importantly, Cora, stay clear of L'Ollon's men. I don't want anything to happen to you."

Cora Star gave a small smile and nodded her understanding. I pulled away from her and trudged through the water to the sand, hurrying to find my friends.

~~~~~~

"Jacob. Over here," called Grant. He was crouching behind a large boulder, clutching his jeweled rapier in his good hand. I rushed to his side. He pointed to the sea, where six longboats swam over the waves, closing the distance between the *Obsidian* and Cerulean Isle. "They're coming. I estimate ten men in each boat. Here, take this and follow me." Grant handed me my Mer-forged sword and led me into the wild of the island.

A wide trailhead opened just beyond the entrance of the crystal forest, making the area look much like a spacious cavern with blue and silver walls. Jagged corners and gnarled boulders cast strange shadows throughout the large, stone room.

"Our crew is hiding behind the stone pillars and atop the high ledges," Grant explained. "We will draw L'Ollon's men into the cavern to surround and overwhelm them. We'll have one chance for victory with our trap."

"What trap?"

"There isn't time to explain. Just fall back and take cover when you hear me call."

We hid behind corners of blue rock on opposite sides of the trail and peered around the stone walls, watching the beach outside the cavern.

The pirates of the *Obsidian* landed on the island. Their

rowboats sliced the white sand. As they grouped, they assessed the island and crystal forest. They were seasoned warriors dressed in dark tunics with skin charred from the sun. Long silver blades gleamed from their belts. From the midst of the mob came an older man with long gray hair.

He wore a dark red cloak over his shoulders that looked like a bloody bed sheet fluttering in the wind. His black tunic was studded with gold. A curving cutlass clanged against his hip, and the smooth stones of the shore crunched under his tall black boots. He stared at the island, his black eyes like nuggets of coal. I watched him pull the sword from his belt. His surrounding men fell silent. The shore lapped behind them and the indifferent ocean stirred.

The gray-haired man gave an order. Although his voice was hoarse and strained, I recognized Captain Jean L'Ollon. "Raid the island." He drew in a long, labored breath. "Kill anything that lives."

The men roared and rushed forth. When the first one entered the cavern, Konopo gave a shrill battle cry and let loose an arrow. The shaft streaked through the air and pierced the man's heart. L'Ollon's men looked in the direction of the shot, but Konopo had moved out of sight. Enraged by the quick death of their mate, they poured into the stone room, trampling their dead comrade and shouting threats.

Nearly sixty men filled the cavern, with swords drawn and eyes blazing. Another tribal call echoed loud and at this, *Destiny's* crew pounced from their places of hiding and engaged the pirates of the *Obsidian*. The clashing of steel on steel rang as loud as the groans and cries of battle. Blades flashed and whirled, sending a faint red mist into the air.

Grant called out over the clamor of war. "Jacob, are you ready?"

I nodded, wringing the handle of my broadsword.

Grant grinned, lifted the tip of his rapier, and hollered, "For the Merfolk, for Grenada, for us!"

Cerulean Isle

He leaped from around the corner and entered the fight; his jeweled sword gleamed like the walls of cerulean stone that surrounded us. He took down three men, moving fast, ducking and shifting from side to side. His deadly weapon stabbed true and chimed as he parried the thrusts of his attackers. Even with one arm in a sling, Grant was a formidable opponent. His curling red hair thrashed like fire. His movements were well practiced and nearly impossible to predict. The enemy, realizing that Grant and his rapier were quickly reducing their numbers, closed in around him.

I rushed in, my azumetalla sword cutting through their blades as if they were wood. My sword was nearly weightless in my grasp, and all that came at me fell fast with fatal wounds. Grant and I stood together, covering one another. My blade sliced and hacked as Grant's stabbed and cut.

Beyond our fight, Waylin fought with precision, his skill more refined than Grant's. He moved away from his attackers' advances and struck them dead when they were off balance. I noticed a pirate readying to attack him from behind. I called out to Waylin, who spun around and stabbed the man in the throat. The bleeding man doubled over, but Waylin took hold of him and shoved him into an oncoming group. They fell back as their dying mate crashed on top of them. Our crew moved over the toppled pirates for an easy kill.

L'Ollon's men could not stop the deadly accuracy of Konopo's arrows. With each kill, Konopo disappeared, only to emerge seconds later atop a new perch where he'd shoot down another, often saving the life of one of our own.

Though we fought well, we were outnumbered. It seemed that for every pirate killed, two more entered the battle. Grant slipped away and moved toward the entrance of the cavern. He yelled to our men, "Fall back, *Destiny!* Take cover!"

Our crewmates peeled themselves from the fight, each man ducking under a stone eve or retreating to nearby tunnels or grottos; L'Ollon's men stood massed in the center of the room.

I pulled my blade free from my attacker's chest and backed away, taking cover under a stone overhang.

Konopo rushed to Grant's side at the forest entrance and pulled back his bow string. He aimed his arrow overhead. I looked up. Above the room hung *Destiny's* largest fishing net filled with sharp broken shards of cerulean stone and jagged lengths of crystal. Konopo's arrow severed the line holding the netting in place.

As the net gave way, the deadly shower began. Screams filled the room as flesh ripped and bodies broke. Long, gleaming spikes impaled the pirates. Blood sprayed over the walls and pooled on the floor. A handful of men survived, only to be killed as Konopo emptied his quiver.

I was wet with blood, some of it my own. Mangled corpses filled the room, but the one I wanted was not among them. Grant ordered the crew to remain in the cavern as he and I made for the beach to find Captain Jean L'Ollon.

Chapter 46

Reunion

The white-sand beach was quiet. As the sun began to set over the water and the warm breeze blew, it was hard to believe that a bloody battle had just concluded. Grant and I paced along the shore of the cove, panning the area for any sign of Jean L'Ollon. The sloop *Destiny* remained ensnared in the shallows and beyond, the *Obsidian* drifted. It was then I heard a rustling on the wind, like a small sail flapping nearby. We looked toward the edge of the cove and from behind a wall of boulders stepped Captain L'Ollon, his scarlet cloak rippling around him.

In addition to the cutlass in his hand, L'Ollon wore two ornate pistols tucked into his belt. The handle of a long dagger protruded from the top of his boot. L'Ollon watched, undaunted, as we approached.

I stopped a mere five feet from him and realized that he did not recognize me. I knew his face instantly, though it wore the weathering of a decade and deep scars from his battle with

James Shanley. The lower lip that was once split in two healed imperfectly. It was now folded and thick with scar tissue. His black eyes were unchanged as he looked at us. His dry mouth formed a crooked smile.

"Stand down, sailors," he ordered. "There will be no heroes on this island." He inhaled, making a long, dry "eeeeee" sound that sent a shiver down my spine. "Come at me if you will, fools. You seem," he wheezed again, "ready for death."

"You will address us properly, L'Ollon. I am Jacob of Rosewing, sworn guardian of Cerulean Isle."

Hearing my name made his dark eyes widen.

"And I am Grant of Rosewing, your old cooper!" He stood at my side with his rapier drawn.

L'Ollon struggled to speak. "Quite the reunion, lads. No longer will I see boys in my memory." His breath whistled. "Nay, I will see men, and dead ones at that."

His swift cutlass slashed in a wide horizontal arch. Grant leapt back, escaping the slice by the grace of an inch. With equal quickness but greater power, I met L'Ollon's blade with mine. The broadsword of azumetalla broke his cutlass in half.

L'Ollon watched the shards of his blade fall to the sand, his moment of distraction giving Grant an opportunity to attack. He stepped in, lunging forward with his deadly rapier. L'Ollon, to my complete surprise, grabbed hold of my blade and pulled me toward him. His palms were cut deeply, but he wasn't slowed. His strong, old arms entwined me and forced my body in front of Grant's attack. There was no way to stop his rapier. The sharp tip entered my side. I gasped as the cold steel went through me. Grant quickly pulled the blade out of me and stared, in horror, at the fount of blood. L'Ollon wheezed and laughed.

"Jacob! I'm sorry… I…," cried Grant.

I fell to the sand, one hand clutching my wound and the other clutching my sword. "Get him," I groaned.

Grant went for L'Ollon. Weary from battle, his offense

was awkward; his broken arm an obvious hindrance. The old captain was quick and slipped away from the streaking rapier. After creating enough distance, he drew his pistols and ordered Grant to yield. I fought the pain in my side, stood up, and charged.

L'Ollon turned a pistol on me. "Halt or the cooper dies," he shouted.

I had no choice. The vile captain stood with his back to the ocean and the falling sun.

"For ten long years," L'Ollon hissed, "I have searched for you backstabbing bastards. You could have had a great career among my crew but, like foolish children, you chose to throw it all away." He sucked in another breath. "Every time I breathe I think of you, Jacob." He touched his chest. "What did you leave me with? One lung and one goal. At long last I will reclaim my fortune and rid myself of your troublesome existence, just as your father did long ago." The breath from his one lung screeched in my ears.

"As for you, Cooper. That old dream of piracy still burns inside you. One time you asked to be an articled crew member; in honor of that memory, I make you an offer. I will give you half of the gold on this island. We will sail up the north coast to meet some allies," he wheezed, "and you can buy yourself a galleon and a crew to sail her. All of your dreams will come true. Just drop your blade and stand by my side. What say you?"

"Half of the gold?"

"Grant, don't listen to him."

"Aye. Think of the power of gold. You lived the last ten years in a hilltop farm bought with pirated gold. You had comfort, food, drink, and women aplenty. Everyone knew your name. It was all from the power of gold. All that was but a taste of what I offer."

"What about protection? I want articled protection from you, your men, and all of your affiliates."

"Grant! No!" The pain in my side was unbearable, but it was nothing to the pain in my heart. *How could he even consider this?* I remembered our old argument as children when I had asked him the question. *"In the end, we get only one chance to choose either right or wrong, the final moment when one decision makes the difference between becoming the person you've dreamt of being or becoming the person you feared. What will you choose?"*

"Aye. You will be fully articled and fully protected. Look around you. See what I see. Aside from the gold and jewels, this land is desolate." L'Ollon breathed. "These men are unworthy of your talent, your passion. Join me, Grant of Rosewing. Stand by me, Jean L'Ollon, and become a master of the sea."

Grant looked at me with tears in his eyes. His rapier fell to the white sand. He turned away and stood next to L'Ollon. The captain wheezed. I stared at Grant, but he would not look me in the eye. My head grew dizzy with confusion. I felt the handle of my sword slip from my grasp. It clanged atop Grant's rapier. My bloody wound pulsed and ached. I was losing too much blood. My knees trembled, and I collapsed.

"Say hello to your mother for me, Jacob," remarked L'Ollon. He lifted his pistol.

My mother. The ocean.

I looked away from L'Ollon. I saw the sun diminishing. The ocean and sky were a swirling mosaic of purple and orange. The water sparkled as it caught the last hues of daylight. Tiny stars drifted on the water...starlight...the Merfolk. They were there, behind L'Ollon and ready for battle. Lord Sydin floated tall and effortlessly, clutching a readied bow of silver and bone. Driften was poised beside Sydin, his bow and arrow aimed. Manta emerged and nodded to me. Then I saw Cora. Her face broke from the water cautiously. It all made sense then—Grant was distracting L'Ollon so the Mer could get in position.

Sydin pulled back the bowstring. I ducked away from L'Ollon's pistol and in that instant, I heard the twanging release of Sydin's arrow and the immediate thud of the shot finding its mark. L'Ollon stumbled forward and clutched the arrow protruding from his chest. Grant moved in and snatched the pistols. He threw one to me, and we turned them on our enemy.

"Impossible..." L'Ollon tugged the arrow and cried out in pain.

Driften's arrows began to appear in L'Ollon's body. Blood sprayed as they drove into him. He staggered and swayed but remained on his feet. Globs of scarlet spewed from his mouth and nose. "No! My gold! I want my—"

The last arrow silenced him as it entered his forehead. Jean L'Ollon, captain of the *Obsidian,* fell to the sand. His cloak draped over his lifeless body, and the white sand around him darkened with blood. Grant put my arm over his shoulders and lifted me to my feet. We turned away from L'Ollon and walked toward the rolling surf.

The Mer swam toward the shore. Lord Sydin greeted me. "Jacob. I would like to apologize. I am sorry for abandoning your people. My heart was crying and..."

"There is no need for apologies. I share the grief for young Brine. I regret that I did not get a chance to know him."

"There will be plenty of time for that once he is fully well."

"You mean that he is not—"

"No. The wound is serious but not fatal. He will survive; he is *my* son after all."

Driften, Manta and Cora joined us. "Jacob, you are bleeding!" Cora exclaimed.

"I will be fine."

"Good," piped Manta. He came out of the water, his powerful lower body coiled beneath him. "There is more that needs to be done. The enemy's ship is still a threat. Cora, how many men did you see aboard?"

"Fifty after one hundred. We have little time. The *Obsidian* is readying her cannon. We have no defense."

"With no defense we have only one option." Manta cracked his knuckles. "Offense."

"Manta," Sydin commanded, "gather the others of your trade. Quickly."

"Yes, my lord." Manta dove away.

"What do you have in mind, Sydin?" I asked.

"Manta is a Wrecker. He and his team will go beneath the ship and pry apart its hull board by board. The *Obsidian* cannot fire if it is underwater."

Bart noticed the blood streaming from my side. He tore his shirt into strips and tied them around my wound, a crude but effective bandage. The deep rapier wound had weakened me and my head ached.

"Should we take you back to the sloop?" asked Bart.

"No. I want to stay on the island."

They brought me to a smooth boulder and helped me sit against it. The blue rock, warm from the day's sun, soothed my body. I wanted to close my eyes and sleep, but the sudden boom of cannon fire echoed over the sea. A wide portion of a nearby ledge was blown to shards. Small boulders smashed into the sand. The *Obsidian* had begun its assault. *Where was Manta? Would the wreckers make it to the ship before the fall of Cerulean Isle?*

The beach quaked from another explosion. A cannonball thundered into the powdery sand behind us. A thick cloud of white fell around us. Our crew hollered to clear the area, but there was no safe place to go. I looked back and saw four of our men run toward the cerulean forest. A horrifying eruption broke the stone entrance over them. Massive chunks of crystal fell upon them.

Waylin motioned for Grant and me to join the rest of the crew in the rowboats. The Merfolk had tied all of the mooring lines together, ready to pull the boats away from the island. Waylin called out to me, but I could not understand him over the roaring cannon and breaking island.

The Water People disappeared under the waves and began to move our boats away from the island. The *Obsidian's* hull flashed as it let loose its firepower. Cannonballs blasted through the surrounding water, each shot striking a random place. I thought this odd. Something had altered their aim.

The ship's stern was falling lower than the bow. The *Obsidian* was sinking rear first. Manta and his team would be deep under the water, Manta's mighty fists pounding the body of the ship, splitting and cracking the old wood, while the other Mer peeled away the planks. I imagined water flooding the bilge and the old barrel hold where Grant and I had spent so many days and nights.

The *Obsidian's* bow lifted higher and the stern sank into the water. A bright orange fire engulfed the main deck. I could hear the screams of the pirates and the creaking of the tilting masts. The Caribbean Sea raged around the ship. Several loud explosions lit the darkening sky. The three masts broke and fell into the water as the sea swallowed the figurehead of the Spaniard corpse. A dark and almost tangible silence fell over the ocean. The *Obsidian* was gone forever.

Chapter 47

Treasure of the Mer

The Merfolk of Cerulean Isle honored us. They worked to ensure that my crewmates and I were comfortable and healing. Cora's brother, Driften, and our tribal seafarer, Konopo, formed a fast friendship, sharing much in the ways of medicine and cultural pride. The two worked tirelessly to tend to the wounds of men and Mer. A soothing paste was concocted from strange seaweed found around the coral reefs and when applied to injured areas of the body, it numbed and closed the skin. Within two days time, I felt like my old self again, having enjoyed meals of fish, clams, and ocean vegetation.

Sydin reminded us of the deal we had agreed upon. The Merfolk of Cerulean Isle needed a new place to store their gold; it could not be certain who else followed in L'Ollon's wake. What enemies hunted him? What bands of seafaring scavengers sought the fabled gold of the Merfolk? We would honor them in turn by transporting their empire and guarding their secrets.

Lord Sydin instructed Cora to lead us to the heart of the isle and show us the reason for L'Ollon's obsession. Grant, Waylin, Konopo, Bart, and I followed Cora Star into the dark chambers that we had stayed away from before. We walked through the twisting damp corridors while she swam beneath us, following the waterways that led to the different rooms.

Each deep cavern and damp grotto was different than the one before it. Some had arching ceilings; others were low with dangerous stone teeth. We entered caverns that were dry with a single, bottomless pool in the center; we came to areas that required us to wade through waist deep water. Cora led us into a small room with a circular pool in the center.

"This is the waterway to the Golden Cavern," Cora explained. "You must swim now, but I fear you will not be able to hold your breath long enough, as the waterway is very long."

Cora thought for a moment, then smiled. "I have a wonderful solution. Please wait here. I shall not be long."

The Mermaiden slipped down into the pool, her lovely purple fin fluttering from the water as she dove away.

After half of an hour, we saw motion in the pool. I looked for the rainbow hues of her hair and the shimmering purple of her fin, but I saw only white and gray forms tumbling and turning in the water. A smoothed gray face with a long snout and beady eyes broke from the surface. Grant leapt back, startled by the creature. The gray face opened its long mouth to reveal a row of smooth white teeth.

"Relax," chuckled Waylin. "It's only a dolphin."

"I know that," retorted Grant. "I thought it was some strange…Mer-thing."

Four more gray faces emerged, and then Cora appeared in the center of the group. The dolphins dipped in and out of the water playfully. Cora caressed their snouts and heads.

"These are my friends," she said. "They will help you

through the waterway. If you take hold of the dorsal fin, the dolphin will guide you wherever you wish to go. It is fun for them and fast for you."

Konopo leapt into the pool with a laugh. The dolphins swam around him, playfully nudging his sides. He motioned for us to join him. "Come now, Captain Grant, or would you rather Cora bring a shark?"

We held tightly to the fins of the dolphins and raced through the waterway. Cora led the way and I could see how she swam. Her fin moved up and down in cadence with her thrusting hips. The gold and purple banner flowed like liquid silk. She was an undersea deity in my eyes, a peaceful female creature who lived in a world of wet crystal light and warm soft sand. In that instant, coursing through the waterways, I felt like one of them. I felt connected to their world.

The magic ended, and we emerged from the water. A vast, domed cavern opened above us. It was filled with riches from near and distant lands. Cora sat at the edge of the pool as we walked around in speechless awe.

Gold, polished and unpolished, forged and raw, was piled, stacked, and crated. Nuggets, coins, statues, jewelry, weapons, all of it made of lustrous yellow gold. Stone tables held heaping piles of jewels, silver reales and eights, shards of gemstones and sacks of diamonds. The cavern was so full of gold that there was scarcely room to walk.

"Welcome to the Golden Cavern," said Cora. "There are many smaller rooms like this throughout the island."

"Cora," I said in wonder, "did all of this belong to L'Ollon?"

"Not all of it. We have collected this cache for many decades. Some of it was recovered from L'Ollon's fallen fleet, but you must remember where he got it. The gold he claimed was his had been taken from other kingdoms of men. Those men took it from others and so it goes. It does not belong to anyone for very long but still, humans keep killing each other for it."

"Perhaps one day," I said, "mankind will see the true wealth in this world and treasure the things that are more beautiful than gold."

"Like what?" Grant asked as he examined his reflection in a golden shield.

"Like the sunrise over a calm sea," replied Cora. "Like the silver moonlight trapped in droplets of water."

"Like the warmth of a fire and the laughter of friends," I added. Cora's amethyst eyes looked deeply into mine. "Like the times of quiet when you can hear the ocean even though it's far away."

"And," added Cora, "when you can hear the voice of the person you never thought you would know, and when you close your eyes so you do not have to see him leave."

"Cora." I went to her. She took my hand.

"I do not want you to go, Jacob."

"When you look at me this way, I am tempted to stay."

~~~~~~

After a return swim with the help of the dolphins, Konopo led us back through the wilds of the island and we came into the main cove. We stopped suddenly as our eyes met an incredible sight.

The sloop *Destiny* waited on the shore. The large and broken bow had been hauled up onto the sand. The stern remained in the water and all around were brawny Merlords led by Manta. Our crewmates looked up at the ship as its planks dried in the sun.

I met Manta in the shoreline. "How did our ship get here, Manta?"

"Ha! How do you think?" He lifted his great arms and flexed his muscles. "And my friends helped."

One of the crewmates ran up to me. "Manta and his team went below *Destiny* and forced her from the stone's grip. I stood here on the sand and watched as our wounded ship sailed toward the island. Never in all my life have I seen a wrecked ship sail."

"And ready to be repaired," added Manta. "Lord Sydin has our smiths working in the deep to forge new beams and reinforcements for the hull. When this boat is done she will be half wood and half azumetalla. A wonder the likes of which men have never seen."

That evening, a fire was set in the middle of the beach. We burned the broken boards of the sloop and reveled late into the night. It was a celebration of Man and Mer. A great victory had been won and an unbreakable friendship formed. We feasted on fresh fish, meaty stews, and spiced ale. The surrounding waters were filled with Merfolk of all colors and sizes. I saw Merchildren leap from the water with their dolphin companions. Lovely Mermaidens, each with unique patterns and colors, curled on the sand and teased the men. Merlords and crewmates grouped together and spoke of common interests and shared yarns. Laughter filled the night, and music rang out as the stars wheeled over us.

Driften sat on the edge of a boulder and strummed an enchanting, guitar-like instrument made from a deep turtle shell. His fingers plucked the strings to create a rippling melody with notes that were light and soft.

Grant and Pearl stole away from the revelry. He came back to the fireside for more ale and stew, then hurried away. Cora and I relaxed in the warm sand near the fire. The light of the blaze made her purple fin shimmer with a rosy glow. Her eyes were violet gems.

"I love the music my brother makes," she said. Her fingers made looping designs in the sand.

"I have never heard anything like it. He's very talented."

"And he is very protective."

"Oh?"

"Well, he was when I was young."

"Tell me more about who you are."

"What would you like to know?"

"Whatever you'd care to tell."

"To start, I am six years after twenty in age. Driften is three years after thirty. Our parents are from the frozen waters of the south. Driften was born there in the icy blue realm of Lord Keltu'wah. Driften was born small and without the thick skin of his folk. Keltu'wah told my parents that he would perish in the cold."

"So they left to save him?"

"The Caribbean Sea is warm, and as you can see, my brother is well. My parents were wise to travel here. I was born seven years later in Cerulean Isle. However, my birth was not joyous."

"Why?"

"Because my father died before I was born. An illness ended the beat of his heart. Not all Mer are able to acclimate to new climates."

"What about Manta? He's from the north and seems well."

"Yes. The northern waters are cold but they are nothing compared to the arctic. The challenge is not only temperature. Plants and animals that also call the ocean home affect us. Something in this sea poisoned my father. Being a female, my mother was able to acclimate and resist the harsh changes. Mermaidens adapt better than Merlords. They must, since they bear life."

"What of your mother? Is she still with you?"

"No. She died two years ago at the age of two years after seventy. We miss her a great deal." Cora sat up a little straighter and put her hand on mine. "What about you? Tell me of your life. Tell me of your mother and your father."

I told her about the day my father sold me to Jean L'Ollon. I told her about my mother's death and the promise she made. Cora listened intently, and her compassionate gaze fueled me on. I told her all about Rosewing and of all the things that led me to Cerulean Isle. She asked me to tell her more about my horses, and when I described the farm, she closed her eyes and imagined it all. She laughed when I laughed, and when my eyes watered from painful memories, hers did too.

The merriment lasted throughout the night. The roaring fire shrank and died to glowing embers. Soon, the stars faded from the rising morning light. Cora Star remained with me. We lay in the soft sand; her head rested on my chest, and her great fin draped over us. With the Mermaiden in my arms, I let sleep take me away.

Chapter 48

A New Destiny

The following day, the Merfolk started rebuilding our ship. From out of the ocean, the Merlords brought long gleaming beams of silver and gold azumetalla. With the ruined bow resting on the beach, the men were able to work easily and safely. Merlords swam in the water around the stern, diving under to make repairs and reinforcements in places that we could not reach.

The designs for the new bow were fanciful and efficient. The ship would be unlike any vessel man had ever seen. The Mer metal was lightweight, buoyant, and resistant to corrosion. The new bow and bowsprit would be strong enough to break through ice and deflect cannonballs. The only weakness was fire. If the azumetalla were touched by flame or searing heat, it would soften quickly.

Within five days, the repairs were complete and our ship was grander than ever. Swirling patterns of silver, gold, and cerulean streamed along the length of the hull. The new bow looked as if it had been dipped in silver and dusted with gold. A sparkling azumetalla bowsprit stretched in front of the ship. Gold bands interlocked with the original wood planks. The keel was a slender blue and silver beam. Our beautiful vessel drifted on the waves gracefully.

"There is no limit to the amount of weight that this sloop can carry," said Sydin. "Her buoyancy is far greater than you can imagine."

"It is the finest ship in the Caribbean," I professed.

"That may be true," he said with a proud smile. "Tell me, have you scheduled your departure?"

"Not officially. Though I know the men are ready to get back to port. It's strange, Sydin, a part of me wants to stay."

He pointed to the beach where Cora sat with Pearl and Driften. "Saying farewell is not something she desires either."

"I mustn't let my feelings come before the welfare of my crew. We can't stay, Sydin. This is your home, not ours."

"I understand well. Our end of the deal is complete. My Mer are prepared to load our cache aboard whenever your men are ready."

"Where should I bring such treasure?"

"I have put much thought in this. Sail north and into the gulf. Along the coast of the mainland you'll find many caverns. I know of one that would be perfect. It rests in the side of a towering stone cliff at a place the humans call Black Water Cove. A normal man would have great difficulty accessing it, but with rigging and a team as skilled as yours, you will be able to get in and hide a large portion."

"And what of the rest of it?"

"Reward your men for their bravery and hardship. Make them rich in payment for their secrecy."

"I will ensure that when mankind speaks of the Water People, they tell only tales of generosity and kindness. Thank you, Lord Sydin, for all that you have done."

Cerulean Isle

That afternoon, two dozen crates, ten trunks, and twelve heaping sacks of the purest gold, finest jewels and the most reflective silver were hauled aboard *Destiny*. The sails were set and the riggings manned. Grant calculated a northwestern course and Waylin took the helm. Bart made an inventory of everything brought aboard. Konopo secured the new store of fresh provisions and tied down the precious cargo.

The men took the rowboats to the ship and were helped aboard. The boats were then hoisted from the sea and battened to the bows. It was time to leave.

I sat on the beach and watched our drifting ship. My rowboat waited in the sand. Cora emerged from the water. The rushing waves brought the Mermaiden to my side. She positioned herself comfortably against me and leaned on my shoulder.

"Grant is a fine captain," she said, "and with Waylin at his side, the two can ride the waves safely. Must you go with them?"

"It's a dangerous matter to sail with such wealth. The crew needs me." I took her hands in mine. "I wish I didn't have to say goodbye."

"I can grant wishes, you know."

I smiled and brushed a strand of purple hair from her soft face. "You already have."

"When your journey is over, where will you go?" she asked.

"Back home to Grenada, to Rosewing."

Cora smiled. "Then that is where I will find you."

"Then that is where I will be waiting."

We held one another tightly. When the embrace loosened, our eyes locked and in her stare shone the glimmer of sunlit waves and the endless depths of the sea. She leaned into me and our lips met. Her kiss was passionate, slow and soft. When it was over, a small tear fell from her cheek.

"I love you," she whispered.

Before I could respond, the surf rushed over us, pulling the loose sand from under me. In that instant, Cora slipped away.

~~~~~~

Destiny's sails inhaled the wind, blooming to look like powerful white clouds. The sloop cut the sea with precision. A cool mist sprayed from under the starboard and port bows. The sun glistened off the metal bowsprit so bright that we had to look away. At the stern, Grant and I watched the island of the Mer shrink from view. Cerulean Isle shimmered like sunlit sapphires before vanishing on the horizon, lost in a mosaic of blue.

Acknowledgements

Special thanks to my circle of readers: Maureen Chabot, Carol Childers, Hannah Fraser, Diane Johansen, Patti Mazzone, Cassandra Mens, Donna Sullivan, Jonathan Taylor and Robb Zerr. Your belief in me has fueled my imagination and it always will. Sincere thanks to good friend Jim Shanley for the use of your name.

Very special thanks to my talented editor, Karen Gowen. You've made me a better writer.

Loving thanks to my wife, Devin, who makes living with a writer look easy. I cannot express how special you are.

Lastly, to Jacob and Grant, thank you for a great adventure. It was fun!

Gardner M. Browning

About the Author

G.M. Browning, known as "Buddy" to his friends and family, is a published author and poet. Born in New Hampshire, Browning resides in a quiet neighborhood along a picturesque river with his wife, Devin.

His first novel, Timeless Love: The Legend of Black Water was published in 2006 by a small Wisconsin press. This novel sold close to a thousand copies just six months after its release. Unfortunately, the publisher closed a year later and The Legend of Black Water fell out of print; the sequel, The Heart of the Cove, never saw publication. This short taste of success motivated Browning to continue pursuing his writing career.

After fourteen months of extensive research, work on Cerulean Isle began. The first draft took eighteen months to complete. Another year and half passed that brought rejections from publishers and agents all over the world. Keeping the mentality of "they can't all say no," Browning found a home for Cerulean Isle at long last in WiDō Publishing.

CPSIA information can be obtained at www.ICGtesting.com
Printed in the USA
BVOW02s1843210115

384373BV00001B/30/P